Kathleen Rowntree's other novels are *The Quiet War of Rebecca Sheldon*, *Brief Shining*, *Between Friends*, *Tell Mrs Poole I'm Sorry*, *Outside, Looking In* and *Laurie and Claire* and she has contributed to a series of monologues for BBC2 TV called *Obsessions*. Her latest novel, *Mr Brightly's Evening Off*, is now available as a Doubleday hardback.

A PRIZE FOR
SISTER CATHERINE

Kathleen Rowntree

BLACK SWAN

A PRIZE FOR SISTER CATHERINE
A BLACK SWAN BOOK : 0 552 99732 3

ORIGINALLY PUBLISHED IN GREAT BRITAIN BY GEORGE WEIDENFELD &
NICOLSON LTD AS *THE DIRECTRIX*

This revised edition first published 1997

PRINTING HISTORY
Weidenfeld & Nicolson edition published 1990
Black Swan edition published 1997

Copyright © Kathleen Rowntree 1990, 1997

Set in 11/12pt Linotype Melior by
County Typesetters, Margate, Kent.

Black Swan Books are published by Transworld Publishers Ltd,
61–63 Uxbridge Road, London W5 5SA,
in Australia by Transworld Publishers (Australia) Pty Ltd,
15–25 Helles Avenue, Moorebank, NSW 2170,
and in New Zealand by Transworld Publishers (NZ) Ltd,
3 William Pickering Drive, Albany, Auckland.

Reproduced, printed and bound in Great Britain by
Cox & Wyman Ltd, Reading, Berks.

Derek's, of course.

And in memory of my father, John Paine.

1

'I am very tired,' said the Prioress.

Margaret darted forward: an extra cushion, a reviving cup of tea?

In her haste to refuse these comforts, the Prioress's teeth became dislodged. Fortunately, her tongue sucked them back into place with well-practised aplomb, but not without a temporary loss of dignity. As Margaret and Catherine turned tactfully away, the Prioress was seized with resentment. She pictured herself as they had seen her. She pictured her fumbling mouth, and gave a twitch of annoyance, which promptly set off her sciatica. She longed to protest that she was not as that picture suggested, that a truer indicator of the inner woman would be her youthful voice. Why, when she was amused (as, for example, at the sight of Sister Hope fleeing from a dangling spider, screeching and clutching her skirts as if a monster were after her with rapacious intent) her laughter rang out in the cloister clear and true as the chapel bell. Yes, in heart and mind she was lively still. 'Sit down,' she commanded, when her mouth felt under control.

Margaret and Catherine sat in two hard chairs placed distantly across the rug.

The Prioress looked from one to the other; from Margaret, pink and glowing with eyes the blue of forget-me-nots, to pale, brown-eyed Catherine. 'Sister Mercy will not recover,' she told them. 'Something will have to be done. Sister Mercy understands her position: that she can never succeed me, that she must prepare to obey a sterner call: more to our point, that she can no longer be responsible for the day-to-day business of this priory. She has therefore indicated her wish to resign.'

From the vicinity of the hard chairs came faint protests.

The Prioress sighed and examined her knobbly hands. 'I am afraid the protracted illness of Sister Mercy has resulted in a serious state of affairs.'

Prominently in the minds of all three women was the thought that even in health Sister Mercy as directrix had allowed the development of a serious state of affairs. Income from the priory's once famous dairy herd, from the vegetable garden and beehives, had dwindled, and there were fewer orders for the sisters' once celebrated needlework. The place had become shabby; important visitors seldom came on retreat. Commissions for the sisters' prayers were few and far between, for the reputation of Albion Priory was no longer high in the world.

Margaret craned forward. 'How brave of Sister Mercy,' she began. Then stopped herself, recalled the advice of Beatrice her friend and lieutenant, and continued in the deep measured tone she had been working on lately. 'How *very* generous, and how typically *selfless* of poor, dear Sister Mercy. Things have indeed deteriorated, and I do so agree that they cannot be allowed to slide further. I know I speak for every one of us when I assure you, Reverend Mother, of our robust support.'

'Hmm.' The thought had slipped into the Prioress's mind – and she wondered if it had also occurred to her guests – that since it was she who had named Sister Mercy as her successor and as a consequence made her directrix of the priory, partly to blame must be her own judgement.

But Margaret's thoughts had cleared this hurdle and

were racing over more profitable ground. Since Catherine had also been invited here this morning, and since Catherine, as Mercy's assistant, was already a member of the priory's hierarchy, Margaret could not jump to any flattering conclusion. She longed to prompt the old woman, but steeled herself to be cautious. 'I imagine it's a difficult task – choosing her successor.'

'Have you considered raising the status of Council?' Catherine asked, speaking for the first time. 'I wonder whether the task ahead requires the skill of more than one individual.'

'Aha, an interesting thought— But Council is overwhelmingly composed of Sister Mercy's contemporaries. No, I have decided to skip a generation. We need youthful energy and fresh ideas. Now then, you two. By common consent you are the most outstanding sisters of the next generation, so give me your views. Sister Margaret, let us hear how you would proceed.'

Oh heavens. The moment had leapt on her without warning, the moment they had hoped and plotted for: she, Beatrice, Agnes and Joan. But they had banked on several more years; in fact, they had thoroughly bemoaned the time that must elapse before their chance could come. One matter they had forecast correctly, however: Catherine was to be the opposition. Margaret steadied herself; she was more than a match for Catherine. She pulled in her chin, flexed the muscles of her throat, invoked her new deep voice.

'We have here' – she threw out her arm as if to include the farthest field in the priory's demesne – 'a priceless jewel. Think of the history, of the artists drawn here by the beauty of the place, of the generations of sisters who have dedicated their lives to preserving and enhancing the reputation of Albion Priory.'

9

Already the Prioress's mind had begun to stray from Margaret's words (for they made her impatient, telling her things she already knew) to contemplation of Margaret herself: an arresting personable figure whose manner of utter confidence would calm many an anxious heart. Indeed, the sisters who were responsible for the priory's accounts had this very week begged the Prioress to pay heed to Sister Margaret's ideas. Apparently, she had drawn up sheets of figures which were nothing short of revelational. The Prioress hoped to do her duty without recourse to the figures.

'And what do we see? Shabby, scruffy interiors. Crumbling, decaying exteriors. Slipshod ways, a pervasive air of defeat. Even' – and here Margaret's voice trembled – 'the Albion Tower declared unsafe.' She screwed up her face in disbelief – 'The Albion Tower in danger of collapse?' – then drew herself up and cried: 'The Albion Tower is known throughout the world. It is a symbol, it *stands* for something.'

Not for much longer, m'dear, thought the Prioress grimly, not unless you really can come up with something.

'We must rethink the ways in which we seek to earn our living. Subsistence agriculture and horticulture will not restore the fabric, nor will a nicely illuminated prayer here nor a well executed tapestry there. Too many people, I'm afraid, engage in activities which are a waste of time – worse, which distract us from more fruitful endeavour. I know this is not a popular view, but the world does not owe us a living. It is absolutely vital to discover what things we can provide for the world that the world is willing to pay for. Nothing in the sad saga of the last few years has so offended against the spirit of this place as the sight of Sister Mercy scurrying to the Church with her begging bowl. How humiliating! The Albion Priory dependent on handouts! Never again, if I have anything to do with it.'

The Prioress shifted in her chair and jarred her sciatic nerve. But sharper than the pain in her legs was the thought that Margaret had a knack of honouring the office of prioress – her deep curtsy, her solicitousness – while managing to convey contempt for the incumbent. It was that bossy tone of voice, that glint in her eye— 'This is all very well, but we're waiting to hear what it is you would actually *do*.'

Margaret put her head on one side and smiled. 'I think I did state what our first priority should be. We should seek to discover services we can provide that will bring us a satisfactory income. Of course, we can take advice on this from many sources, but some of us have been thinking along these lines and have come up with an idea – backed up by figures, let me hasten to add, which I am sure will interest you.'

'Yes, yes—'

'You see, it is *rarity* that makes a commodity valuable. Can we provide the world with a rare commodity? Indeed we can. We can provide *tranquillity*. And, more rarely still, we can give that tranquillity an aura of spirituality. Peace and quiet in an uplifting atmosphere. The setting is perfect: acres of privacy, glorious buildings, our music, our art, our daily religious observance. We can provide a refuge from the world—'

'Really,' cried the Prioress. 'Is that your great plan? But we've always taken visitors on retreat.'

'The wrong sort of visitor,' Margaret all but snapped. 'I'm talking about the wealthy visitor. We need to attract powerful important people able to pay handsomely for our hospitality. The thing would have to be done properly, of course; everything geared towards it. Superfluous, counterproductive activity would cease, thus freeing resources to service our new endeavour—'

'Well, thank you, Sister—'

11

'I realize this may take some getting used to, but I assure you, once you have seen the figures—'

'Quite. But now—'

'And if it seems a rather radical proposal, do bear in mind, Reverend Mother, that radical measures are required if we are ever again to hold our heads high in the world.'

'I'll hear Sister Catherine now.'

Catherine smiled.

At once the Prioress's heart softened. How right Catherine looked in her habit, her face neither diminished nor thrown into cruel relief, as was the fate of so many behabited sisters. Rather, the white and grey frame became her, coif and veil seemed natural appendages, she was all of a piece like a sculptured madonna. Catherine was now speaking, and the Prioress steeled herself to pay attention. However, as happened very often, her own thoughts proved too alluring and she was soon reflecting that the woman at Catherine's side who was merely listening appeared the more active of the two. Margaret craned forward to miss not a word, her eyes darted, her arms hugged her body. Did Catherine find her eagerness intimidating? wondered the Prioress. Certainly Catherine was hesitant.

'But when I remember our purpose – um, that we should live a good life – to the glory of God, um, and share all that we have in the common good – well, I really can't think we've strayed far from our goal. After all, we're a loving and caring community. By and large, every member is happy and fulfilled—'

Bless the dear girl. She was her heart's choice. Mercy's choice, too. Hadn't she and Mercy stood together at the great oriel window watching Catherine below in the garden? Hadn't they nudged one another and confided: 'There she is. Yes, Catherine's the one'? In less complicated times there'd be no question about it. To observe her in Council smoothing feelings and encouraging compromise, to hear her glorious mezzo giving the anthem at evensong, to be cheered by her smile, was to know she was special and that in due course she would succeed them.

'I must admit Sister Margaret's talk of activities being unprofitable worries me rather. Because profit can't be the only yardstick. When you think about it, these activities define what people are; people would be quite lost without them. And they're part of the fabric of the place, we relate to them. The riches of our lives – music, art, writing – flow from them. I admit the need for change,' – she gave a nervous laugh; 'heavens, we're certainly up against it at the moment. But let it be change with safeguards for all the good things we've built over the years. Margaret,' she said, turning diffidently to her companion, 'you talk about freeing resources. Please remember you're talking about people. And you said— You implied Sister Mercy has mismanaged our affairs. Well then, so have I, since I've been her assistant for the past five years. And I do concede it may be so. I'm not trying to wriggle out of anything by pointing out that many of our difficulties are due to matters beyond our control, to changes in the world outside—'

'Exactly,' cried Margaret, unable to hold back a moment longer. 'And we must change too if we're to survive, because it's from the world that we seek a living.'

This silenced Catherine briefly. Then, 'I'm sure there's a lot in what you say,' she said. 'And maybe your ideas do contain the answer. I admit I'm not sure what we should do beyond improving the things we do already. But so long as we never lose sight of our purpose.'

'There can be no higher purpose than restoring our beloved priory to its rightful place in the world.'

'But the priory is *us*, we sisters. And I'm not sure we can claim a right to any particular place—'

'It's more, much more. It's those who have gone before and those who'll come after. More still. It's an *ideal*, a thing in its own right.'

During this exchange, the Prioress, as she afterwards recounted to Sister Mercy, was visited by the Holy Spirit. Suddenly, blazingly, she was enlightened. She saw clearly what it was she was called upon to do, which was to choose not one or other, but both. Plainly both were needed. Catherine had admitted she had no radical solution, and Margaret was so sure of hers that she seemed to have lost sight of those precious things which Catherine had remembered to value. Their gifts – Margaret's practical drive and Catherine's spirituality – were complementary. 'I have it,' she cried, nearly ejecting her teeth.

This time her guests were too full of suspense to feign blindness. They stared frankly while the Prioress struggled with her mouth behind her hand. 'You are both to be directrix. You will help one another. That way all sides will be considered and nothing overlooked.'

'But which of us—?'

'Who—?'

'Don't even think of the succession,' cried the Prioress airily; 'there's plenty of time for that. I'm sure God intends me to endure this pain for many years yet – I've hardly begun to come to terms with it. Later, when the time draws near, I shall name my successor. In the meantime your brief is to devote all your energies to restoring the well-being of our community. Take advice and assistance from Council; if necessary appoint new members. I leave it to you. Now, kneel.'

Exhilarated, the Prioress gabbled a blessing. Not only had she come to a decision, she had been innovatory;

for never before had the office of directrix been held by other than the nominated future prioress. She had excelled herself this morning, and had earned, she considered, a restorative measure of elderberry wine.

2

Margaret went at once to the chapel. 'Dear Heavenly Father,' she prayed.

In her private devotions she always began with Dear Heavenly Father; never Dear Lord Jesus or Almighty God, which might be another's personal choice. There was something about Father that felt very good to her, and Heavenly Father was even better. Her earthly father, of whom she had been enormously fond, though modest in his calling (a small-town grocer, in fact) had been famous for his strict adherence to the virtues of prudence and thrift and for striving to establish their practice in civic matters through his position as a local councillor. Margaret had taken his strictures seriously, and become as passionate an advocate for sound housekeeping as he. She was altogether a satisfactory daughter. Whenever his eyes rested on her, satisfaction covered his face. Dear Father, she had thought, observing this. And so it was a natural progression that later, sensing a loftier paternal approval, Dear Heavenly Father should spring to her mind.

When she had completed her communication she got off her knees. She walked briskly from the chapel and through the corridors to Agnes's room. 'Brr,' she cried, bustling in, the cold adding impetus to her customary haste. She sat on the edge of Agnes's bed and surveyed the waiting ones.

On the rug lay Beatrice, sprawled on her stomach and propped on cushion-pillowed elbows. Beatrice exuded physical strength – her rangy body, jutting chin, prominent cheekbones. Rather attractive strength, thought Margaret, meeting her friend's violet eyes with affection and also with a stifled sense of misgiving. But she forgave Beatrice for whatever it was that inclined her to be secretly uneasy, because Beatrice, as well as possessing great charm, showed herself time and again to be a first-rate tactician. If she was a little— (*exotic* was the word Margaret's rather limited imagination invariably settled on), never mind; Beatrice had an unequalled nose for strategy.

Agnes, too, was a considerable strategist; certainly in her own estimation. But Margaret felt her value to be somewhat diminished by an uncertain temperament and a repulsive countenance. She sat now at her desk, her sallow skin drawn into a scowl over half-moon spectacles. There had been occasions when their careful plans, nursed along by artful reasoning, had very nearly been blown sky-high by an intemperate public outburst from Agnes. And sometimes she gave unnecessary offence by referring disrespectfully to the Prioress. Agnes, sound as a bell on matters of policy, lacked a reliably politic manner.

Joan – wild-eyed tortured Joan sitting tensely in the easy chair – was their theorist. A highly strung creature, but brilliant; able to produce a legitimizing Biblical reference or historical precedent at the drop of a hat, possessing a dazzling facility for matching strategy to goals and for conferring high-minded authoritativeness on mundane expediency. Unfortunately, Joan's talents required a degree of ideological sophistication to be appreciated; her handicap was that of many an intellectual: it was only to the already initiated that she could properly communicate.

At this point in a consideration of her colleagues, Margaret became acutely conscious of her own worth. They had honed their ideas and developed their plans as equals, but gradually it had become clear that if they were to win others to their cause, Margaret must be their front woman. Equals they might be, but Margaret was indisputably first among them.

'For pity's sake,' cried Beatrice, seizing Margaret's right ankle and pretending to sink her teeth into it. (Margaret smiled, but nevertheless primly removed her foot.) 'Hurry up and tell us what happened.'

'Well, our information was correct. Sister Mercy has resigned.'

Their gasps were fierce as snakes' hisses.

'And the Reverend Mother has appointed myself and Catherine jointly as directrix.'

'Jointly?'

'Both?'

'But which—?'

'She declines to name her successor for the moment. She reckons there's plenty of time before it becomes an urgent consideration.'

'Probably is, the tenacious old bat.'

Margaret, recalling that barely an hour ago the old bat had been good enough to elevate her, said: 'I'd rather you didn't speak disrespectfully in my hearing, Agnes. I am now directrix of this priory.'

'*Joint* directrix, for heaven's sake. What a stupid idea. How exactly did it come about? Both of you were closeted with her. Was she trying to choose? Were you and Catherine in competition?'

With raised eyebrows and lowered lids, Margaret began a sweeping examination of the floor – a sure sign that she was thinking rapidly. 'No-oo. I wouldn't say—As a matter of fact, the Reverend Mother gave no indication of having any motive other than to seek advice. Probably, were it not for Sister Veronica pressing her to see me, Catherine alone would have been summoned there this morning. Catherine, I understand, was with the Reverend Mother at Sister Mercy's bedside yesterday evening.'

'That's true. I had Sister Hope keeping a lookout,' Beatrice confirmed.

'There you are. For all we know, the Reverend Mother was about to appoint Catherine and suggest merely that I advise her.'

'So you think you swayed her. In which case there *was* an element of competition.'

Margaret's eyes were now wide open; they seemed to jut towards her inquisitor as she boomed: 'I think my words did sway her, yes! She was very, very impressed. Whatever her plans had been prior to that interview, she made a decision then and there to include me. There was no doubt whatever that I advanced our position. I presume you wouldn't have wished me to turn down the opportunity?'

'Perhaps,' mused Agnes, not in the least intimidated, 'you ought to have held out. Insisted on being sole directrix, with Catherine to advise you as necessary.'

Redness rose in Margaret's cheeks. But an intervention from Joan saved further argument: 'Too risky. Margaret might have lost everything.'

'In any case, Catherine won't be a problem,' declared Beatrice. 'The important thing is, from now on our hands are on the wheel. Any hands pulling in the wrong direction: well, they'll have to be dislodged.'

'Catherine was awfully vague, quite out of her depth,' Margaret recalled. 'More of the same but done a bit better seemed her only solution.'

'Catherine won't be a problem,' Beatrice repeated, then rolled onto her back to gaze at the ceiling. 'We must find a way of packing Council with our sort of people.'

'Absolutely. We can't afford to waste time arguing. At last we've a chance to accomplish our dream of a truly great Albion Priory. Joan, come to my room and help me with my speech, will you? Got to get all the facts and figures off pat.'

'Never mind the facts and figures. Give 'em one of your rousing turns. Throb on about Albion.'

Margaret smiled. (Beatrice was a tease, but *staunch*.) 'Come along, Joan,' she called pleasantly.

The silence following their departure held for some minutes. Agnes stared at her desk, Beatrice stared at the ceiling.

'Well, I'm off,' Beatrice declared at last, and rolled over and got to her feet. At the door she looked back. 'Oh, Ag?'

'Uh?' said Agnes.

'Do guard your tongue in public from now on, sweetie. Margaret will want us to raise the tone.'

A mean look came into Agnes's eyes. 'Thanks for the advice. Perhaps I can reciprocate. You'll probably find this hard to grasp, but Margaret's an idealist; she's not in this just for the power. But the trouble with idealists is they can't stand being let down by people they trust. Know what I mean? Let's say a close associate turns out to have a sordid side which could become public knowledge. Now that would be really upsetting. If I were you I'd watch my step from now on.'

Having listened carefully, Beatrice turned the door handle and slipped softly from the room.

3

It had begun to snow when Catherine sped through the cloister. Moonlit flakes spat in through the open archways. Head down, keeping close to the solid wall, she hurried to the chapter house door. There, she grasped the iron ring, turned, pushed, and thrust herself inside. On her right was the lobby giving on to the chapter house. Briefly, the scene in the chapter house this afternoon played in her mind's eye, a meeting of Council during which many of her assumptions had been challenged and demolished. She dismissed the memory, and, skirting the lobby, hurried along a vaulted corridor to the hospital.

Sister Luke came to meet her. 'She's asleep. But come in and wait. She was asking for you earlier, hoping you'd come.'

In a narrow bed at the far end of the room lay Sister Mercy. A chair stood by her bed. Catherine sat in it and peered about her through the gloom. Her eyes met those of another patient, who inclined her head then looked away. The small obeisance – which Catherine understood to be an acknowledgement of her newly conferred status – again brought this afternoon's meeting to mind, for the meeting had heard the Prioress announce that Catherine and Margaret were now jointly directrix. Catherine reflected that the promotion may have gratified and surprised Sister Margaret, but as far as she, Catherine, was concerned it had felt like a vote of no confidence. Sister Mercy had always seemed to take for granted that one day her assistant would inherit her position. And throughout Mercy's illness, senior sisters close to the Prioress – Cecilia, Monica, Anne and Elizabeth – had whispered that she should prepare herself because very soon the Prioress would appoint her. Catherine had vowed to dedicate herself to the task ahead. She had asked a blessing. She had gathered the resolution to believe that one day she would succeed in restoring the well-being of Albion Priory. In the hospital's gloom she remembered all this and marvelled at her naïvety. For apparently, without immediate radical change, the priory was beyond saving. At least, that was the proposition put forward at this afternoon's meeting. *There is no alternative*, Margaret had bellowed, and evidently people had believed her. For a moment Catherine had almost believed it herself. It had crossed her mind that her understanding of the matter had been inadequate, and nothing would suffice short of revolution. But then, rising to reply, her former con-viction returned: that basically the convent was run on the right lines and simply required some adjustments and greater effort all round. 'We have the promise of further funds. We have so much goodwill, a wealth of advice to call on. Why hurry?' she had asked. 'Why not accept help gratefully, and restore what we have to the best of our ability? Above all, let us have faith in our traditions.' But this hadn't answered their mood. They were dazzled by Margaret's picture of a glowing future. Outvoted, Catherine had asked about the position of those unable to change. Would Margaret's solution accommodate them? 'We must all learn to adapt,' Margaret had replied, and a sense of fore-boding had entered Catherine.

She raised her eyes and looked to the head of the room where Sister Luke sat at her desk. Glare from the desk's lamp illuminated the coiffed jowly face so that it seemed to float unattached in the darkness.

Then a hand rose and jabbed the end of a pen into the mouth (Sister Luke bit on the pen and frowned in thought) and at once the face became anchored to an invisible whole. Catherine returned her attention to the form in the bed. There seemed little chance tonight of a word with Mercy. She decided to pray for her instead.

Sister Mercy was thinking: She's here. I must speak. But though the need was urgent, the effort defeated her. Soon Sister Luke would suggest that, the patient being apparently settled for the night, Catherine might as well leave. Mercy's body felt deadly heavy and her feet were frozen. Stay, she silently begged, and strove to utter her visitor's name.

Sister Luke put down her pen and came softly along the aisle between the beds. 'I should go now. No point waiting any longer. I don't think she'll stir before morning.'

Wait, silently cried Mercy, making a supreme effort to break through the heaviness.

'I think she's waking. But she's cold, Sister, she's shivering.'

Sister Luke snatched a blanket from an unoccupied bed. 'Put this over her. I'll get a hot water bottle.'

Sounds broke from Mercy's mouth. 'Don't try to talk,' Catherine murmured, pressing the blanket round her.

Darn it. Darn, thought Mercy. She had known this would happen; that if she managed to speak, her words would be sabotaged by wilfully chattering teeth. It was because she was so dreadfully cold. At last heat was placed at her feet. Warmth stole through her. 'Ah,' she sighed. And a moment later, 'I knew you were— I've been trying—'

'It doesn't matter,' Catherine soothed.

But it did matter. She needed to say it. 'I'm sorry. It's my fault. If I hadn't – made a mess of things – Reverend

23

Mother wouldn't— It would be you, Catherine – not Margaret.'

'It isn't your fault. It's just that things are far more difficult than we supposed.'

'I can't bear it. Knowing I've failed. Having to – take that with me.'

Catherine thought for a while. Eventually she said, 'It takes courage to know what we are. And I imagine even greater courage to take that knowledge with us honestly, without flinching from it.'

'Courage,' muttered Mercy. 'That's – something.'

'A great thing. Rare.'

Mercy closed her eyes.

'Goodnight,' Catherine whispered, kissing her.

In the cloister, snow was beginning to settle under the arches. Catherine walked quickly, hugging her waist inside her cloak. She had singled out a virtue and made a present of it to the dying Mercy, she remembered, and wondered if she could summon a sufficient measure of it herself.

By morning, the snow lay thickly. On their way to chapel the sisters hurried through dark corridors, clutching their cloaks closely round them. Prayers were offered in voices thick and cracking, yawns stifled behind clasped hands. After the service they shuffled and pressed through the doorway, nerving themselves to face the working day.

There was a small commotion.

'Excuse me.'

'Do you mind?'

'I do as a matter of fact. One of my lay sisters is in bed with flu.'

The last speaker was Sister Mary John, the senior herdswoman. 'I'll come and give you a hand,' called Catherine.

Margaret caught her arm. 'Here is one aspect of our religious observance you might usefully attend to – if that is to be your province. This shuffling in and rushing out of chapel is quite disgraceful.'

'Um— Look, I must go and give a hand with the milking. They're short-staffed this morning.' She was glad of the excuse. Her spirits always rose at the prospect of a few hours in the cowshed. In the cloakroom she hitched up her skirt and pulled on wellington boots and a waterproof cape. Then she set off through the snow.

Steam hung over manure mounds in the yard, making the first light ghostly. Reeking ammonia cut the air.

'Oh, Sister Catherine!' said a lay sister. (There were many lay sisters attached to the priory, specialist workers whose freedom from spiritual obligations allowed work to continue without interruption.)

'Right. What do you want me to do?'

The lay sister was embarrassed; she had expected more lowly assistance. (Sister Catherine had often tended the cows, she would set her hand to anything, but now she was directrix.) 'Sister Mary John,' she called.

Mary John removed her head from a cow's belly. 'There's the hay to be put out, and the sluicing.'

A cowshed is the cosiest place, Catherine thought, pitching hay into mangers, shaking each forkful to make it airy and appetizing. Dust flew, heady-sweet, mingling with the milk smell and the pungent steam from the cattle. The throb of machinery and the cows' munching were steady as heartbeats beneath the clanging and spattering and swishing. She tossed pailfuls of water across the floor and drove the broom in sharp thrusts, taking pleasure in her working limbs. She rested briefly on a bale of hay, and a tabby cat came mewing and wove between her ankles. She caught it up, tucked its head under her chin, played its tail through her fingers; its contentment reverberated against her throat.

Afterwards, she did not go with the others to breakfast, but set out along the broad tree-lined path to the woods.

The way ahead rose steeply. Here and there, spray misted through the trees like isolated snowstorms and small avalanches of sun-warmed snow fell in thick clumps from the highest branches. A mass of snow struck her shoulder and splintered softly over her cape. When she passed through the wood, snow beat spasmodically on her head like the patting of friendly hands.

Soon she came to a wicker gate. She let herself through, and entered a meadow – a sea of snow, its surface gleaming with crystals. She hesitated, reluctant to mark the flawless expanse, but then scrunched briskly across to a five-bar gate, swept snow from the highest rung, climbed up and sat down.

To her left, the priory lay spread in the valley, its ancient stones yellow-warm against the whiteness, its twisted chimneys grouped like conspirators about the gleaming roofs. From the old chapel rose the famous tower with its famous statue of Our Lady of Albion, snow-capped this morning and dazzling in the sunlight. The place was beautiful, she thought, and Margaret's passion to save it commendable.

Her eyes watered. She lowered her head, and a wave of the previous night's misery rose in her, stale as a shameful dream. The thought came that her pride had been hurt. And maybe because of this she had sensed ill in Margaret where none existed.

Across the meadow, her footmarks came to meet her. She sprang down and began to make the returning set with clean, strong strides.

4

In the sewing room, Sister Cecilia put down her work, pressed together the tips of her long fingers and sighed: signals that she was about to speak and anticipated attention.

Sister Monica turned from the tapestry frame and peered over her half-moon spectacles, and Sisters Anne and Elizabeth, who continued to wrestle with a completed tapestry they were stretching over damp cloths on the floor, managed to convey nevertheless that they were all ears.

'I do wonder whether the Reverend Mother has done the right thing.'

'But you agreed with it, Cecilia. You voted that Sister Margaret be allowed to get on with it.' (At the mention of Margaret, Cecilia raised her fine eyebrows and screwed up her papery face.) 'Whereas I had the good sense to abstain,' Monica added triumphantly.

'My thinking was: after such a catalogue of woe, let the gel do what has to be done and then we can get back to normal and have Catherine as directrix as we always supposed. That is why I gave the proposal my blessing. However, I have misgivings, I must confess.'

'At least the Reverend Mother forbore to name her successor.' The clarity of Anne's observation was hindered by teeth clenching a drawing pin. 'By the time she gets round to it, Sister Margaret, one fervently trusts, will have outlived her usefulness.'

'Oh, there's no question of *that* one for the succession,' Cecilia said with an air of being privy to

Authority's thinking. And her friends accepted this implication, for it went without saying that no-one did anything at Albion Priory without first consulting Cecilia. One of her ancestors had founded the community; bequests from later ancestors were a source of support; a great-aunt had once been prioress; indeed, the present prioress was a childhood friend of Cecilia's mother, and Mercy, who had been chosen to succeed her, was a distant cousin. Cecilia, though technically without power, had high status in the priory; she was a receiver of confidences and very generous with her advice. Generally, Cecilia and her intimates were not resented for always knowing best. Their very loftiness, it was felt, preserved them from the self-interested manoeuvrings that detracted from the weight of lesser sisters. Those whom they took up flourished, and from her days as a novice Catherine had been their particular pet. 'Mercy, then Catherine,' they had decided with regard to the succession. But Mercy, it now appeared, had sadly let them down.

'Well, it's done now. Let's hope this gel Margaret really does know her stuff. Veronica seems to think she does,' said Monica, turning again to her tapestry frame.

'Sister Veronica is inclined to take too much on herself these days. And I fear she has a tendency to get things out of proportion.'

'Speaking of things out of proportion: have you seen the way Our Lady is leaning from the tower? I happened to look up yesterday as I came through the courtyard, and she gave me quite a turn. For a moment I thought she was about to topple down. It really is shocking, you know. A bit of a gale—'

'Yes, they ought to do something about the tower.'

'Not to mention the east wing. Those poor creatures who have to live in there— None of their doors fit. The draughts are lethal. I don't know; things really are in a bad way.'

Cecilia hugged her spare body. 'So long as they maintain the boiler. I nearly died when it broke down last winter. I can stand most things, but not the cold.'

'Oh, I'm the same. Starve me, deprive me of every convenience, but please not the heating,' cried Monica with the complacency of one who expects to retain all her comforts.

'I do so agree,' said Elizabeth. 'Food I can cheerfully do without, but warmth is essential. Anne, if I pull here, can you stick in a pin between my hands?'

With a sigh, Cecilia took up her embroidery ring. But then she recollected the point she had been leading to. 'It was something Catherine said in her speech. More of an impression I gained, really. I wonder. Is it possible that Sister Margaret is a bit of a bully?'

'A bully?'

'Oh, surely—'

'Well, we'll have to watch out. We can't have her pushing the poor things about.'

'Certainly not. The lay sisters, for instance; they do such splendid work.'

'A thoroughly decent bunch of women.'

'We must ensure their position is safeguarded in all this. After all, they have no say—'

'But they've got *us* to speak for them. We've always dealt with that sort of thing.'

'And there's Catherine.'

'Of course. Things can't go far wrong with dear Catherine as directrix.'

They lapsed into a comfortable silence, which was eventually broken by a squabble between the tapestry stretchers whose knees and backs had begun to ache and whose thumbs, violently imprinted with the tops of drawing pins, were by now very sore.

'Drat,' said Elizabeth, shuffling sideways and getting caught up in her skirt.

'Elizabeth,' tutted Cecilia.

Anne was cross. 'You've wrinkled it. Really. I'd just got that bit straight.'

'Well, if you'd stop hogging the pin box—'

'And if you weren't so clumsy—'

'Sisters, Sisters. The novices may come in at any moment.'

But when the door opened it was Margaret who came in, followed by Agnes carrying clipboard and pen.

'The sewing room,' Margaret announced, and proceeded to a thorough examination.

'Good afternoon,' Cecilia said severely. But Margaret appeared not to hear. Her eyes lighted on a pile of folded silk, and she darted forward.

'This, I take it, is the altar frontal commissioned by Devereux Abbey?'

Monica agreed that it was.

'And you are presently engaged on—?'

'Oh,' Monica said airily, 'this is a piece I'm doing for myself. Frightfully tricky, actually.'

Margaret walked over to the tapestry stretchers. 'And what is this?'

'It's for the refectory. Reverend Mother thought it would cover that awful crack.' Elizabeth put her head on one side. 'We think it's turned out rather well.'

Margaret and Agnes moved to the window, each talking exclusively to the other.

'This is what we're up against. There are probably plenty of commissions to be had if only they'd get a move on.'

'Of course, the tapestry for the refectory's a good idea – once the plaster's been attended to. We could do with lots more about the place, great big ones, they're so impressive.' Margaret looked over her shoulder and enquired: 'Where are the other needleworkers this afternoon?'

'Well you see, we can't get on with the altar frontal

30

because we're waiting for more of that gold thread,' explained Monica. 'So they've gorn orff somewhere—'

'Leaving you four with a cosy little setup of your own, eh?' Agnes suggested rudely. She turned back to Margaret. 'What they *do* is all right; it's very good by all accounts. The trouble is, they lack direction. We're coming up against that time and again. Every area needs someone in overall control.'

'Mmm.' Margaret began to pace about. She came to rest beside a tapestry frame and leaned her arm along it. 'You see,' she told the needleworkers patiently, 'this area of work will be expanded. We anticipate many, many orders for vestments and altar frontals. And our own priory requires a great deal of embellishment. So you'll have to take on more help. Don't worry, you'll have plenty of people to choose from; several other areas of work are closing down. Now, do you think you can deal with that?' Since they remained silent, she addressed her further thoughts to Agnes, and together they moved towards the door. 'The first priority here is to put somone in charge.'

'Certainly. And that applies everywhere. We'll have to sort out some suitable people.' Agnes pulled the door open.

'*Our* sort of people,' murmured Margaret, sweeping through to the hall.

For a time the sewing room was still and silent. Eventually, without stirring, Monica said in a small voice, 'Did someone say something about her being a bully?'

Cecilia could not at once respond. It was being suggested, she slowly grasped, that *they* – not the lay sisters or the humbler *religieuses*, but *they*, members of *their set* – might be susceptible to bullying. 'Don't be vulgar,' she snapped.

*   *   *

Apart from the light in the organ loft, the chapel was in darkness. Catherine ran up a flight of stone stairs and slipped on to the end of the organ bench. 'Sorry I'm late.'

Angelica smiled and played on. The fugue went ponderously on solid diapason.

Watching the music, Catherine waited for the start of a new episode and just before it began leaned forward and smartly changed the stops. Now the sound was thin and high like the toy piping of a merry-go-round. The fugue began to build and Catherine pulled new voices into play: a round tone, a reedy tone, a low growling in the bass. For the valedictory statement she organized a blaze of sound, and when Angelica released the final chord it hung for a second among the rafters.

'Oh, John Sebastian—'

'The lovely man,' Angelica agreed. She studied her friend. 'You look happier.'

'I think I am. I've had a good discussion with Margaret. Perhaps I've misjudged her. She listened carefully to everything I said, seemed to appreciate my anxieties and assured me she wants us to work closely together. We decided that I'd be responsible for our religious observance. Of course, she's absolutely correct about the need for action. I'm determined to be constructive, Angelica. I'm determined to get on with her so things are put right without hurting people.'

'You have changed your tune.'

'To be fair, many of her criticisms are justified. Not just about the general decay, but about our slipshod behaviour. Take for instance the way we all push and shove through the door after morning prayer. And the way we leave the clergy to wander in. The Reverend Mother used to make quite a ceremony of receiving them and bringing them into chapel.'

'It's her sciatica, poor thing.'

'I know. But one of us could do it. Look, I realize Margaret's got an eye to the impression we'll make on all these hoped-for visitors, but even when no-one is there to see, we ought to behave respectfully.'

Angelica began to search through sheets of music. 'Well, I'm glad you're feeling happier. But Sister Cecilia is most unhappy, let me tell you. Apparently, Margaret and Agnes burst into the sewing room this afternoon and started throwing their weight around. Cecilia and co. were not amused.'

They laughed. Angelica propped up a piece of music. 'Here's the solo I had in mind for you.' She began to play. Catherine, following the notation, listened and hummed. After a time she sprang to her feet. 'Let's try it.'

'*As the hart pants for the waterbrooks, so longeth my soul for Thee,*' sang Catherine, her voice soft and intense over the beating hum of the organ, bell-like when the melody rose from its chordal bed.

A nun hurrying through the cloister below paused to listen. She was still there, motionless in the moonlight, when silence came.

5

In the gleam from an unshaded light bulb, Sister Hope sat tensely on the edge of her bed, hands pressed between serge-covered knees, eyes fixed to a spot on the floor, ears straining. Her pounding heart made her feel feverish. She shivered, and the involuntary movement unfixed her eyes; they slid towards the uncurtained window, but the diamond panes of navy-blue glass revealed nothing.

Minutes passed. She again studied the floorboards. Then all at once she knew – though there was no light outside other than pale reflection off the snow – that a figure had clouded the window glass. She prepared to look towards it, urging herself not to start when she did so. Slowly her head rose, slowly turned; but despite the check she had put on herself, her heart leapt and her mouth flew open.

On the other side of the window Beatrice grinned and thought what a simple matter it was to rouse pathetic little Hope to a state of terror.

Hope rose to her feet. A hulking head and shoulders filled the window space. She took a step towards it and saw a face – Beatrice's face – grinning at her steadily.

Hope undid the buttons of her robe. She untied the knot of her girdle. The girdle dropped to the floor; the robe, freed from her slight body, hung straight and loose. She pushed the robe over her shoulders and down over her arms and let it fall to her ankles. Next she loosened her coif, then snatched off coif and veil in a single movement. Standing in her shift, Hope raised hands to her head and explored her clumpy hair. Her hair felt longer; there were now five or six inches of growth, though it was still nowhere near as long as Beatrice's. She shook her head to loosen it and plunged her fingers through its silkiness.

When Hope looked up, Beatrice had gone. She closed the curtains, and went to the switch by the door and turned off the light.

.

'Where the dickens is Beatrice?' thundered Margaret. 'It's too bad of her. Joan has come up with a marvellous scheme and I want us all to hear about it. Well, we can't wait for Beatrice all night. So welcome, Sisters Veronica, Clare and Imogen, to our little group. Agnes will take notes, but our meeting is quite informal; it's an opportunity to try out ideas on one another, and to spark off new ideas. Joan's brainwave, for example. Will you tell them, Joan, or shall I? Well, put simply, we sell the dairy herd. You see, to operate profitably the dairy operation would need to expand; which would require heavy investment; which would mean running the dairy at the expense of other less capital-needy undertakings. Hardly a sensible option, I'm sure you'll agree. And quite frankly, dairying on a large scale is not an appropriate venture for our community. Joan proposes therefore that we sell off the herd and realize a useful capital sum; but – and here comes the brilliant part – we let the pasture and cowsheds to the buyer for rent. In other words, we continue to derive income. And I'm pleased to report that we have already had some enquiries. Marvellous work, Joan. Now, Agnes: you were looking for means of improving the guests' accommodation.'

Agnes scowled and drove the point of her pencil along a groove in the tabletop. 'Haven't had time. I've been stuck on confounded room offices all week. I don't know who was supposed to clean this corridor last, but they didn't pull the beds out. There was dust half an inch thick.'

One of the sisters tutted sympathetically, otherwise there was silence.

When Margaret spoke, her voice was low and exasperated. 'This is *nonsense*.' She looked from one to the other. 'Don't you see? It's *sheer lunacy*. Inefficient. A waste of resources. You can't have someone like Agnes sweeping out rooms, clearing up after people who— Well!' She shrugged and left it to their imagination. 'These archaic practices stifle initiative.'

'It's supposed to be valuable,' Veronica pointed out. 'I mean, Jesus washed the disciples' feet—'

'Correct me if I'm wrong,' Margaret said kindly, 'but I don't think Our Lord made a habit of it. It was just the one occasion, I believe.'

Agnes chortled.

Joan craned forward. 'I think Margaret has a valid point. There are plenty of people who can do the cleaning, but only a few with the intelligence and imagination to make this place viable.'

'And as people become more productive and more specialist – the needleworkers and artists, for example – they simply won't have time for domestic chores. I can see we have a job of education to do. We must try to get as many people as possible on our side before a formal proposal is put to Council. Agreed? Right. Next I want Beatrice to tell us— Oh, confound the woman! Where the dickens is she?'

Beatrice lay with Hope on Hope's narrow bed. Their bodies and Beatrice's streaming fair hair were silvered by a ghostly glow coming through the curtain crack. All else was in darkness. They were perfectly still now, drifting towards sleep.

Presently Beatrice stirred and shifted her arm on which Hope was lying and which had become numb. They rearranged themselves and settled comfortably. But Hope's eyes remained open, staring into the dark. Soon fears and horrors began their familiar chase through her mind.

'What's the matter now?'

Hope stuffed a fist in her mouth.

'Can't make you out,' mused Beatrice. 'I mean, you expected me this evening, you'd have been pretty disappointed if I hadn't shown up. You were waiting for me, I saw you. So why for heaven's sake did you jump out of your skin? For a nasty moment I thought you were going to yell out. I nipped straight down the corridor and into your room and blow me if you didn't start jumping and trembling all over again. Beats me. If I hadn't shown, you'd have sulked for days. Admit it.'

'I know,' moaned Hope. But inside she was gloating. Fat chance of Beatrice not turning up, she thought. Beatrice couldn't resist her. She pictured herself, weak and fearful, drawing powerful Beatrice to her bed. It was a potent combination, her drawing power and her helplessness. And Beatrice, she recalled, had become more powerful than ever since Margaret's elevation. Margaret— A new thrill formed hazily. She fluttered her fingers over Beatrice's stomach. 'You know, I've a feeling Margaret likes me.'

'Margaret?' Beatrice frowned. 'I'd be surprised if Margaret's more than vaguely aware of your existence. Oh, I get it,' she laughed. 'But I shouldn't bother. You're barking up the wrong tree there.'

'I wasn't— Oh, you are horrid. What do you take me for? You're the one who's— I was totally innocent before you—'

'Aw, shut up, Hopeless.'

Hope started snivelling. 'If you knew what I go through. My stomach leaping, my heart going mad—'

'But what *at*, for heaven's sake?'

'Anything. Nothing.' She thought for a moment, then whispered: 'Things.'

'What things?'

'Sudden things. Shadowy things. Oh, I don't know. Things that are ordinary to most people I can have a horror of. Don't ask me why. Sometimes I have this nightmare—'

'Go on, you can tell me.'

'Can I?'

'Course you can.' Beatrice made a cooing sound, breathing languorously over Hope's face. 'Tell me.'

'Well, I'm shut in this room; there's a sudden scuttling and a, a *thing* runs over my foot.'

'You mean a—'

Hope clamped a hand over Beatrice's mouth. 'Don't say it,' she cried.

'A *mouse*?' got out Beatrice disbelievingly.

With a scream, Hope shot forward into a ball.

'Shh, idiot. Do you mean you've got some sort of phobia?'

'I don't know. But in the dream I'm so terrified I fling myself out of the window. Once something like it really happened. I had to go to the shed for potatoes and— No, I can't tell you. But I screamed and ran and screamed and ran and—'

'Shh, take it easy. Fancy being frightened like that, you poor duffer. Come here.' She pulled Hope back into her arms and smiled contemptuously into the dark.

6

The Prioress pushed her teacup to one side. 'I know nothing of the sort.'

'That's because you've cut yourself off,' said Cecilia serenely. 'If you would leave your room for longer than it takes to attend chapel, if you would sometimes come to the refectory, if you would just stand about and *talk* instead of hurrying back to your room at the earliest opportunity, you would discover what I say to be true. People are quite wretched.'

The Prioress recalled that even Cecilia's mother had at times found Cecilia hard to bear. Her placid assumption of speaking for all sensible folk was enormously irritating. 'I dare say some of them are disaffected by all these changes.'

'There have been too many changes, far too quickly, without – and this is the burden of my complaint – proper consideration for people's feelings. Take, for instance, the sisters who ran the dairy. They've been deprived of their role and are now merely at the beck and call of the bullies. And it's no use sniffing: if you don't care for the word you should come and watch that officious Sister Imogen giving her orders. Imagine it: Sister Mary John, a respected senior sister, obliged to report daily to that sourpuss Imogen. Told to clean up after everyone else because we no longer take our turn to do the offices. It's outrageous. And because there is now no dairy interest to be represented on Council, these sisters have lost their ability to speak up for themselves. They're not likely to get it back, either.

Apparently, there are to be no new regular jobs. Something to do with *freeing resources*, which seems to mean they are free to do the skivvying.'

'I dare say something'll be done for 'em. Rome wasn't built in a day.'

'The gardeners are in the same predicament. Their numbers have been drastically cut. From now on there'll just be the flower gardens and enough vegetables grown for the house. Such a pity. People came from miles around to buy Albion Reds, and Sister Martha's Purple Wonder—'

'Didn't pay. None of it paid, I gather. Besides, potatoes and purple sprouting don't convey the right image.'

'Image? What do you mean *image*?'

But the Prioress was not entirely sure. It was the word Margaret had used when she attempted to explain why bee-keeping, though not strictly profitable, was to continue whereas cow-keeping and the more robust forms of horticulture were to cease. 'You'll have to ask Margaret. I haven't time to go into the technicalities.'

'Hmm. Well, Sister Martha is making a terrible fuss. And have you heard the rumour about a plan to convert the east wing into accommodation for all these new paying guests they hope to attract? They won't get away with it. There's tremendous feeling. The lay sisters have always lived in the east wing.'

'I suppose they can live somewhere else?'

'As far as I know there's no indication where the poor things might live. That's the trouble. These people do as they please and damn the consequences for those who are discommoded. I think you must do something Reverend Mother. You must put your foot down before things get worse.'

The Prioress looked bleakly into her empty teacup. She was not entirely out of touch, she reflected, thinking of the sisters who had recently visited her sitting room. Some of these had lavished praise on the new regime. This very morning Sister Veronica, seated in the chair in which Cecilia now sat, had given a confident account of the latest financial situation. Even Elizabeth, having first secured the Prioress's promise not to breathe a word of it to Cecilia, had expressed great satisfaction with the achievements of her newly expanded needlework department. On the other hand, the Prioress had glimpsed that good soul Sister Mary John wiping tears from her eyes during vespers, and Catherine's strained face (paler than ever with bruised wells under her eyes) warned her of worry and trouble abroad. Catherine had already confided all that Cecilia now conveyed, though she had fallen over her words in a scrupulous attempt to be fair to Margaret. Well, Catherine had been accorded an equal share of authority. It was up to Catherine to fight her corner. The Prioress wagged her head vehemently and thought it too bad that, having made an arrangement calculated to achieve the best of all worlds, still more was expected of her. For she was tired, quite beyond it—

'Are you in pain, Reverend Mother?'

The Prioress scowled. Did the idiot imagine it a painless condition to be twisted and bent as an old hawthorn?

'Some fresh air might buck you up; it's awfully stuffy in here. Come outside for a while, take a turn round the cloister. Do come. It's spring.'

'The air's still sharp.'

'No, no, it's quite mild today. I'll go and fetch Monica. She and I will take an arm each, then you'll feel perfectly safe.'

The Prioress summoned a picture of herself shuffling round the cloister between Monica and Cecilia, and decided she did not care for it. 'Not today, I think.'

'Dear, dear. Will you come and see Mercy, then?

41

Apparently, she's a little bit brighter. Sister Luke said she sat in a chair for over an hour yesterday.'

'I don't suppose it'll last,' the Prioress sighed.

Mornings were the worst, thought Sister Mary John as she knelt in her pew. By evening, fatigue permitted the comfort of a few weak tears. Impossible to weep in the harsh void of early morning when desolation gripped her, and her body functioned in a state of shock so that her movements were slow and her breathing laboured. In the days before the blow had fallen, her thoughts had been no more engaged by the early morning service than they were today; they would slip to the task ahead, to the medication she must prepare for a cow with mastitis, to the cart she must despatch to the barn for fresh hay. Recalling such thoughts now, she saw they'd been those of a satisfied woman. It had not occurred to her to treasure the mundane routine of her life. But she should have done, oh, she should.

Morning prayer proceeded, and the half-heard familiar canticles, working treacherously on Mary John's mind, conjured a lost world. With a sense of craving she recalled the touch of warm creatures. Throughout her life there had been some animal at hand, to stroke and fondle and melt life's troubles away. As a child she had nursed her cat by the fire, she'd curled up with the dog basking on the doorstep. Cats, dogs, cows, taking life as they found it, showing contentment with the fire, the sun, the hay, had drawn her into a stream of well-being never seriously penetrated by hardships and irritations. Whatever the calamity, she'd had only to put out her hand and know that life was fundamentally good.

Perhaps her worst moment had come when the herd's new owners experienced staffing problems. The community could assist, Sister Joan had decreed (for a price, of course). But only the lay sisters had been directed there. Religious sisters were to concern themselves solely with matters endorsed by the new regime. The memory of her dashed hope returned so sharply that she was obliged to clutch the prayer book ledge for support. And she noticed then that the pews were almost empty, the service over.

She struggled to her feet. Sister Imogen would make life even more uncomfortable if she were late reporting for her allotted office of the day.

A hand on her arm detained her. Looking up, she met the eyes of Sister Catherine. For some seconds they held the other's glance.

'Are you all right, Sister?'

Mary John could not reply. She disengaged and hurried from the chapel.

Catherine watched her go, then ran up the steps to the organ loft. 'Got pencil and paper?' she asked Angelica, who was putting sheets of music away in a cupboard. Angelica produced these items. 'Thanks. Now, about this afternoon's meeting.' Her voice was fierce. 'This time it's clear a majority of sisters are on our side. But we won't take chances. We'll play it their way and do a canvass. So let's make a list, put down every single sister who might support us. Because over the east wing issue, I'm determined we're going to win.'

Beatrice was the last to arrive in Agnes's room. She closed the door and leaned her back against it. Just the four of us, she thought; new friends not invited. The reason was clear: having this afternoon suffered their first setback, they wished to lick their wounds in private. Beatrice looked from one to the other, noting how their bodily attitudes gave them away. Joan's

43

posture – she was sitting forward with her head in her hands, her fingers stiff and outspread – seemed to bewail how impossible life was; that however neat the idea, human beings would always muck it up. Agnes was hunched over her desk, writing up notes and bearing too hard on her pencil. Her free hand was clenched as if, thought Beatrice, Agnes ached for a scrap.

Margaret was angry – though only someone who knew her well would guess it. She sat primly on the edge of the bed with her knees and ankles together and her hands folded in her lap. But her brows bulged and her eyes darted. She was going over it, Beatrice knew, recalling every word uttered at the meeting, on the lookout for a loophole that might yet yield advantage.

Beatrice, who secretly didn't give a fig whether they won or lost, who had allied herself with the group out of boredom, sensing in their schemes a coming drama and the chance of a thrill, stepped forward and snapped her fingers. 'It was a hitch, that's all. Keep a sense of proportion.'

'But we'd only just begun,' Joan moaned.

'Dear me. Talk about defeatism.'

'Quite right, Beatrice,' said Margaret, visibly rousing herself. 'We can't be diverted by one setback. No, I've been thinking. The matter of the east wing: we'll let it drop for the time being.'

'We can't, you know. The roof leaks, the timbers are full of rot,' Agnes pointed out. 'The only question is: do we patch it up for the lay sisters or completely refurbish it for paying guests? The decision may have gone against us, but something still has to be done.'

'I said, let it drop.'

Agnes, Joan and Beatrice stared at Margaret.

'Let 'em stew for a bit,' she told them.

Evidently conceding that Margaret's thinking had

44

jumped ahead of her own, Agnes shrugged. 'Right you are. Actually, in my own mind I *had* let it drop. I'm more concerned with the mechanics of the thing, trying to work out what went wrong for us this afternoon.'

'I think it was the majority voting against us,' mocked Beatrice mildly.

Agnes briefly closed her eyes and then continued. 'I doubt whether we've ever commanded a majority of opinion. We've simply made the better job of presenting our case. No, the new thing, the thing that went wrong for us today, is the opposition's woken up. They've taken a leaf out of our book. Catherine and Angelica were canvassing in the refectory earlier, you know. They're going to be less of a pushover in future.'

'And some of the young ones are quite bolshie. Yes, we've got a problem. We must all *think*,' said Margaret, her glare indicating the ferocious degree of thinking required. And Agnes, wanting to advance the thinking along the right lines, reminded them:

'What we need is a way of controlling opinion.'

Beatrice sighed, pulled a pillow from the bed, threw it to the floor and arranged herself, stomach down, on top of it. After a time she sat up and announced that she might have something. The trouble with Council, she pointed out, was their inability to control it. So why not establish regular open meetings for the whole priory: ostensibly as briefing meetings to explain what was going on, what the aims were of each innovation and so on, but with the primary purpose of presenting each new plan in the best possible light. Their own people could be planted strategically in the audience, briefed beforehand to ask helpful questions, coached in the proper reaction to criticism and shown how to encourage support for the right line. If the need arose they could divert attention to side issues. The point was, they would be in control and Catherine always on the defensive. And Council, of course, would then feel constrained to bow to popular opinion—

'Brilliant,' cut in Margaret, who had been sitting very still and listening intently. 'It's the perfect answer. Just what we need.'

Joan sighed. 'I don't know how you do it, Beatrice. Again and again you come up with amazing schemes.'

'Thanks,' said Beatrice.

'Of course, the thinking behind these open meetings must remain entirely *entre nous*,' Margaret warned. 'Though we take our people aside from time to time and explain what is required, we must deal with them singly and in the strictest confidence; none but we four must know the thing is stage-managed. You know, it's a wonderfully fertile idea. It widens our scope considerably. We could drop suggestions about certain people—'

'Oh yes, we can cook Catherine's goose,' said Agnes.

Margaret bounced to her feet. 'I'm going to leave it to you' – she waved a hand towards Agnes and Joan – 'to work out the details; what to call the meetings, how often to hold them, and so on.' She turned to Beatrice. 'Come along. I need some exercise. Let's take a walk.'

Catherine and Angelica came running down the path from the wood. They leaned into the wind which held them like firm hands till it dropped suddenly, sending them staggering and laughing. 'What?' yelled Catherine, seeing her friend shout. But nothing could be heard above the wind's rush and the flapping of their streaming veils.

Behind a tall yew hedge bordering the garden, they found shelter. Panting, searching in their pockets for handkerchiefs to mop dripping eyes and noses, they flopped on an iron seat and spread their legs out straight. The blustering wind had added zest to their excitement following the afternoon's success. Now they basked in the sun and thought how good it was that right and reason had prevailed, and how amazing that they had ever doubted it. The dislocation of the last few months could now be viewed in perspective: simply, an over-reaction to the alarming financial situation. Catherine even allowed that Margaret's new broom had worked to some good effect, but from now on, she promised, its sweepings would be inspected to ensure people's feelings weren't cast aside. There would be no more innovations unless they were accompanied by mitigating measures.

Angelica was still savouring their victory. 'The best moment was afterwards, when that group of young sisters came up and grabbed our hands. I'd always thought there were people who felt as we did, but I hadn't understood how passionately.'

'It surprised me, too. After all, a lot of people have done well out of the changes. They love not having to take their turn with the chores. Being waited on makes them feel valuable and important. I'd begun to dread that people's support would depend on whether they stood to lose or gain.'

'That's hardly fair. Take Sister Cecilia—'

'I know. Even so, Cecilia may have done well as a needleworker, but in terms of prestige you could count her as a loser with Elizabeth now in charge of the sewing room.'

'You've become cynical, Catherine.'

'This afternoon they proved me wrong. I happily admit it. No-one had a thing to gain by sticking up for the lay sisters.'

In another part of the garden, Beatrice and Margaret were battling with the wind.

'This weather alarms me,' shouted Margaret. 'I wish

we had the money to go ahead with the tower.'

'What?'

'The tower. We must make it a priority. It'd be a tragedy if the statue came down.'

'Don't worry, I fixed it. Roped Our Lady to the buttresses.'

Margaret came to a halt. 'You went up onto the top of the tower?'

'Good job I did, eh? This wind.'

'But the tower's unsafe,' screeched Margaret.

'Make up your mind. You said the statue's of paramount importance. A symbol of the priory.'

'So it is. But let others see to it. You're indispensable. What an idiot thing to do, Beatrice.'

Beatrice grinned, showing her even white teeth. And Margaret's wrath dissolved. She thought what a charmer Beatrice was, and suddenly the reason for Agnes's nasty little hints came to her. The woman was jealous, being herself so frightfully plain. In the middle of being put out over another matter, Margaret was pleased nevertheless to mentally tick off this item. 'It was rather splendid of you,' she called forgivingly. 'But don't ever do such a risky thing again.'

Grinning to herself, Beatrice went charging ahead. Rounding a corner, she spotted Catherine and Angelica on a garden seat. She waited for Margaret to catch up. 'The opposition's over there,' she warned. 'Want to take a different route?'

Margaret hesitated, but then walked briskly forward. 'Just the person,' she called. 'Sister Angelica.'

So full of embarrassed surprise was Catherine at the approach of her adversary – her vanquished adversary, she endeavoured to recall, inwardly shrinking before the eagerly inclined head, the avid blue eyes and the china complexion wind-whipped to rosiness – that some moments elapsed before she made sense of what Margaret was saying.

'These endless arguments put it clean out of my head, but I've been meaning to suggest it ever since evensong on Sunday. Tell me, what was that delightful piece you played at the end?'

'Oh, the Fauré—'

'*Mar*vellous. Well, it came to me then that an organ recital after Sunday evensong would be just the thing for our visitors' programme. What do you think? You could plan a series of recitals in advance. Sister Prudence could make some programmes with a few notes about the music and so on.'

Going red in the face, Angelica got out that she thought it an interesting idea and wondered if Sister Catherine agreed.

'Absolutely.'

'And Sister Catherine, of course, has such a fine singing voice,' Margaret informed Beatrice: Beatrice, who knew this already, said nothing but continued to smile amiably. 'One does hope that all the argument and debate we seem stuck with lately doesn't overtax it. Perhaps Sister Catherine should sing a solo at some point during the recital? I'll leave it with you, Sister Angelica. Draw something up and let Sister Beatrice have it.'

She and Beatrice continued their walk.

Too late now for the clever, softly spoken phrase to put them on an equal footing, thought Catherine, furious with herself.

'What do you make of that?' asked Angelica.

'She's recognized what a good musician you are.'

'It was sporting of her, wasn't it? I mean, she didn't have to come over, never mind say something nice.'

'Truly magnanimous.'

'I must say, I'm attracted to the idea.'

'So am I,' said Catherine, smiling brightly to prevent her friend guessing that her newly found confidence had unaccountably taken a blow.

7

In the top greenhouse, Sister Martha (she of Purple Wonder fame) was busy propagating *Begonia rex* from leaf cuttings. She was ruefully observed from the potting shed doorway by Sister Lazarus. (The name 'Lazarus' was a mark of gratitude to God who had restored her after a debilitating illness.) By tradition these two sisters were close friends, Martha the senior vegetable grower and Lazarus the chief flower gardener. But when vegetable growing on a large scale ceased and Martha became redundant, their friendship entered a testing phase, for Martha refused point-blank (and there was an immovable quality about Martha) to consider any occupation save gardening, and it was not unnaturally assumed that her services would be welcome in the extended flower garden. Unfortunately, Martha had grown accustomed to directing others and reserving her own energy for the more interesting tasks. And herein lay a difficulty, for the propagation of *Begonia rex* was one of Sister Lazarus's joys; it was a treat she saved up for herself during the June rush with rose and lily spraying, with bulb lifting and staking out and weeding in the borders.

It's not that we don't need extra help, but that Martha's the wrong sort. We need more strong girls to weed, rake and mow, Lazarus told a faceless, imaginary friend, aware that the friend in whom she would normally confide was the very subject of her complaint. Lazarus bit her lip and returned to the bulbs that needed cleaning and storing and stacking in trays.

Taking a razor blade, Martha severed a prominent vein junction on the underside of a large leaf. She worked slowly and deliberately, making an arc of judicious cuts, then pinned the leaf with half-hoops of wire onto a dish of peat and sand. In her mind's eye arose a specimen of *Begonia rex* hitherto unknown, its leaves spotted orange and silver. Sister Martha's Spotted Beauty, perhaps? She was full of optimism as she sliced and pinned; her rage at the slighting of the Purple Wonder only dimly and infrequently recalled. For that's me all over, she liked to tell herself whenever she thought about it: quick to blow up, but quick to calm down, and then there's no-one in the world more easygoing. Not that she was ashamed of her outburst and refusal to work anywhere but the flower garden. Not likely. Catch her eating humble pie and meekly going wherever Sister Imogen had it in mind to send her. Like poor old Mary John, for instance. But Sister Mary John was an idiot. She, too, should have taken a stand.

All in all, thought Martha, things had turned out well. It was companionable working with Lazarus, and the flower gardens were beautifully sheltered, unlike the exposed acres where Purple Wonders were sown. 'Oh, it's you, Laz,' she said, looking up as some-one opened the greenhouse door. 'I thought it might be the lass wi' the coffee. What's up wi' 'em, this morning, d'you reckon? We had to stand kicking us heels waiting for breakfast, and now there's no elevenses. It's all right for them inside, helping theirselves whenever they feel like it, but for us stuck out here working in all weathers, well, yer get peckish—'

Martha settled into sprightly Us and Them talk, while Lazarus, who usually supplied the Mmm and I'll Say accompaniment to this theme that had so de-liciously bonded them over the years, remained silent. Lazarus ran her eyes over spilled peat and sand, over tools encrusted with old dirt, over a coffee mug with a ring round its inside and soily fingermarks and dried-on drips on its outside, and asked herself how any gardener could behave so uncleanly in a greenhouse where pests and infections were a constant hazard. She tried to recall the state of the vegetable greenhouses, and then remembered that Martha had always wandered down to the shelter of the flower gardens for one of their chats. *And then I cleared up after her*, recalled Lazarus, picturing herself carrying two dirty coffee mugs back to the house.

'I came in to ask if you'd mind giving Sister Barbara a hand with the weeding,' Lazarus suddenly blurted.

Interrupted in full flow, Martha blinked and said reproachfully, 'But I'm busy in here. I'm doing the *Begonia rex* for you. Anyway, I couldn't face all that stooping today,' she added with a certain look to indicate a certain condition.

Prickly heat broke out over Lazarus. Martha had a nerve. If anyone had a right to claim indulgence it was Lazarus. But no-one ever heard Lazarus complain, in spite of recurrent attacks of pins and needles and frightening numbness. To relieve her feelings, Lazarus reached under the bench for a dustpan and brush, vigorously swept up the spilled peat, emptied it onto waste paper and rolled this into a parcel. Then she stood, twisting and kneading the paper, and imagined herself confronting Sister Imogen with a demand that Martha be exchanged for a more compliant sister. Only – and at this point she almost dropped the parcel – how would it be if Martha put up a fight (as she surely would) and it somehow fell out that she, Lazarus, were the one removed from the garden?

'You're not listening to a word I say. What yer doing wi' that paper? What's up wi' yer this morning, Laz?'

'I need that coffee. I'll go and see what's happened to it.'

*　　*　　*

The kitchen had encountered setbacks. The place was in turmoil, and it was all due to Sister Mary John, Sister Lazarus discovered when she stepped in at the scullery door. A sister scrubbing potatoes at the sink described in breathless undertone how Sister Mary John had been clumsy from the moment she had begun work this morning. At this very moment Sister Imogen was within, deciding what was to be done with her.

It was thought, it soon became clear, that Sister Mary John would wreak less havoc outside. The chastened one came into the scullery and began to hunt for a yard broom. 'Excuse me, Laz,' she said shamefacedly to her old friend who was standing in the way.

Lazarus, seeing Sister Imogen watching from the kitchen doorway, affected an offhand manner towards Mary John, thus shielding herself from any association with that luckless sister's fallen status. 'What's happened to the coffee?' she called brightly, pretending, in Imogen's presence, to a confidence she did not feel.

'Just coming,' someone called.

'I'll take mine and Sister Martha's with me, then. Not that I'm desperate. It's Sister Martha. "Can't tackle another leaf wi'out me coffee," she declared; so I thought I'd better come for it. Got to keep the workers happy,' she added daringly. But Sister Imogen had her eyes on Sister Mary John and evidently didn't hear.

An unpleasant taste rose in Lazarus's mouth.

'Great,' said Martha, when Lazarus arrived in the greenhouse with two mugs of coffee. 'Find out what the delay were about?'

'No,' said Lazarus. She gulped her coffee and hoped it would clear the sourness from her mouth.

'Well, it's good and hot, I'll say that fer it. Couldn't half go a bicky, though. Have we got any, Laz?'

53

'No.'

'Ah well. Grateful for small— I say, I been thinking. When I've done the begonias I might try me hand wi' the African violets. Same method, after all. You can get some smashing colour variations—'

'When you've finished your coffee I'd be glad if you'd help me with the bulbs. That is, if you're still too delicate to lend a hand with the weeding.'

'I told you, Laz—'

'Right. Drink up, then. I want those bulbs finished today.'

Martha stared thoughtfully at her over her coffee mug.

After a while, Lazarus stood up and waited pointedly.

'I'll just—' began Martha.

Lazarus opened the greenhouse door. 'Come on.'

Closing the door behind them, she found her hands were trembling. A great longing for someone to talk to stole over her, as in the old days she had talked to Martha.

Margaret and Catherine were doing the rounds of the priory in the company of a surveyor. They had already studied his report; the problem now was to decide on priorities. Margaret could have done very well without this excursion, for she had already settled on the immediate restoration of the Albion Tower, but Catherine was more worried about the danger to the lay sisters in the east wing, and the surveyor was inclined to agree with her. The kitchen area, its sculleries and outhouses, also required attention, particularly in view of an anticipated influx of visitors. It was a matter of what could be afforded, Margaret reminded them whenever they paused to examine stonework, suck in their breath, and refer worriedly to the report.

Sister Mary John was sweeping the yard. She drew their eyes as they paused there to discuss the out-houses. The head of her broom refused to go neatly into a dirt-stuffed corner. Fascinated by Mary John's ineffectualness, Margaret stared and listened and detected that Catherine and the surveyor seemed already to have forgotten the requirement to bear in mind what the community could afford. She was preparing to remind them of this – for she had no shame in constantly repeating herself – when her patience snapped, and she marched forward and snatched the broom handle. 'Like *this*,' she boomed, getting down to it.

Sister Mary John seemed to shrink. Catherine watched as Margaret deftly cleared the corner and then, appearing exasperated, held out the broom for Mary John to retrieve. A look of sullen stupidity now covered the face of Mary John; the look, Catherine recalled, adopted by habitually unsuccessful school-children.

Catherine went forward, took the broom and propped it against the wall. 'Sister, I don't think you're up to this today. You need a rest. I'll finish the sweeping later. Is there anyone here who can help us?' she called towards the scullery door, and when a sister appeared drying her hands on an apron, continued, 'Take Sister to her room. Make her lie down.' To Mary John she said, 'As soon as I've finished here, I'll be along to see you,' and she squeezed her arm and pushed her gently away.

Each of Margaret's cheeks bore a bright red spot, Catherine noticed, turning again to the matter in hand. 'Now where were we?' she prompted the surveyor.

The moment she was left alone, Sister Mary John rose from her bed and went to sit in her chair by her open window. She was sitting there calmly when Catherine came in. Having got her breathing under control, she was reluctant to speak, so smiled instead and put out her hand.

'You look more like your old self,' Catherine commented, retaining the hand and kneeling on the rug beside the chair.

Quietness fell. A breeze lifted one of the curtains. In the distance, voices called.

Catherine studied the hand in her own. It was large and rough, stringy-veined and scarred; an industrious, turn-to-anything hand. It was not that Sister Mary John worked unwillingly at her present chores, she guessed, but rather that Mary John was encumbered by a heavy heart.

'Do you know, I've really missed the farmyard, the cattle and the cats. We've been so busy reconstructing this place there's been no time for normal things, like taking an evening stroll, for instance. We're missing one of our summer treats. Let's do it tonight, eh? After evensong.'

Mary John looked away.

'What's the matter?'

'I'm not sure we'd be allowed—'

'Allowed? It's still our land, you know. They only lease it. Really I ought to keep an eye on it. Come with me tonight, and then perhaps I can ask you to make a regular inspection.'

'Oh – well.'

'Meet you after chapel, then.' Catherine rose. 'I'd better go and finish the sweeping.'

'I'd rather you didn't. I'm better now, I'll do it myself.'

'Nonsense. Stay where you are. The rest is doing you good.'

But Mary John looked flustered.

'I don't understand,' Catherine said slowly. 'We've

worked side by side over the years. I've often helped you to muck out, cart the feed. It's not out of the way, surely, for me to sweep the yard?'

'Things are different now.'

'All right, I'm half directrix,' said Catherine, attempting a joke. 'But you'd often see Sister Mercy doing the weeding, and the Prioress liked to clean the chapel brasses before her sciatica became too much. We're still Sister Catherine and Sister Mary John, members of the same community. We help one another. No-one here is above the rest.' But her companion continued to look doubtful. 'It's true. That's how it is,' Catherine persisted. 'I know I don't do as much around the place as I used to, but that's because I've so many new things to do these days. But maybe you're right, I ought to do more.'

'Heavens, I didn't mean— You do enough as it is,' cried Mary John. 'Don't take any notice of me. I only understand dairying. I can't get the hang of this new routine.'

'Well, it'll be nice poking round the farmyard this evening.'

'Yes,' agreed Mary John. 'It will.'

Pink and yellow already streaked the sky when Catherine and Mary John strolled down the track. From up the bank on the far side of the hedge came sounds of snorting, tearing, chomping. The scent rose of bruised meadow grass, as amiable cattle savoured a summer evening. Arriving at the gate, the sisters paused to lean over.

Soon the curious ones arrived, abandoning their cud to push and nudge and become transfixed. Their eyes – huge, black, liquid – offered a frank exchange from the living to the living. They would go on watching for ever, thought Mary John.

At length, the women moved away and continued towards the farmyard. The cattle watched them go.

The yard was still warm from a day's basking, but new chilly air was stealing in between the buildings. A cat and her kitten came running. Mary John explored the cat's empty flap of a belly and estimated five or six kittens had been carried. She was glad one of them had been spared. The cats squirmed under their hands, lifted their heads and gave stabbing yowls. 'Next time we'll bring something for them,' said Catherine.

The shadows were lengthening rapidly. Sniffing night, the cats widened their eyes and stalked away.

And Catherine and Mary John also retraced their steps. In the cloister, drowsy and peaceful, they wished one another goodnight.

8

'My *head*,' cried Cecilia, pressing three stiff fingertips to her temples. 'Open the window, someone. It's so close I can't breathe.'

But when Anne opened it a ferocious wind blew in, dashing curtains to ceiling, sending paper patterns flying. Anne promptly shut the window and began to gather up the patterns.

Monica seized one of them and began to flap it in front of Cecilia's face. 'Lie back and I'll fan you.' Cecilia tipped her head as far as possible from the crackling paper. 'Or would an aspirin do you more good, do you suppose?'

'Possibly—'

'I'll go and get her one,' said Elizabeth, removing her spectacles and laying them down on an open record book with an air of resignation. Thinking that the sooner Cecilia was pacified, the sooner would Monica and Anne settle down to their work, she marched from the room.

'That gel has become so disagreeable,' Cecilia marvelled. 'Thank you, Monica, I think that'll do.'

Monica and Anne exchanged looks. By 'disagreeable' they understood Cecilia to be referring yet again to Elizabeth's unfortunate elevation. By virtue of her superiority as a needlewoman, Elizabeth had been put in charge of the department. Naturally this had offended Cecilia who, by general consent, was the most superior of their little band of superior personages. What one could *do* hardly came into it.

'I'm not sure having to write everything up in a book really suits her,' Monica said, sending a reproving glance towards the record book. 'I rather think it is gone over with a fine-tooth comb by certain people. Life isn't entirely hunky-dory for those who have recently enjoyed preferment. The strain on Elizabeth is beginning to tell.'

'Mmm. I happen to know—'

'Yes?' prompted Cecilia, suddenly alert, for Anne was closer to Elizabeth than she was or Monica.

'You know she had tea upstairs today?'

'Yes, yes?'

'Well, apparently it emerged over the Royal Worcester that the Reverend Mother is at last thinking seriously about the succession. A deputation of some of the young ones called on her yesterday to complain vigorously about Margaret. Soon afterwards, the Reverend Mother made an impromptu visit to the east wing. And we know what the poor things there are having to put up with.'

'We do,' Cecilia confirmed, thinking of damp and draughts, of wormy beams and crumbling plaster.

'I have a feeling – from what Elizabeth told me of the Reverend Mother's reaction – and bear in mind, this does not give Elizabeth pleasure – that the experiment may soon come to an end.'

'*Well.* Though I must say, Margaret has become thoroughly unpopular lately. I know *we* never liked her—'

'But now they all seem to detest her. People are fed up with the changes. They've gone too far.'

'Quite. So I shouldn't be at all surprised—'

Cecilia got no further, for just then Elizabeth returned with aspirins and a glass of water.

'Thank you, dear,' murmured Cecilia with unusual tenderness.

'My goodness, the wind has got up,' Elizabeth

reported. 'Shouldn't wonder if we have a storm.'

'Good job too, clear the air. Has anyone seen Catherine lately, by the way?' Monica wondered.

No-one had, it was agreed thoughtfully between Monica, Anne and Cecilia.

'Why?' Elizabeth asked sharply.

'Just wondered, dear, just wondered.'

Martha was holding forth in Lazarus's easy chair. 'Don't get me wrong,' she said, raising a hand and an eyebrow, evidently addressing the crucified Christ on the wall above the desk. 'I'm not still hurt or owt, it's just me heart bleeds for all them poor folk as can't get their Albion Reds. It's the flavour, yer see; quite unique. Baked in their jackets, yer can't whack 'em: lovely waxy earthy-tasting flesh and the skin all crisp and toasty— Properly cooked, mind. We know a few cooks as could manage to ruin a simple baked spud wi'out really trying, don't we eh, Laz? No, as I were saying—'

Is it coming back? Please God, don't let it come back, prayed Lazarus, staring down at her hands. Then she told herself not to be ridiculous, she'd had this numbing sensation before, and it always went as mysteriously as it came. And in any case, it didn't necessarily mean a loss of function, did it? She looked at the prayer book that was lying open on her bedside table, and decided to set herself a test. She would put out a hand – her right hand, the hand that seemed to be giving the worst trouble and that she most depended on – and deftly turn the prayer book's uppermost page. She would do this with a casual air so that Martha would think she was merely keeping up to date with the day's collect. She would turn the flimsy page cleanly and then she could laugh at her fears.

61

Her hand went forward. It wobbled a little, but not significantly. Her fingers met the delicate paper. They went to take hold, but became thick and fumbling as though clothed in gardening gloves, and a wodge of pages mounded up, refusing to separate. It *is* coming back, thought Lazarus, snatching back her hand.

'Something on your mind, Laz?' asked Martha with a coy glance at the prayer book. 'You can talk to me, you know. Or what about Father Dawson? Meself, I swear by Father Dawson. Remember that time I had scruples over the slugs?'

Will I ever forget? Lazarus groaned to herself, remembering hours spent listening to Martha on the subject. But then, striving to be fair, she recalled her own fascination: it had seemed an interesting dilemma and she had followed closely every turn of the argument. Why, she wondered, was she now so keen to stoke up resentment against her friend? Martha hadn't changed and neither had she. But of course the priory had changed. The priory had changed and turned her friend into a threat. Because, if her paralysis were indeed returning—

Lazarus tucked her hands in her skirt and began to hunt through a range of gardening jobs, panicking at the thought of fiddly ones, dwelling hopefully on others that even the cackhanded might tackle. But would she, as a handicapped gardener, retain her authority? Once, a tradition of respect would have made it certain. Sister Marjorie, for instance, their most talented illuminator of sacred texts, had continued to be revered as the senior artist even when her sight had failed. The matter had been managed with delicacy and tact. And when Sister Mercy, the Directrix, fell sick— Ah yes: that had been the start of it. Deference to an ailing Sister Mercy had culminated in their present troubles. Even so, by putting things right in a harsh and uncaring fashion, they were changing the very nature of the community. And no-one had been consulted about *that*.

No, there would be no crippled head of the flower garden, Lazarus concluded, looking hard at the garrulous one whom she imagined succeeding her. And all at once she understood how very much the position meant to her. Not because she was proud or bossy, but because it gave her life meaning and dignity. And because it earned her people's respect. The thought of losing all that made her jump to her feet. 'Look, Martha,' she said, 'as a matter of fact, I'd appreciate a bit of time to myself. To be quiet, you know,' she added, looking meaningfully and untruthfully at her prayer book.

'Right y'are,' said Martha, getting up. 'By gum, hark at that wind. I should stuff yer rug under the door – ain't half a draught. I'm sorry for them poor souls in the east wing tonight, God help 'em. That reminds me. Did you hear the Reverend Mother paid 'em a visit?'

'Yes, I did,' said Lazarus, opening the door to encourage her visitor's departure. As it came unlatched, the door swung violently inwards.

'Whoops. Told you there was a draught. Well, night night, sleep tight— Though how any of us'll get a wink wi' this racket—'

'Good night, Martha,' said Lazarus, pressing home her door.

Mary John could not sleep. She lay staring at her agitated curtains, listening to the wind battering her window. She could not sleep because she dreaded to wake. Mornings had become more desolate than ever after her evening stroll with Catherine. The cowshed and the meadows seemed to call her with renewed insistence. Sometimes her misery reached an unbearable pitch. She recalled such a moment a few days ago, brought on by the chanting of the psalm at morning prayer: *Save me, oh God, for the waters are come in, even unto my soul.* Her heart turned over remembering it.

And now, of course, she was obliged to assume a false brightness before Catherine: who meant well, who was anxious on her behalf. She had taken to avoiding Catherine.

Mary John sat up. She listened attentively, measuring an increase in the wind's ferocity. Then she climbed out of bed, removed her nightrobe and began to put on her clothes.

'I suppose,' Beatrice said, 'I really ought to go.'

Hope whined complainingly.

Then an even stronger wind-blast shook the building, and Beatrice bounded out of bed. 'Listen to that. I hope the tower's still standing.' She began quickly to dress.

While Beatrice was sightless with a skirt over her head, Hope slid her hand to the floor and felt for an item of clothing which she secreted under her body.

'Where's my girdle? Drat. Where is the blessed thing?'

Hope gave a squeak.

Beatrice promptly seized and raised her and retrieved the girdle. She gave her a clout.

'Ow, that hurt.'

'Serves you right for messing about. I suppose it hasn't occurred to you the damage this wind might be doing? Damnation. Wouldn't it just have to happen when we were all set to make the tower safe? Another month and it wouldn't have mattered.'

'Shall I come too?'

'Please yourself.' Beatrice knelt to tie her shoelaces. 'Though you'd probably be a liability. I mean, if the tower does come down there'll be hordes of homeless bats.'

Hope yelped and stuck her head under the pillow.

Beatrice put her foot against the door to prevent it from lurching inwards; then unlatched it and looked outside, stepped into the corridor, fastened the door, and sped away.

9

'Where have you been?' Margaret roared.

They had met – collided almost – in the cloister; Beatrice running from one direction, Margaret, Agnes, Joan and several others rushing from another.

'Is it the tower?'

'The tower's all right, apart from some fallen masonry, but—'

'The statue's wobbling. The ropes have come free.'

'If it falls, that'll be the end of it. It's so fragile.'

'The statue will *not* fall. We can't allow it.' Margaret with the moonlight on her face seemed to command more than earthly assistance.

'I'd better take a look,' said Beatrice.

They gathered in the courtyard below the tower, a continually enlarging group of grey-veiled sisters, their robes driven like bunting. Wind-sped clouds over a brilliant moon cast alternating blackness and shine. For long moments the light revealed her: Our Lady of Albion on her platform at the top of the tower, framed by four open arches rising from the corners to meet at the middle point above her head. She had watched over the courtyard for centuries. Her outstretched arms invoked a blessing on the sisters as they went about their duties below. For some months she had leaned precipitously, and Beatrice had made her temporarily secure with anchoring ropes attached to the arches. Now, gazing upwards, holding veils from their faces, they strained to count the flailing ropes. 'Every rope's come loose,' Beatrice decided at last, and a groan went up.

Suddenly, during a particularly ferocious wind-gust, the watchers saw the statue move. There was an instinctive flinching and averting of eyes. But Margaret charged forward. 'No,' she yelled, hands raised against the invisible threat. 'You shan't!' She turned back to address her companions. 'That statue is known throughout the world. If we let her fall, we might as well pack up and go. Sisters, the spirit of Albion is under attack. What are you going to do about it?'

There were gasps, shuffles, cries.

'It seems not everyone is bothered,' shouted Agnes. 'At least half of 'em are messing about in the east wing.'

'The *east wing*?'

'Yeah. Trying to evacuate it.'

'You hear that?' screeched Margaret. 'Half our members are more concerned with their creature comforts than preserving Our Lady of Albion. Go and fetch 'em. Go on. Bring 'em here now.'

The sisters looked at one another. Imogen and Clare slipped away.

Beatrice went forward and put her mouth against Margaret's ear. 'Leave it to me. I know what I'm doing. I'll get up there and fix the ropes.'

'You will stay *here*,' insisted Margaret, jabbing a stiff finger towards the ground. 'You're the only one with knowledge of the conditions. You must direct operations, but from a *safe place*. I've told you before, you're indispensable.'

'Steady on, Margaret,' Joan warned, catching her arm. 'I don't know what you've got in mind, but for heaven's sake be careful. Our stock's low enough as it is.'

Margaret jerked her arm free. Their waning popularity was large in her mind also; indeed, the imminent loss of the statue seemed to presage their downfall. But if Joan imagined caution could ward off an already beckoning defeat, she, Margaret, knew better. This was the moment to take a chance. 'Aha,' she cried as the party arrived from the east wing. 'I see you've managed to rouse the comfort-lovers. Sorry, you lot, but your arrangements will have to wait. We've got a *crisis* on our hands.'

'There's nothing we can do about that, surely?' Catherine shouted. She had been organizing an evacuation of the lay sisters from the east wing when Imogen and Clare arrived and more or less dragged her off. Her arms still clasped a bundle of bedding. 'The tower isn't safe. No-one can go up there.'

There were murmurs of assent. They drove Margaret wild. She examined the white-faced woman with her homely bundle and almost spat her contempt. 'Yes, we might have expected that from you. You never have been able to grasp anything beyond the safe, the ordinary, the pedestrian. "But we always do such-and-such so we had better go on doing it for ever and ever, even if the place is crumbling round our feet,"' she mock-mimicked unpleasantly. 'Well, I say there *is* something we can do. I say the Sisters of Albion are not cowards; they will do their duty gladly without flinching. I say—'

Many of her words were drowned by the wind, but their gist was plain. A prolonged blast sent the sisters staggering. When it relented there was an anxious peering towards the top of the tower, but for the moment Our Lady of Albion held her ground.

'The wind'll beat us to it if we don't get a move on. Tell us what needs to be done,' roared Margaret to Beatrice.

'She has to be roped again to the arches. But it's dodgy in the tower. Some stairs are missing, there are lumps out of the wall—'

'Who'll volunteer?' Margaret shouted. 'I'm sure you feel as passionately as I do.'

'Why don't you, since you feel passionately?' one of the younger sisters screamed. (One of the bolshie ones, Margaret noted.)

'Let me assure you, Sister, were it not for my onerous duty to run this convent, I shouldn't hesitate.' A gust almost knocked Margaret over; she recovered and looked anxiously upwards. 'I must say I am sorely tempted.'

Her ardour was palpable. Most sisters believed her.

'I'll do it,' cried Sister Mary John.

They turned and craned their heads to look at her.

For months Mary John had found eye contact impossible with her former peers. And she'd noticed other sisters, downgraded like herself, experiencing a similar difficulty. It was an affliction of the redundant, she'd decided; like the bells of lepers, their downcast eyes signalled to those who retained their self-respect to keep a safe distance. Glorious it was now to stare brazenly, to watch amazed confusion dawn in the face of Sister Imogen.

'Sister Mary John!' cried Margaret, her very tone seeming to confer honour, dignity and respect. She clasped Mary John's hands.

Agnes began to clap. Others followed suit.

Catherine pushed through the gathering. 'What is all this? Have you gone mad? Listen, Sister.' But Agnes, in her eagerness to cry 'Who else?' jostled Catherine, setting her off balance.

'Me!' a lay sister cried, catching the mood.

'Me!' cried another.

Each cry met with applause.

'Wonderful, come forward.' Margaret beckoned. 'Yes, you and you. Well done.' She shook their hands. 'I feel sure Albion Priory will have reason to honour you for this night's work.' And in an aside to Beatrice, she added, 'Take 'em off and tell 'em what to do.'

'You mean, this lot?' said Beatrice disbelievingly.

'Go and get on with it.'

'Sister Mary John, wait,' cried Catherine. She struggled to get near her, but Mary John disappeared with Beatrice. 'You're putting their lives in danger,' she screamed at Margaret. 'I insist you call them back.'

'They're going of their own free will. Who are you to stop them?'

'To do what? Save a lump of stone? A bit of metal?'

'To save our reputation!'

'What absolute rubbish.'

The sister who'd suggested that Margaret herself ought to perform the saving deed, now spoke up in support of Catherine. Some others also joined in. But most eyes were on Margaret, who was continuing to roar praise for Mary John and her companions, and contempt for those who did not acknowledge the pre-eminence of Our Lady of Albion.

Disengaging from her supporters, Catherine said she must catch up with Mary John and attempt to dissuade her.

'I shouldn't bother,' her new champion said. 'If she's fool enough to get herself killed it might even do good. There'd be a scandal: it'd put a stop to *her*.'

Horrified, Catherine pushed through the crowd. But the way to the tower was barred by Agnes and Imogen. She considered the matter quickly, then hitched up her skirt and charged off in another direction. She ran harder than she had run in her life.

But the Prioress was not in her apartment. Several precious minutes later, Catherine discovered her in the hospital at Sister Mercy's bedside. Also present were Sisters Cecilia, Monica, Anne and Elizabeth. As Catherine burst in, Sister Luke caught her arm. 'Shh,' she hissed. 'The end's very near. She's about to be taken.'

Mercy, Mercy, thought Catherine. What a time to choose. She stood hesitantly in the aisle, thinking of the peril facing Mary John and her companions, looking towards the bed where one of the little band of friends lay at the point of death. Could she really violate this moment, break the concentration of their prayerful vigil? It seemed monstrous even to consider such an act. Yet only the Prioress could prevent a probable catastrophe. Undecided, Catherine approached the bed.

Monica saw her and smiled. Cecilia followed her friend's glance and shuffled to one side, touching the bed to signal Catherine to join them.

For just one minute, Catherine promised herself, and obediently sank to her knees between Monica and Cecilia. She closed her eyes and prayed rather perfunctorily for the easy passage of Sister Mercy's soul, and then for forgiveness for the disruption she was about to cause. When she looked up, the women on the other side of the bed – Elizabeth and Anne kneeling, the Prioress in a chair – smiled at her sadly, and Cecilia, who was holding Mercy's hand, took Catherine's and wrapped it round the nearly lifeless one.

Awe filled Catherine. Awe at the presence of death. That, and her companions' expectations, destroyed her last trace of resolve. She had no notion of what she should do, but continued to kneel there, strong for neither Mercy nor Mary John.

'Dear God, what a shower,' said Beatrice, finding her fears well founded concerning the volunteers' competence. 'We'll have to bring her down. The idiot's blocking the stairway.' She referred to one of the volunteers who had fallen after failing to negotiate a gap. 'I warned them,' Beatrice complained to Agnes. 'I said, Watch out just after the sixth window.' She leaned into the stairway. 'Can you hear me up there? Have you got her? Well, get a move on. And mind you keep away from the wall.'

Now and then when the wind dropped, Margaret's voice came through like a foghorn. 'All pray,' they heard. 'Our brave sisters.' 'Inspiration to us all.'

Agnes, her political acumen as sharp as ever, went off to warn Margaret to remain with the main group in the courtyard to avoid having to reconsider the operation in the light of an accident.

With much heaving and panting, the rescue party emerged. Imogen bustled forward to examine the injured one.

'How many are still up there?' Agnes, returning, wanted to know.

'Three,' replied Beatrice. 'And not one of them's arrived on top. If they had, they'd have been spotted from the courtyard: Joan's on the lookout. The thing is, Agnes, it's all very well for Margaret to make stipulations, but she doesn't seem to realize the need for someone with a bit of savvy up there. I think I ought to go up. At least I can find out whether the others are still functional.'

Agnes thought it over. 'All right. We don't seem to be getting very far as it is. Go on. With a bit of luck, Margaret need never know.'

Mary John, nearing the top of the tower, began to whistle her milking tune. She was exhilarated, triumphant to be showing her mettle while others collapsed around her or became gibberish with fear. She had clambered over one inert sister, evaded the clutching hands of a terrified other; she had negotiated gaps, scrambled over rubble, ducked from falling masonry, and when sucking draughts came at her through gaps in the wall she had laughed and pushed upwards. The skills acquired in her tomboy youth had come into play as naturally as if she had never ceased from their daily practice. And now she had done it, she had reached the top.

She pushed the trapdoor open. Moonlight flooded. Clouds raced. Mary John blinked, clambered upright, gazed around.

The night was wild and wonderful: gold-streaked indigo, a rushing river of air. Mary John screwed up her eyes and saw, in the gleam and dazzle of a swinging spotlight, delirious snakes leaping and slapping, and the outstretched arms of a ringmaster: instantly, a trip to the circus, the most magical evening of her life, had returned to her. The spotlight was fading. Darkness fell over, enclosed her in a booth of black velvet, while noise pounded, growing louder and louder. Oh, but now came the brilliance flooding again. Enchanted, Mary John moved over the floor, Beatrice's warning about broken boards and keeping strictly to the sides of the platform gone clean from her mind. When the boards gave way and she plunged downwards, her strong arms circled a beam and she threw herself with her tree-climber's ease onto firm floor beyond the statue. 'My, my,' she spluttered. 'Whatever next?'

On the stairway, Beatrice had stumbled across the unconscious sister. Dear God, not a corpse, she prayed, certain that such a catastrophe could not be weathered. She stepped over the inert form and climbed on. Her skirt became a hindrance. When it was safe to do so, she eased upright, pressed against the central pillar, and bloused the garment over her girdle. For good measure she tore off her coif and veil. Should have done it sooner, she thought, resuming her cautious circuitous crawl.

The sound of the storm was muffled inside the tower. Beatrice's ears were therefore able to detect a low animal noise some time before she arrived at its source. It was the frightened sister successfully avoided by Mary John. She was huddling by a gap in the wall through which the wind licked spitefully. Her hysteria had reduced to a manic whimpering.

'Get hold of yourself, for Pete's sake,' muttered Beatrice, climbing gingerly over her, praying the woman wouldn't latch on to her and cause them both to hurtle downwards. Finding she had cleared the obstacle, she let out her breath.

Like Mary John before her, Beatrice crawled from her dark confinement and emerged, unfolding, into windswept space. The vista took her breath away: swelling waves, racing smoke, the brilliant moon. She threw out her arms and felt the wind in her sleeves; it streamed her hair and, as she tipped up her face and whooped, rushed warmly to fill her mouth and throat. Fantastic, she thought, as the clouds sped by and the tower rocked. Maybe the way she was feeling was like the charge people sought from illicit drug-taking. They spoke of getting high, didn't they? Beatrice felt she couldn't be higher. Nothing could dampen her mood, not even the discovery that half the floor was missing and poor old Sister Mary John was marooned on the other side. Well, good for Mary John, she had actually made it. What's more, she appeared to be enjoying herself. 'Yoo-hoo, Sister. What a night, eh? See you're in a bit of a pickle, but don't worry, we'll think of something. Gotcha,' cried Beatrice, catching one of the tossing ropes. 'Had an idea,' she yelled. 'I'll grab another and swing over. We'll tie one rope to the statue and ride back on the other. Come here, you blighter. *Whey-hey.*'

Mary John heard not a word.

Once, when still a child on her father's farm, Mary

John had wrestled herself from a bog. A moment ago she'd remembered that occasion, and the thought had come that down there from where she'd just climbed was something very similar; something that sucked at her and drew her down, a mire of pitch where there was nothing but indescribable misery. She would never go back. She would stay up here in this gaudy tent, reliving the happiest times of her life. One of those times took possession of her now. It was soon after her evening at the circus. She was at home in the paddock, practising bareback riding and some of the tricks she'd seen a lady in a tinsel dress perform on the back of a circus pony— Now she was teaching her Jack Russell terrier to jump through a hoop— And now turning somersaults on a plank instead of a tightrope— And now flying through the air on a tree-borne trapeze. And now— Mary John clasped her hands and gaped, for here flying towards her through the spangled night, with her moon-coloured hair and her pink and white laugh, came the trapeze lady in person.

'Damnation, missed!' cried Beatrice. 'Hang on, Sister, I'll try again. Get ready to catch me. One, two, *three-ee*.'

Here she came again. But now Mary John saw it wasn't the trapeze lady. Because, look at her hair, her golden hair, and the wings billowing from her shoulders. It was the angel of the Lord! God had sent his angel for Mary John. What a reception, she thought. Who would ever fear dying knowing it was to be like this? 'I'm coming,' she cried, and hurled herself forward into the angel's arms.

In the area of the Albion Tower, time entered three dimensions. For the watchers in the courtyard below there was no time between the moment when the fall began and the moment of impact. There was no point when they could say, 'The body is there, then there, now there,' for time was too swift for their cumbersome perceptions. Later, they would imagine the form's flight. But were it not for the smack on the ground, repeating again and again in their inner ears, the form so eternally still might never not have been lying there.

Beatrice wrestled with time. She crouched against the parapet clasping the rope, willing time to play over again. Come back, you idiot. *Stay.* Her mind recovered Mary John. It set herself flying again. But though she struggled to correct the moment when her feet struck and launched her companion, it remained unchanged, slipped ever further from her mind's grasp.

Time has become infinite for Mary John. She floats smoothly on to where time has always been drawing her. Old friends lift their heads, gaze with huge black liquid eyes. They will go on watching for ever.

10

Catherine awoke with her temple burning. It was difficult to raise her eyelids under its fiery weight. At the thought of going further and raising her entire self, nauseous pressure rose in her throat. This had not happened to her since her early twenties; she had supposed she'd grown out of migraine attacks, but here she was laid low by another. She sought the reason, and it fell over her dully like an iron-weighted blanket: Sister Mary John had fallen to her death. It had really happened.

She recalled foreseeing that it might, and shouting this to Margaret, and finally (when it was already too late) urging the possibility on the Reverend Mother. But her foreseeingness in recollection seemed unreal. Her immediate reaction to the news had been disbelief, and now it felt more believable than not that she would bump into Mary John some time during today.

She was not the only one to have foreseen an accident. That young outspoken sister, the one who was so against Margaret— What did she say: 'If she's fool enough to get herself killed it might even do good: put a stop to *her*.' Catherine heard the words again, and wondered whether their speaker was as shocked as she was now they'd come true.

Shocked, dazed. Hard to take in that the situation in the priory had spun out of control. Had come to this.

She eased to the edge of the bed and put her feet to the floor. Slowly she rose, reached for her cloak and pulled it round her shoulders. She hurried barefoot along the corridor, and in a cubicle in the bathroom leaned over a lavatory bowl to vomit.

The sentiment contained in those words which had so offended Catherine, though less brutally expressed, was often repeated in discussions over the following days. Several of the younger sisters were convinced that Margaret had miscalculated and could not survive. They even doubted her strident confidence, speculating whether it covered guilt.

But a majority in the convent did not know what to make of the tragedy. They remained confused, waiting to have its significance explained to them.

Far from experiencing guilt, Margaret in fact was buzzing inside with a sense of triumph. In her judgement, her conduct of the affair had been magnificent. No-one but she, not Beatrice, not Agnes, could have summoned the guts to see it through. Anyone less would have allowed the consequences of failure to inhibit her. And with the fall of Mary John the stakes had certainly rocketed. But even then, in her very worst moment – the body on the ground, the Prioress sent for, the weeping, the beginning of recrimination – she had kept her nerve. She was helped considerably by Beatrice of course, who, while everyone in the courtyard awaited the arrival of the Reverend Mother, had completed the task at the top of the tower attempted by Mary John. Hearing that the statue was secure, Margaret had immediately pronounced the death well vindicated. Encouraged by Agnes, this had actually brought applause. And when objections were voiced Margaret had turned on her critics: 'The statue is safe. Rejoice about *that*.'

The exhortation had shut them up and earned her time. But even then she'd been obliged to keep her wits about her. First Joan had become hysterical, imagining some aberration in Beatrice's headgear, and then Agnes had deserted her, rushing off (it was explained to Margaret later) to ensure that when Beatrice reappeared she would be decently attired. It had given her a jolt to learn of Beatrice's disobedience, though in the circumstances of course she did not complain. Beatrice was a heroine. So too was the fallen Mary John. This was the message she tirelessly sought to instil in the minds of the uncertain majority.

Margaret's own mind turned to plans for a suitable celebration: a service of thanksgiving, and later on, when the tower had been restored, a procession to the courtyard and a service of dedication, the scene presided over by a newly gilded Lady of Albion. Imagining it, Margaret's heart swelled with pride. It was a fitting way, she told herself, of demonstrating to the world that the Albion Priory was back in business.

In the meantime there was work to be done. They had won a marvellous victory, and it should, it must, be sustained. With Mercy gone, the Prioress would feel more than ever obliged to consider the succession. And the succession could not be allowed to go the wrong way.

Agnes, she found when she dropped in to her room, was thinking along similar lines. 'This mood of mourning,' said Agnes, doodling a tombstone in the margin of her notes, 'has gone on long enough. It's not doing us any good. As soon as Mercy and Mary John are decently buried, I suggest we try to lift the atmosphere: call a meeting, arrange a rousing service.'

'Presumably it'll have to be a meeting of Council,' Margaret mused regretfully. 'Catherine will insist. And we can hardly call it a briefing meeting.'

'No, I've thought of that. Our line is, that in view of the momentous happening we think the whole convent ought to be present. After all, Sister Mary John wasn't even a member of Council, not since we sold her cows.'

'Mmm. I should think that'll work.'

Agnes smiled sardonically. 'You'll have to come on strong,' she warned.

Margaret pulled in her chin and bellowed: 'This is a moment when the entire community must draw together—'

'That's the sort of thing,' Agnes agreed, cutting her off. 'Now, according to reliable sources, the other side assumes we're on the defensive. They're gearing up to put the skids under us. That being the case, we'd better get together and plan every detail.'

'You know, Agnes, I've been thinking. Why not admit one or two trusties to our inner circle? Imogen, for instance. I'm enormously impressed by Imogen. And Veronica's sound. That spunky little Clare's one of us, wouldn't you say?'

'Oh, certainly.' Agnes began a new, spikier doodle.

'Us four plus those three.'

'Just Imogen and Clare, I'd say,' countered Agnes. 'They've got the right idea. Veronica's useful, but too old and stodgy. I don't see her grasping the finer points of strategy.'

'Perhaps you're right. One other thing.' Margaret carefully removed a speck of fluff from her habit. 'I suppose, mm, I suppose Beatrice is *all right* if you take my meaning? It's going to be necessary to talk up the positive side of the affair – meaning Beatrice's accomplishment – to counter the negative effect of Mary John. Which will put Beatrice rather in the spotlight.'

'Mm.' Agnes doodled and Margaret waited. 'Yes, Beatrice'll be all right, I should think. I'd give her a pep talk, if I were you. Tell her she's our trump card and she's got to live up to it. You know the sort of thing.'

80

'Quite. But you would tell me, Agnes, if there were something I ought to know.'

'Absolutely, Margaret.'

Often Catherine went back over the events of that night, and often examined how far she herself was responsible. Those twenty minutes of indecision at Sister Mercy's deathbed gave her particular trouble. Even so, she was doubtful whether greater decisiveness would have changed the outcome. After all, the Prioress could not have mounted the tower steps, and neither with any speed could Catherine if the Prioress had ordered her up there to fetch Mary John down. Catherine was by no means happy with her role: the tragedy might have been averted if she had done more for Mary John during the preceding weeks; but she did not delude herself: Margaret's new rule had bred Mary John's fatal despair. For the sake of others in Mary John's position, Catherine steeled herself to work for Margaret's defeat. It was time to put a stop to her.

She prepared for the meeting with confident composure. The sisters in the main were horrified by Mary John's death and the injuries to her colleagues. They would surely back Catherine. It could not be otherwise.

'Now, I'd like you all to take a look at this.' Margaret, nearing the end of her speech, waved a yellowed card before the noses of those occupying the front seats. 'An old print of the Albion Tower. And do you know where it came from?' She paused, craned forward and showed her teeth to say, '*Italy*.' The card was put down and a book taken up. 'And here again.' She held up an open page to show an illustration. 'Our Lady of

Albion. You can read all about it in here. In *German*.'
Her audience duly gasped, and Margaret went on to
predict that the world would soon thirst again for news
of the Albion Priory. People would clamour to visit. If
all went according to plan, and Margaret did not
foresee any delay, the visitors' programme would
come into effect this very autumn. 'That is why it was
vital to secure the statue. Imagine the effect of an
empty space on visitors expecting to see a well-known
landmark. Thanks to our brave sisters that humiliation
will not occur. We can continue to take pride in Albion
Priory. When you next look up at Our Lady of Albion,
let the events of that night remind you that we are a
vibrant force. That we have a *future*.'

There was hearty applause. Even some of the un-
converted members of her audience felt Margaret's
words had given meaning to Mary John's death. Her
version was a more comfortable memorial than one
suggested elsewhere: that the death was a useless
disgrace. But a minority of sisters remained angry.
They waited hopefully for Catherine's reply.

Her voice came out evenly. 'I have a question for
Sister Margaret. What are the *means* by which these
great things will be accomplished? We need to be told.
Will she please tell us plainly what they are? I ask
because when her original proposals were put to
Council she did not explain that many sisters would be
deprived of their way of life; she did not explain that
these sisters would then have no function other than
that of cleaning up after others; she did not explain that
those unfortunate enough to bear the burden of these
"improvements" would lose their voice in Council and
thus any means of countering their distress. She did
not explain that some of us would become less than
others—'

Oh yes, thought Lazarus, becoming excited, that is
exactly what happened. They asked us whether we

wanted our affairs to be put in order. But they didn't explain it would change the very way we live with one another. No-one asked us if we wanted that. Resolving to speak in support of Catherine at the first opportunity, she shuffled to the edge of her seat in readiness. But then her mouth went dry, and the tension of the moment brought on an attack of pins and needles. Someone else would have to do it; it was too much for her in her state of health. She edged backwards, slumped lower and lower. And a premonition stole over her that she would indeed lose her cherished position.

'It would not be so bad if it was frankly admitted that some sisters have been placed at a disadvantage,' Catherine was saying. 'Then we could ensure they were compensated. That would be the honest, the moral thing to do. After all, it's no-one's fault, it's quite arbitrary, that some forms of work are now considered more profitable than others. Will Sister Margaret please respond to that?' she asked, and sat down.

Agnes smirked. Beatrice grinned. Margaret heaved a sigh of relief. What a novice was Catherine, playing the ball right back into her opponent's court.

Once more on her feet, Margaret inclined her head and raised her eyebrows. 'Sisters, I confess to a certain disappointment. Was that *really* the carping tone we expected to hear this afternoon, so soon after our triumph? And, yes, we *have* had a triumph. For goodness' sake let's rejoice about it!' Her eyebrows fell. 'Now, to answer the points raised by Sister Catherine. She says, some of us have become less than others. Less than others? Because of a change of work? Look, I believe Sister Mary John was one of those whose working life had changed. Is it seriously proposed that Sister Mary John could have acted as she did, believing we did not value her? What nonsense. Sister Mary John *knew* she was a valued member of this priory; that is why she gave her life for it. It is true, some people are doing work they were not used to. Well, times change. The world has changed. We must change. I tell you, sisters, *there is no alternative*. Are we frightened of change? I say to my critics, *you* may fear the challenge of change, but please don't stifle *our* initiative.' She craned forward, preparing to make things plain even to halfwits. 'You see, it was *vision* that inspired Sister Mary John. It was *vision* that inspired Sister Beatrice. Let us, also, have *vision*.' She softened her voice and threw out a hand to indicate Beatrice who was sitting beside the lectern. 'Sisters, many of you watched Sister Beatrice on that terrible night, risking her life for our beloved statue. If every one of us here can summon a small portion of that fearless spirit, between us we shall restore our beloved Albion Priory to its former glory.'

Beatrice smiled her widest smile. So overcome was one sister in the front row that she darted forward to kiss the hem of the heroine's robe. 'Sisters,' Margaret cried, shooing the emotional one, 'I think the proper response is a prayer of thanks to Almighty God. It would be fitting for Sister Beatrice to lead us.'

Help, thought Beatrice, looking wildly round. But Joan, never at a loss for a suitable text, handed her a book and pointed out a place.

Beatrice rose. '*Stir up, we beseech thee, O Lord, the wills of thy faithful people*—' My goodness, this is going well, thought Beatrice, enjoying the hush in the hall, and the ringing words, and her voice voluptuously delivering them. '*That they, plenteously bringing forth the fruit of good works, may of thee be plenteously rewarded.*'

'Amen,' sonorously intoned Cecilia, thinking that the gel had a charming voice and such a nice, frank smile. Plucky, too. It was a pity she was in with that frightful crew. Perhaps she should take an interest in her. Perhaps the needlework room should entertain Beatrice to tea.

'Amen,' Catherine said hastily, wondering whether to jump up and try again.

But Margaret was too prompt for her. Even as the Amens died away, she was giving her opinion that it was a shame after that to add so much as a word. 'However,' she went on apologetically. 'Sister Joan has an important matter to bring to your attention. Sister?' she prompted. Agnes nudged Joan to get on with it, and Joan, fingertips stabbing her creased forehead, hurried to inform them of an innovation: a bulletin which would be brought out at regular intervals and pinned to a notice board specially erected on the refectory wall; its purpose to keep everyone *au fait* with the many changes going on. Anyone with thoughts to convey to the whole community should get in touch with her with a view to including them in a further issue. By now Margaret was halfway to the door, mouthing Hellos and reaching to clasp hands.

Two sisters rushed up to Catherine. 'Margaret evaded the question. Why didn't you pin her down?'

Cecilia, who happened to be standing close to Catherine, and had no idea why these impolite women were making a fuss, answered in Catherine's stead. 'Perhaps it was not the right occasion.' She turned away to address her friends. 'Wasn't Sister Beatrice splendid?'

Angelica took Catherine's arm and steered her to the door. She led her to the chapel. Without exchanging a word they went up into the organ loft. When Catherine failed to break their silence, Angelica tactfully opened up the organ and searched through some sheets of music.

'Shall we practise the anthem for tonight?' she suggested after a while.

'Anthem?'

'I've found a really joyous setting of *O sing unto the Lord a new song.*'

'Are you mad?' asked Catherine. 'We buried Mercy and Mary John less than twenty-four hours ago.'

'But Sister Theresa specifically asked for that psalm. And I thought a new setting would make a change. After all, it's a service of thanksgiving.'

'Look, tell Sister Theresa from me: all due respect, but I'd like her to think again. Thanksgiving by all means, but in a context of remembrance. And maybe contrition, too. You'll do that, won't you, Angelica? I'm going for a walk. I need to think.'

When Catherine had gone, Angelica closed up the organ and left the loft. She went doubtfully to the Precentor's office, recalling the Sister Precentor's uncompromising manner earlier when she'd handed Angelica tonight's order of service. Sighing, Angelica wondered if it would be possible to please everyone. Perhaps, if Sister Theresa remained adamant, she could satisfy Catherine by finding a chant that would moderate the psalm's triumphant tone.

'What d'you mean, camped it up? I put heart and soul into that prayer,' cried Beatrice.

'I thought you read it beautifully,' soothed Margaret. 'Please do not always be finding fault, Agnes. Joan dear, is everything in order for tonight's service?'

'Yes. And I discovered the perfect psalm. *O sing unto the Lord a new song: for He hath done marvellous things. With His own right hand, and with His holy arm, hath He gotten Himself the victory.*'

'Wonderful. By the way, when you write up the bulletin you will try to slip in how very much faster we'd all get on if it weren't for all this carping and whining?'

'How about a catchy postscript: "Moaning minnies sap our strength"?'

'"Moaning minnies" is good.'

'If it doesn't do the trick, we can go for something stronger.'

'Perhaps not so much stronger, as suggestive,' Beatrice said thoughtfully.

'Good, good. Plenty of ideas. Now, Beatrice, I'd like a chat. Let's go for a walk. And while we're at it we can chivvy those gardeners.'

The low sun beamed towards the sanctuary, blinding and haloing those in its path, divorcing them from their shadowy sisters. In the chancel, the sun singled out Catherine, and beyond her, on the gilded altar frontal, a lamb bearing a cross. By Catherine's side, the Prioress squinted at the sun-splashed page of her prayer book as though she did not know by heart every word of the liturgy. To the left of the Prioress knelt Margaret, apparently rapt in prayer.

Margaret was thinking what a dismal start to the service it had been; the organ muted, the responses half-hearted. She looked forward to the psalm, though it was apparent from the lack of music on Catherine's desk that no anthem was to be made of it. How small-minded of the woman! She, Margaret, had enjoyed a brilliant success, so Catherine must sulk and decline to lend her voice to the celebration. Well, people would draw their conclusions.

The congregation rose to say the Gloria. The organ gave out the chant.

Soon, a red spot dawned in each of Margaret's cheeks. In the nave, Beatrice stole a glance at Joan and grinned to herself, for Joan, finding her intentions sabotaged once again by human incompetence, had thrust a clenched fist to her brow. Unnoticed at the back of the chapel, Agnes slipped quickly from her pew.

Angelica, keeping a careful eye on the psalm's

pointing, was thinking how clever she had been to find this blameless little chant in F major. It had just the right air of innocent cheerfulness, and voiced by the light bright stops she had selected conveyed nothing of a thumping victory. Catherine would be reassured. Fondly, Angelica pictured her in the chancel singing with a clear conscience.

When a hand appeared from nowhere and snatched out the eight-foot diapason, Angelica almost fell off the bench. 'What y'doing?' she hissed, fighting to control her suddenly dithering fingers.

'Just keep playing,' Agnes said in her ear.

'Get out, you fool!' Angelica steadied herself and stared hard at the text, fearing she would lose her place in the pointing.

But Agnes not only remained, she pulled out further stops: the four-foot principal, the two-foot, the oboe, the trumpet. 'Come on, put a bit of life into it. This isn't a funeral.'

'Will you stop? You must be mad.'

Angelica ploughed on, wondering what on earth her friend would be making of this uneven and crude crescendo. 'That was diabolical,' she hissed at the psalm's end. 'I don't know what you think you're doing, but will you please clear off?'

Unmoved, Agnes reached forward and turned over the pages of the psalter. 'What have you got for the Magnificat?' she asked.

'What's it got to do with you? Please go.' She turned to the correct page.

Agnes, who could not read music, frowned at the chant with suspicion. 'Just make it loud and lively, right?'

Below them at the lectern, a sister announced the end of the first lesson. It was Angelica's cue, she had no choice but to play. 'Leave things alone or I'll be bound to make a mistake,' she warned.

'Better,' murmured Agnes at the Magnificat's close.

'Look, I suppose Sister Margaret sent you up here. Well, Sister Catherine's going to be pretty annoyed, and I dare say the Prioress—'

'Shh.' Agnes put a finger to Angelica's lips and leaned her mouth close to Angelica's ear. 'How's that pupil of yours coming on? I hear she's good. If you've lost your appetite for this work, maybe she's ready to replace you. Pity, though, 'cos Sister Margaret was really taken with the idea of your Sunday evening recitals. Nice capable hands you've got, Sister Angelica. I bet Sister Imogen'd be glad of your help in the housekeeping department. Think about it, eh?' She raised her head – 'What's next?' – and peered at the psalter. 'Of course, the Nunc Dimittis. Fair enough, that's always a quiet one. But see what you can do with the hymn. *Now thank we all our God*: I'll expect something really rousing for that. See you later.' She slid from the bench and disappeared round the side of the organ.

The chapel fell silent. Angelica realized she had missed her cue. Hastily, she played through the chant, managing to slow up her fingers just in time for the voices to enter. '*Lord, now lettest thou thy servant depart in peace*,' they sang. *Depart* stuck in Angelica's brain, ominously echoing Agnes's threat. She imagined packing her music away for the last time and having no further right to enter the organ loft. Never again those winter evenings when the chapel was empty and the only light was the light on the console, and the only sound was the piping music set off by her fingers and feet. She imagined coming into the chapel for services for which her pupil was playing. She imagined listening in her pew and knowing the instrument she regarded as her own was out of reach.

She blew her nose. She turned to *Now thank we all our God* in the hymnal. She pulled out every stop and opened the swell box. They demanded noise: let the noise blast them.

At the end of the service, Catherine hurried up the stairs to the organ loft. She waited for the last brilliant notes to die. 'Whatever got into you?' she demanded. 'It was going so well, then all hell broke loose. Did you have a brainstorm, Angelica?'

Angelica pushed home the stops, removed her music, closed the console doors.

'Answer me,' cried Catherine, seizing her friend's wrist. Angelica averted her eyes.

Released, Angelica stacked the music away in the cupboard.

Catherine sat down on the bench and put her head in her hands. 'What's going on?' she asked.

Angelica hesitated. 'Sister Agnes came up.'

'Up here? During the service? You mean, she forced you to play like that?'

'Please, Catherine, don't make trouble.'

'Oh, dear God,' whispered Catherine.

11

'I do get tired— And rather stiff,' admitted the Prioress. Her guests – Margaret and Catherine – tutted sympathetically. 'However, *inside* one is tireless. Vigorous, even.'

Her words seemed to hang in the air. She turned her head to look irritably at a jug of ox-eye daisies. But they made her think of Sister Lazarus and feel crosser than ever, for Lazarus had brought her the flowers this morning and had insisted on making them into 'an arrangement'. As she worked, she had twittered nervously and incessantly, and largely unintelligibly. Then when she'd gone, the Prioress had discovered a mess of green slime on a favourite tray cloth. Why in heaven's name hadn't the woman fiddled with her flowers somewhere safe like the draining board? the Prioress wondered for the umpteenth time. Forgetting her guests, she hauled herself up and went across the room to poke at the cloth that she had put to soak in a bowl of cold water.

Behind her hand, Margaret coughed discreetly. 'Aren't you delighted with the refurbished refectory, Reverend Mother?' she asked brightly. 'The tapestries are splendid, they lend such a wonderful atmosphere. I'm sure it will prove a most attractive room for our visitors.'

'Mmm, very nice.' The stain did not appear to be shifting. She pushed the cloth back under the water, then dried her hand on her skirt.

'It's all coming along spendidly,' continued Margaret.

'The kitchens and outhouses are nearly finished. Next week we start on the tower.'

At the mention of the tower, the Prioress frowned. It had been a shocking thing, that Sister Mary John business, and it quite bewildered her the way it had all turned out. She had expected an uproar and a laborious inquiry. But not a bit of it. Evidently, a great thing had been done, and Margaret, the escapade's instigator, was proclaimed a marvel. 'Seems a rum thing to me,' she muttered, thinking of the people who had come to her door all bursting to lavish praise on the woman. Even Cecilia seemed to have lost her head over that tall girl who had survived the incident: the one with the eyes and the grin: what was her name?' 'Sister Beatrice,' she told herself aloud.

'Sister Beatrice?' repeated Margaret. 'Did you expect her also this morning? Forgive me, but I thought you summoned only myself and Sister Catherine.'

'Yes, yes.' Arriving back at her chair, she gingerly lowered herself into it. 'You see, by now I had hoped—' Her eyes dwelt reproachfully on Catherine. There was no need for her to complete the sentence. Her guests understood perfectly.

You'd hoped, thought Margaret, oh yes, you'd *hoped* to be naming your precious Catherine as your successor. Well, we can all *hope*, only some of us prefer to roll up our sleeves and set about creating our own destiny. How furious the Prioress must be that one of her own select little band had proved such a let-down. And how full of chagrin at the prospect of making Margaret – not one of *them* – her successor.

'But I've decided there's no hurry. With so much going on you will both have your hands full. You have quite enough to occupy you without the burden of an added responsibility. No, no. As I said just now, I may get tired, but I am still a vigorous woman.'

You can't bear to do it, thought Margaret angrily. It

really goes against the grain. Well, we shall see, but I rather think you'll come to it, m'lady.

Catherine leant forward. 'Reverend Mother, you must follow your conscience. Don't think of my, um, our feelings.' Looking into the old woman's face, Catherine felt ashamed. Dimly she understood that the Prioress felt obliged to ignore her heart's prompting and follow the advice she was undoubtedly receiving to name Margaret as her successor. So she had decided to hang on.

Once the financial recovery is assured, things will change again, the Prioress was promising herself. This made sense. Margaret was more suited than Catherine to money-grubbing and fabric mending. Catherine's qualities were spiritual; they had been noticed by the Prioress and her friends when Catherine was a mere postulant. Of course, Catherine's mother was Anne's first cousin. Or was it Monica's?

Deciding little was to be gained by extending this visit, Margaret rose to her feet. 'I'm afraid I must go, Reverend Mother. There's a tremendous amount of work to be done down there.'

The Prioress dangled her fingers from her sleeve. Gravely, for she prided herself on her formal manners, Margaret touched them with her lips and dropped a deep curtsy. 'Reverend Mother,' she murmured, before bustling away.

'You see,' Catherine burst out when the door had closed, 'I'm not sure I'm ever going to do any better. I'm not sure what's going on. Words don't seem to mean what I think they mean. For example, Sister Margaret's having a great campaign to re-establish our traditional values. Wonderful, I thought. But it turns out to mean that people shouldn't run or talk in the corridors, but walk with their heads bowed and their hands together; and that we shouldn't chat during supper but listen to readings from scripture: that sort of thing. Things to impress the visitors, I can't help thinking, but maybe that's cynical. *I* want us to remember that we are all equal in the sight of God and get back to treating people with care and consideration.'

'Have patience. As soon as our affairs are in order people will discover Margaret's limitations.'

'But I rather fear, Reverend Mother, that by then our community will be irrevocably changed.'

'Nonsense. How could that be? Really, Sister, you had better buck up. That reminds me: will you call in at the needlework room and ask one of them to come up? There's a nasty green mark on my tray cloth. Monica or Elizabeth, I should think; they're awfully clever about stains and so forth. If it doesn't shift soon, I'm worried it may take hold.'

12

'About the arrangements for tomorrow,' said Sister Luke to Sister Joan.

Joan jumped. Margaret had entrusted her with the arrangements for tomorrow's ceremony to mark the restoration of the Albion Tower, and she dreaded she would overlook some small but essential detail.

'Obviously, the paraplegic, Sister Brenda, will be wheeled along in her chair,' Sister Luke continued. 'Thinking it over, it might be sensible if the other two who were injured were also in wheelchairs. They are not incapable of walking, it's true, but Sister Ellen can't stand for too long with that damaged hip, and poor Sister Grace is so unpredictable I think it'd be easier if she were strapped in a chair: for her own protection, of course. And they'd look more of a piece, don't you think, the three injured ones in wheelchairs? I suppose they'll be positioned near the head of the procession, with Sister Beatrice?'

'Sister Joan,' called Margaret, who happened to be passing and had paused to catch the gist of this. 'Excuse Sister Joan for one moment, Sister Luke. I must borrow her. The memorial tablet has arrived.' She led Joan from the cloister and the ever-present danger of well-meaning but time-wasting interruption. (It had always puzzled Margaret that such a draughty place should attract lingerers and gossipmongers.) She led through the vaulted hall and out into the autumn sunshine.

Their shoes crunched over the gravel. By the

creeper-clad wall a sister was picking up leaves that had fallen since the previous day's tidying.

'Over my dead body,' growled Margaret.

Joan clutched herself in fright. 'Oh, you mean the wheelchairs,' she gasped, suddenly comprehending. 'Yes, I thought they sounded a bit off. I thought myself they would draw attention—'

'Not the wheelchairs, the injured. I won't have the injured anywhere near the ceremony. They'd detract from its purpose, which after all is a celebration. Those negative-minded people would leap at the chance to bring in a wrong note. No, shut the injured away for the afternoon. In fact, not to put too fine a point on it, Joan, I'd prefer it if they were shut away somewhere pretty much most of the time. I'm sick to death of the way they're handed round like overgrown babies. Sister Luke and her lot are always at it. Do you know, I was actually invited to congratulate the revolting dribbly one—'

'Oh heavens, you mean Sister Grace—'

'Yes, yes. I was expected to make a fuss of her because she'd managed to tie her own shoelaces.'

'Sickening, Margaret.'

'Can't a room be found for them?'

'They've got one, the old lumber room in the hospital corridor. It's been made very comfortable.'

'Then why the dickens don't they stay in it? As for tomorrow: not a hint of an injured nun, not a glimpse of a wheelchair. Do I make myself clear?'

'Perfectly,' said Joan, making a note of it on her clipboard. 'Did you say the stone's arrived?'

At once Margaret's face cleared and her voice became tender. 'Over here. Come and see. They're going to lay it this afternoon and drape something over until the ceremony. There.' The finely etched script and the polished granite gave her deep satisfaction. '*In memory of Sister Mary John, who gave her life for this*

96

Priory,' she read lovingly for the second time that morning.

'Very nice.'

'Nice?' frowned Margaret.

'Um, fitting.'

'*Inspirational*, Joan.'

'Oh, certainly inspirational, Margaret.'

Like a chisel embedded in the left side of her brow, the dug-in pain very slowly turned. Her lips parted, and she moaned very quietly.

'Not another migraine?' Angelica exclaimed in dismay. She'd come to Catherine's room to discover why Catherine had not been seen that morning. 'What a pity. I suppose this means, if it's anything like the last attack, you'll miss the ceremony tomorrow.'

Through her eyelashes, Catherine observed the arrival, dismissal and obstinate return of an embarrassing conclusion on the face of her friend. Angelica suspected, she guessed, that the migraine was self-induced. Well, that was understandable. Until recently most people here were not aware she was prone to suffer from migraines. Furthermore, she had made her misgivings about the proposed ceremony pretty clear. And it was true, thought Catherine, that the whole idea filled her with disgust: a parade to the foot of the Albion Tower, the unveiling of a memorial tablet, an act of dedication. So maybe her sickness and headache *were* unconsciously self-induced. Maybe they were a form of protest. Maybe it was her body's way of saving her from attending. However— Angelica had asked if she could bring her something or do anything for her, and the slight gesture Catherine now made to decline the offer set off a nauseous wave in her stomach. Lights flickered under her eyelids; the chisel started turning again. And she knew, given the choice, she would put

97

up with any ghastly charade of a ceremony just so long as she could stand upright and free from pain.

She heard the door close. She lay very still. The lights beneath her eyelids converged to form a stream. The stream gathered momentum, became a flood tide, roaring forward and pulling back over shingle. Amid the noise in her ears she heard voices gloating; gloating and glorifying; and a picture rose of the people and the water rushing towards the Albion Tower. Everyone here is swept away, she thought. Then the noise in her ears died down, and she corrected herself. Not everyone, not Sister Luke who had care of the injured; not young Sister Christa who still spoke out bravely against Sister Margaret; not Angelica— Though lately Angelica had developed a most annoying habit of qualifying every critical remark they made, as if Sister Agnes were nearby and able to eavesdrop. 'Of course, it's very pleasant to see the place looking so much smarter,' she would say, or 'Though I do think the Albion Tower episode restored people's pride.' Heavens, why were people so witless about the saving of a statue? What good had it done? Hadn't it done irreparable harm? Apart from Mary John's death and the injuries sustained by Sisters Ellen, Brenda and Grace, there'd been a great welling of emotion that had swept people up beyond the reach of reason. It had changed their perceptions. She thought of how certain vainglorious hymns, once sniggered at and avoided, were sung these days with passion; and how the old custom of arguing for a change of mind or an alternative proposal had become sacrilegious.

The pain ebbed a little. She hoped she might sleep. It occurred to her in her weariness that maybe the effort it cost her to constantly argue against the changes was not worthwhile. Maybe those sisters who were forced to bear the burden of the priory's recovery deserved their fate, were despicably meek and accepting. But this line could not be held for long. Soon she recalled that a large number of the disadvantaged were lay sisters, and although the community had taken pride in good and gracious behaviour towards them, membership on a footing equal to the *religieuses* had always been withheld. So an evil of the present had its roots in the snobbery of the past, for the very existence of a lesser class provided today's élite with a ready dumping-ground.

A rapping on the door sent shock waves through her, and brought her painfully alert. Sister Christa came in and leaned over the bed.

'So it's true, you are ill,' she conceded grudgingly. 'I thought you were copping out. Anyway, you may as well hear the latest. I've just heard from Sister Luke that the injured nuns are not to take part in the ceremony. Did you hear that?' she asked, when there was no reaction from Catherine.

'Mm,' Catherine managed.

'Honestly, what a time to get a headache! Can't you take something for it? We need your help. Why should they get away with it? The injured, above all, have a right to be there. They *ought* to be there, to remind everyone of the cost.'

Catherine peered at the youthful face. Anger made no impression on it: deep lines creased the brow, then fled; lips pursed, then were shiny and unshrivelled once more. Christa's energy wafted to her, and she shivered at her own enervation. Immediately a wave of her nausea rose. Now she was obliged to swallow, to gulp, to cry, 'Water.'

'Where? Oh, here. Come on then, I'll hold your head.'

Catherine sipped, then was lowered again to the pillow.

'You all right? Look, I'm sorry you're so ill. I really shouldn't have bothered you. Hope you're better soon. I'll leave you in peace.'

Catherine heard the door open, but was not conscious when it closed.

'One hardly knows whether to laugh or cry,' said Margaret. 'Still, at least our guests will be spared the sight of her doleful face, and for that one is grateful. But really, you know, for the joint directrix to give in to some trifling indisposition at such a solemn moment in the priory's history— Well, it's hardly the stuff of leadership.'

'She's a bad loser. That's the long and short of it,' Imogen declared, thus earning the indulgent smile with which Margaret acknowledged support of a robust but impulsive nature.

Beatrice, who had pictured herself being praised before an audience of enemies as well as admirers, felt some of the zest had gone out of the occasion. 'I'm fed up with her attitude.'

'We can use it,' Agnes said.

'Ah,' said Margaret after a pause, and they all became extra alert.

Agnes explained: 'Each of us – not Margaret, obviously – but the rest of us should make a point of confiding in one other person. Pick that person carefully – someone who can't keep a thing to herself. The line is: "Catherine is licking her wounds, which is understandable, but unfortunately reflects badly on the priory." Our concern is that she is letting the priory down. Speak in a burst of anxious confidence. It'll spread like wildfire.'

'Very good, Agnes.'

'Bit tame, though,' said Beatrice. 'No more than our usual stuff. And personally I reckon it's such a thorough-going snub that she deserves something sharper.'

'Such as?' drawled Agnes.

'Don't know yet. But never fear, I'll think of something.'

'All right,' agreed Margaret in a tone that urged caution. 'Let us know what you come up with. But Agnes's plan is well worth implementing. Got it, everybody?'

'You've got a smashing little bum, Hopeless,' said Beatrice with calculated flattery.

'Oh, do you think so? Why?'

'It's round and downy. Like a strongly indented peach.'

Hope was entranced, but quickly recalled her manners. 'Yours is pretty good, too.'

Beatrice agreed absently. 'Hopeless, pet,' she went on, 'I wonder if you could do something extra specially clever for me.'

'Course I could.'

'Can you do a Welsh accent?'

'Welsh? Indeed to goodness!'

'Mmm. Well, I've thought of a rather good plan.'

Hope listened, and it soon became clear that this was no ordinary scheme. More, much more, than simply spying or eavesdropping or asking a cunning question was required – the sort of thing Beatrice usually put her up to. So she could start thinking in terms of more than the usual recompense. 'Yes, it could be done: if you're quite sure that's where she'll be.'

'I'll check it out about an hour before the ceremony. It'll be simple enough to go outside and see whether her curtains are still drawn.'

'And no-one else will be about?'

'Not a soul. Everyone will be in the procession, except for the sister delegated to stay with the invalids in the hospital wing.'

Hope drew her fingers through Beatrice's long fair

hair. 'It'll take some nerve, but I'd do anything for you, Beatrice.'

Beatrice sat up.

'You're not going already?'

'Got to, I'm afraid. I'm on show tomorrow, so I need my beauty sleep.'

'Oh, stay a bit longer.'

'Look, tomorrow night when it's all over I'll stay for hours. Now, have you got every detail in there?' she asked, seizing and shaking Hope's head.

'I won't let you down, promise. And by the way, Beatrice: I've noticed you're pally with Sister Clare. Be a love and ask her to make Sister Prudence put me in charge of the souvenir prayer cards, will you? I'm the best artist in our group, but they never let me be in charge of anything. It's not fair.'

'Do a good job tomorrow, and I'll see what I can do.'

Catherine was feeling somewhat better. The nausea had stopped, the headache was less dwelling. Sister Monica had been with her, had fed her soup, cake, and tea. Afterwards, she'd helped her to the bathroom and put fresh sheets on her bed. So long as she was left in peace for twenty-four hours, to lie perfectly still between cool sheets with the air coming softly through the curtain crack, all would be well. Soon, very soon now, she would drift into sleep.

How good was Monica, thought Catherine drowsily, with her coddling motherly ways. And for all that she remained under Cecilia's thumb, how intrinsically wise. For Monica could persuade the most painracked and done-for of sufferers that life, after all, might be worth the candle. Catherine was almost ashamed to think that she proposed to harry the good soul, to make her thoroughly uncomfortable by insisting she face up to the idea of rottenness at the heart of Albion. Now that she was feeling soothed and comfortable, Catherine shrank from the idea. Wasn't it strange, how, on the morning after, even a nightmare supported by reason faltered a little, put its head on one side and seemed to suggest: 'Ah, go on, not worth it, is it? Hardly the end of the world. Bit embarrassing, y'know, all this fuss you're making.'? It would be so much cosier to give in, to take the best life had on offer – worship, beauty, friendship – and forget the rest. Tea in the needlework room, imagined Catherine. Always a dainty occasion. With the Rockingham china, and Cecilia pouring, of course—

When the bell summoning the sisters stopped ringing, Hope stepped out of her room. She gathered her skirts and ran through the empty corridors, then mounted the flight of stairs leading to a wide landing over-looking the courtyard. Here she waited, her heart's drumming the only sound, only the dust moving in sunlight pouring through the glass of a stone-carved window. Below, the visitors were waiting on a patch of ground near the foot of the Albion Tower: covering the very spot, she thought idly, on which Sister Mary John had fallen. They waited, orders of service in hand. Hope waited, tingling with readiness.

Soon, the faint singing of a canticle reached her, and then came into view a simple cross borne by a sister; next, a smattering of visiting clergy, then the main body of women, their silver-grey robes flowing like smooth water, their pristine coifs and cuffs white as fresh snow. She raised her hands to the window catch, stealthily released it, and pushed the window wide.

The scene was set. Gathering her skirts, she raced back through the corridors.

In the south wing, she thrust open a door, crying,

'Sister, wake up! Sister, I'm needing your help. Urgent now.'

Catherine woke with a start, and as the voice penetrated her consciousness, turned her head towards the door.

Squinting through the dimness and seeing that Catherine was roused, Hope gabbled out the information in a rehearsed Welsh accent. 'Sister Grace has got out. I found her on the landing over the courtyard: the ceremony caught her eye, I shouldn't wonder. Leaning out of the window, she was. I tried to pull her away, but she wouldn't budge. And I've Sister Ellen taken terrible poorly; I shall have to go back to her. Will you go to the landing for Grace, Sister Catherine? I'm at my wits' end. There's no-one else I can ask.'

'Yes— Don't worry, I'll go.'

Hope fled.

Catherine pulled on her robe and tied the girdle; she fastened the first button of her veil over her coif. She did not wait to put on her shoes. Lurching through the corridors, she might have been at sea: levering herself from the walls, fighting for balance. Going upstairs, she hauled on the banister rail, and nearing the top cried, 'Sister Grace, Sister Grace!' But the landing, when she arrived there, was empty.

Her heart leapt as her eyes fell on the open window. She rushed to lean out of it, raised herself on tiptoe to crane further: but no crumpled nun lay sprawled below on the grass. Across the courtyard the ceremony was in progress. A voice intoned a prayer. Squinting, she saw Beatrice: who could miss her? And Margaret— And yes, there was Angelica, sharing her order of service with Sister Theresa. Then a nun, who had inclined her head confidingly towards her neighbour a moment ago, suddenly looked up and stared at Catherine. It was Sister Agnes. And the nun whom Sister Agnes had been whispering to also looked up:

104

Sister Martha. It was an unreal moment, containing only that silent, long-held stare. When the bright light sickened her, she stepped back and fumbled with the catch to close the window.

Unsteadily, her hands supporting her along the wall, she went through the gallery above the cloister and then into the corridor leading to the hospital. Her vision swam. Her head started throbbing. Even as she opened the hospital door, an easygoing voice reached her, a voice she recognized. She staggered in. And Sister Luke, who was encouraging Sister Grace with her knitting, looked up. 'Over . . . round . . . and through,' she was saying. 'Good girl! And look who's come to see you. It's Sister Catherine. Sister?' Sister Luke rose and hurried over to Catherine who was swaying in the doorway.

'Where's your assistant?' panted Catherine. 'That Welsh nurse?'

'Come and sit down. I decided to stay here and let Sister Megan go to the ceremony. Thinking it over, I found I preferred to be with our sisters here.' She led Catherine to a chair near to where Sisters Brenda and Ellen were contentedly sewing. 'Are you feeling worse? Let me take a look at you.'

'No, I'm fine,' Catherine said, as blood rushed from her head.

Sister Luke caught her as she fell.

'I were sharing me order paper with Sister Agnes' – Martha mentioned this fact casually, but it was the most exciting feature of her story, for she had been tremendously flattered to find herself on chummy terms with so powerful a figure – 'when she whispers in me ear: "Can that be Sister Catherine at the window?" And, do yer know, it *were*: Sister Catherine, staring down, cool as a cucumber. Or bold as brass, yer might say, seeing as how she'd made out she were too ill to attend the ceremony.'

A most satisfactory gasp erupted in the potting shed.

At that moment in one of the laundry rooms, several nuns were clustered round Sister Maud. 'Honestly, if you don't believe me, ask Sister Imogen,' she was saying above the hiss and pop of a steam iron. 'It was Sister Imogen first saw her. She was so surprised, she gave me a nudge. "That surely can't be Sister Catherine up there?" she whispered. So then I looked up, and saw Sister Catherine, plain as I'm seeing you now.'

Over the washing-up – and there was plenty of it: over a hundred visitors to tea, not to mention the two dozen guests in residence – Sister Virginia was explaining how she had been diverted from the prayers of dedication that afternoon and found herself staring up into the face of the joint directrix. 'Sister Clare was beside me. She suddenly gave a gasp. I followed her eyes, and there she was: Sister Catherine, leaning half out of the window. I could hardly believe it, because when Sister Monica came for her tray this morning, she said Sister Catherine was so poorly she had to lie still and keep her curtains closed.'

Beatrice slipped into the art room. She leaned over Hope's easel. 'Nice work,' she murmured. 'I shall be having a word with Sister Clare about your promotion later on.'

Waving over her shoulder, Beatrice went on her way, Hope's shining eyes following her.

*   *   *

In the hospital, Sister Luke was applying a compress to Catherine's brow.

'Any better?' she asked anxiously.

Catherine could not reply.

13

After all, this is very pleasant, Anne thought, taking a Viennese finger from a dish of cakes. With her lips standing delicately from her teeth, she bit off its end. Sugary crumbs showered over her chest and lap. She noted where the larger crumbs fell so that later a moistened finger might convey them to her mouth. Cecilia, she recalled, had been sniffy about her coming here this afternoon, peeved, no doubt, because it was Anne whom Elizabeth had invited rather than her good self. Cecilia purported to despise the Blue Sitting Room; having no official right to enter it, she had made an inspection, nevertheless, the moment the room had been declared ready for use. 'So vulgar, my dear. All velour and tassels and deep-pile carpet.' 'Well I think it is delightful,' Anne imagined herself saying to Cecilia later on. 'The chairs are the last word in comfort, and the colour scheme, keeping strictly to blues, most restful.'

That the Blue Sitting Room should be restful was the precise intention of its creator, Elizabeth had explained. 'You see, Margaret felt that with the pressure of work currently placed on us heads of department, facilities for our relaxation ought to be set aside. The greater one's responsibility, the greater one's need to unwind: in order to be refreshed and able to continue performing effectively. Because if the heads of department are performing well, the priory as a whole benefits.' It had made sense to Elizabeth, and now, sampling the facilities, it made sense to Anne. Her view was reinforced by Elizabeth having confided an intention to make Anne her deputy: there was sufficient work to justify such a move, goodness knows. This of course would confer on Anne also the right to use the Blue Sitting Room.

When she had finished her cake and raised most of the crumbs from her habit, Anne licked her fingers and reached for her teacup.

'Can I top you up, Sister?' the attendant sister hurried to ask.

'You may,' Anne kindly corrected her. 'Thank you.' She took her cup and settled back to sip its contents.

In fact, a decision had been taken at the highest level to allow heads of all the larger departments to appoint deputies. This had provoked lengthy and sophisticated deliberation. The likeliest candidates were not automatically chosen, for the coming of privileges had bred in those who enjoyed them a fierce desire to preserve them for their own use. Even Elizabeth, who had wondered in the early days of her elevation whether the honour was worth all the work and worry, now desired above all else to safeguard her position. A hardworking deputy was one thing; a challenging deputy quite another. But Anne was a comfortable choice and would surprise no-one, since Anne was her closest friend.

Surveying the occupants of the Blue Sitting Room, Anne was surprised to see one or two who were present on the same terms as herself. She was not surprised to see Sister Martha: on the contrary, it was always a jolt to recollect that Sister Lazarus and not Sister Martha was the head gardener; but she was surprised to see Sister Prudence of the art department with Sister Mark in tow, for Sister Mark was a mousy little thing with hardly a word to say for herself; surprised, too, that Sister Veronica of Accounts had not chosen as her proposed deputy someone with more about her than Sister Faith. And Sister Imogen's choice of bland Sister Joy seemed a trifle eccentric. Still, people were getting along very well together, and Anne supposed that a convivial atmosphere could only assist in the business of relaxing. For her part, it was not just the right to wallow in luxury that she found so pleasing (her attention at this point was caught by the handy placing in the walls of push-button service bells), not at all; it was knowing how useful she could be to dear Elizabeth who, until now, had been most frightfully overworked.

'Look, there is Sister Beatrice,' breathed Cecilia, coming to an abrupt halt and causing scones to slither on the tray she was carrying. 'Let's ask her to tea.'

'I dare say she'll have tea in the Blue Sitting Room. She is eligible, of course, as Margaret's chief aide.'

'Well, she's not *in* the Blue Sitting Room. She's *out there*.' Cecilia and Monica had come to rest in front of window overlooking the garden. 'Go and ask her.'

'But you know very well Elizabeth asked us to stop taking tea in the workroom. It's forbidden to ordinary workers.'

'Monica, do not be so – grubby.'

'Dear one, I'm only repeating what is said.'

'Well, phoo-ee! If you won't ask her, I shall. Only you can see I'm carrying this tray,' she pointed out piteously.

Monica considered the fact of the tray.

'Dear, I must be able to swank a little when they come back from their horrid Blue Room tea. If we can say we had a bit of a party, too—'

Monica hastened without more ado to the garden door. 'Sister Beatrice. Will you take tea with us in the needlework room?' she called.

Beatrice, with her fascinating smile, came slowly down the path.

It was the way, when she smiled, her cheeks pushed up and emphasized her feline eyes, thought the waiting Monica, trying to assess the precise nature of Beatrice's pulchritude.

'Well, how nice,' Beatrice agreed affably. 'Are we going to use that pretty china I've heard so much about?'

'You mean the Rockingham? Oh yes, we always use it: when it's just our group, you know,' laughed Monica deprecatingly. 'It was Sister Cecilia's mother's tea set. Though I suppose, strictly speaking, it now belongs to the priory.'

'Strictly speaking,' laughed Beatrice.

Cecilia, who had gone ahead to fill the kettle, was setting out the tea service when they arrived. 'Hello,' she cried gaily. 'How kind of you to come. Particularly when superior comforts are to be had elsewhere.'

'But not presented with your élan, Sister Cecilia.'

'Sister Beatrice was saying how pretty she thinks our china.'

'Then she shall come and use it as often as she likes. One lump or two, Beatrice, dear?'

The beneficence of the Blue Sitting Room was not universally effective. Sister Lazarus sat edgily in her chair. Thrice she had declined tea and cake. 'No, no; I never partake between meals.'

Martha, holding forth as usual, had paused long enough to overhear Lazarus's remark and to mouth behind her teacup an explanation to her neighbour: 'Wobbly hands; hates to show herself up.' Lazarus had lip-read this with ease. Resentment flooded her. This was Martha's first visit to the Blue Sitting Room and already she had the manner of a long-standing habitué.

With an effort, Lazarus removed her eyes from Martha and covertly examined others in the room. The Sister Precentor was breaking the rules by talking shop with Sister Angelica. Lazarus deduced this from the fact that they were looking at a score. Sister Prudence of the art department was another offender; retaining her sociable smile, her words to Sister Clare were more redolent of complaint than relaxation. 'That funny creature, Sister Hope. I know you recommended her, but she has managed to upset the entire group.' Sister Clare did not appear to be enjoying the exchange; her eyes searched about for escape. Sure enough, when Sister Joan came in, Sister Clare sprang up. 'Sister Joan, take my seat; I'm just leaving.' Smiling grimly to herself, Lazarus began to eavesdrop on a group near the fireplace. After a while she deduced that these particular sisters were trying out new personae: one would have to call them Blue Sitting Room personae, Lazarus supposed, for she had never before encountered this sort of talk in the priory.

'Have you seen the carpet samples for the north wing?'

'Well, no, but—'

'*I* have. Sister Imogen brought them round to ask my opinion. I recommended the willow green.'

'Perhaps khaki would be safer, the way some sisters barge in through the north door.'

'Oh, she means *dirt*-coloured. Hee-hee!'

'At least they're pulling their socks up in the kitchen. Breakfast has been on time—'

'But the supper on Thursday! Whatever was that concoction, do you suppose?'

'Apparently, the poor dears are trying to be adventurous.'

A hush fell as the door opened and Margaret came in. She glanced appraisingly round, appeared satisfied, then launched into a noisy fuss – for she knew herself to be the centre of attention – over which cake to choose. Presently she sat down and spoke civilly to her neighbours; and with half an ear to the great one's conversation, the occupants of the Blue Sitting Room gradually resumed their own.

In the scullery, tension was building. Sister Kirsty, one of the redundant sisters who had been directed for the time being to labour in the kitchen, had been obligingly helpful this afternoon to an almost unbearable degree. 'No, no, I'll do it, Sister,' she had cried, seizing the slop bucket; and on her return from the yard had all but hurled the bucket to the floor, so avid was she to substitute her own body for Sister Michael's at the top of the stepladder. 'Mind yourself now, Sister. Why not come down and let me reach for it? I've got longer arms.' And at the conclusion of every chore, 'What next?' she cried breathlessly.

It was driving them mad. It disturbed their rhythm. It appeared to imply, Sister Ruth considered darkly, that some people were getting past it. Sister Rachel, putting on her 'voice' – thus signalling to those in the know a meaning beyond the sense of her words – called, 'Sister Kirsty, it's time we were doing the vegetables. Go into the shed and weigh them out.'

'Right y'are, Sister,' Kirsty cried eagerly, dropping a teacloth in her haste to obey.

'Now look.'

'Sorry. There. It hasn't hurt, there's no dirt on it.'

'Into the laundry basket, if you please.'

'Right-oh. I'll go and be weighing the vegetables, then. Shan't be long.'

'As long as it takes to do the job properly, I trust.'

But Kirsty had gone. They exhaled vigorously.

'Thank goodness for that.' Sister Rachel pulled in her chin and raised her eyebrows. 'You know what she's about? Trying to worm her way in.'

They considered this over the washing and drying of baking tins, their hands slowing to their normal pace.

'Well, I hope Sister Florence doesn't fall for it,' said Sister Michael. 'It'd be a mistake to start letting any of that lot in permanent.'

'It would. Because what if the number of visitors dropped off for some reason? They might have to cut down on the kitchen staff.'

'But they wouldn't pick us. We've got years of experience.'

They worked silently for some moments, but it soon became apparent that the remark about years of experience had not entirely reassured.

'You never know,' Sister Michael said thoughtfully. 'They might see advantages in keeping the young ones.'

'Young ones!' scoffed Sister Ruth.

'I'm only saying. Who knows who they'd move?'

Sister Rachel dried her hands on the roller towel. 'I think we ought to put Sister Florence straight. I mean, Sister Kirsty tries to create a good impression, but take that teacloth business—'

'Slipshod,' pronounced Sister Ruth. 'We'll get the others to back us.'

Outside the Blue Sitting Room door, Catherine hesitated. She disapproved strongly of this method of setting the most powerful people apart. Margaret's reasoning had not impressed her. 'But we all work hard according to our individual abilities,' she had protested when the idea was mooted during a meeting of Council. 'And we all need a measure of rest and recreation.'

'Of course,' Margaret had agreed in a reasonable tone, before raising her voice and launching upon a diversionary tirade – which was her usual response to any attempt to argue with her. 'But don't, please, talk to me about "we all". Some people are working incredibly hard: for the benefit of everyone else, I might add. Yes, those with responsibility *are* being encouraged to rest. Yes, a place has been set aside for them. And I think it is petty and small-minded in the extreme to begrudge it. Instead of stirring up envy, it's a pity these carpers and moaners don't look at what's *right* with the priory for a change. My goodness, just look at the improvements. Just look at the change in morale. Why don't these people stop trying to stir up trouble for the sake of it, and start thinking *positively*?'

It was impossible to argue with her, Catherine concluded. Margaret would never stick to the premise. She scuttled instead to a premise of her own instantaneous devising, and clung to it so belligerently that her opponents were left open-mouthed and reeling.

Catherine had resolved to cold-shoulder the Blue Sitting Room. But the Prioress, when acquainted with her decision, took exception to it. 'Do you want to lose every vestige of your popularity? Because you're going the right way about it, Sister. People can't abide a sulkysides; and from where I'm sitting, that's what you appear to be.'

So now, her heart knocking unpleasantly, Catherine opened the Blue Sitting Room door.

Her entrance met with silence: but it was short-lived, buried by conversations resumed in an animated manner which seemed to deny knowledge of anyone's having entered the room. Only Angelica greeted her. 'Sit here, Catherine,' she called, 'I'll pour you some tea.' She rose, half pushed her friend into her chair, then hurried to elbow the attendant sister away from the teapot. 'I'll get it for Sister,' she insisted in a low voice, knowing it would embarrass Catherine to be formally waited on.

Theresa, the Sister Precentor, looked at Catherine. 'Will you sing the solo part in this arrangement of Sister Angelica's? It's charming, and bang in the middle of your range. I must have something new for Sunday.'

Catherine, with Angelica perched on the arm of her chair and humming in her ear, studied the score. 'All right,' she agreed, though she was aware that her voice was off form these days. She remembered the words of the Prioress, and thought she had better be obliging. Angelica and Theresa chatted across her. Their proximity seemed sheltering to Catherine as she sipped her tea and broke small pieces off the cake that Angelica had laid in her lap. Eating, smiling, sometimes interjecting, her attention wandered.

Eventually, murmuring that she would return, she rose. Across the room Sister Lazarus looked ill at ease, and no-one appeared to be paying her notice. 'How are you, Sister Lazarus?' Catherine asked, perching in friendly fashion on the arm of Lazarus's chair. When no answer came, she went on, 'I must say the chrysanthemums look splendid in the chapel. Specially those big golden blooms—'

Lazarus could hardly credit her misfortune. It had been a terrible afternoon, and now to cap it all she was being singled out by Sister Catherine. She felt marked; as if Failure had recognized and claimed Failure. Lazarus looked round. Yes, they were all watching. Pretending otherwise, of course, but their darting looks were like glancing wounds. She struggled from her chair and hurried, weaving and stumbling, out of the room.

'Duty calls,' said Martha, stretching.

Something seemed to be going wrong, thought Elizabeth, sending a look to Anne. Who understood her at once; and from long practice, the old friends achieved a simultaneous rising. Elizabeth, passing the

116

chair where Catherine still perched, said kindly, 'Come and see the St Peter's reredos. We've hung it in the gallery to check the weighting. It's turned out well; though we had doubts at first, never before having undertaken a modern design. It's a sort of seascape: fish and shells and seaweed: quite daring.'

'Yes, do come and see what you think,' Anne encouraged her.

In a dream, Catherine followed.

14

Agnes was addressing the company in the Green Sitting Room, a facility brought into use soon after the opening of the Blue Sitting Room. Agnes was a popular speaker here, for the Green Sitting Room had been her idea. It was a room where the second rank of workers, those who could boast five or more years' continuous service in one of the flourishing areas of work, could gather and exchange views in a convivial and comfortable atmosphere. Needleworkers would learn how the art department fared, cooks hear the thinking of accountants, and thus would be engendered a feeling of everyone pulling together. Those eligible to use the Green Sitting Room took pride in their membership, and Sister Agnes was their favourite visitor. They heard her respectfully, disposed to agree with her every word.

Agnes's mode of delivery was not exciting; her tone was flat, her choice of phrase homely. Yet her message often contained breathtakingly vindictive asides aimed at named persons. Sister Agnes did not mince words.

'I suppose,' she was saying, 'Sister Catherine feels an extra sympathy for those with no particular job because, in a way, she's got no particular job. She excused herself from taking one because she doesn't like hard decisions. She's afraid of responsibility, and that's her problem. But if she starts interfering with the rest of us who have to do the jobs she can't or won't do, then that could get dangerous. People understand what we're doing and they want us to get on with it.'

'Hear, hear,' they cried, as Agnes sat down.

By the door, Beatrice, who had been commissioned by Margaret to keep an eye on what Agnes got up to, smiled and slipped away.

In an anteroom off the chapter house, Margaret was talking with members of the Forward Planning Committee. 'Beatrice shouldn't be long,' she said, checking her watch. 'I want you to give her a nice hand when she arrives, because she's brought off a magnificent coup: two large gifts in as many months. She's making a tremendous success of liaising with the visitors, who are thrilled to be talking to the heroine of the Albion Tower incident. Particularly the men: well, I suppose men do warm to bravery, and Beatrice certainly has plenty of that commodity. Ah, here she is. We were just talking about you.'

'Well please don't stop,' Beatrice beamed, and they broke into gentle applause.

'Beatrice, we're proud of you. Now, as I was saying, our latest benefactor – the gentleman in room eleven, by the way; please be especially gracious in your dealings with him – proposes to hand over the cheque this afternoon. I have to go and brief the Prioress in a minute. She's giving him tea.'

'But I thought you said "Never again" after her teeth dropped out that time.'

'I know,' Margaret sighed. 'I shall be on tenterhooks. But where else in this place can one find decent china? Imogen, please make sure it's not rock cakes again.'

'Talking about decent china,' said Beatrice, 'that old trout Cecilia's got some really fine stuff. Keeps it in the needlework room for the exclusive use of the snobs. Of course, officially it belongs to the priory; she's got no business hanging on to it.'

They had listened with sharp attention. Now there

was a pause, broken by Margaret. 'Most interesting. Thank you, Beatrice. One for Agnes, I think. Ask her to look into it, will you? Now where were we?'

'About the gift,' put in Imogen. 'If there's more money coming in, isn't it time we did something about the east wing? Those cracks in the ceiling look ominous.'

'No, I don't think so.'

They darted looks at one another. Margaret's refusal to discuss repairs to the east wing contrasted strangely with her keenness to tackle every other deficiency.

'Let's get to the problem of the old vegetable fields. Joan has come up with something.'

Joan clapped a hand to her head. 'Mmm. Yes. Well, I've found someone at last who might be interested, but only if we include the field where we grow vegetables for the house. But I think we could strike a good deal, and it occurred to me— Whoops!' In her excitement an expressive gesture sent her notes flying and further explanation was accompanied by a scrabbling over the floor to retrieve them. 'Why not let him – ah, thanks – grow the vegetables for us, rather like – excuse me; under your foot – the deal we have with the milk? I've got the figures somewhere—'

The figures were found and passed round.

'Brilliant idea,' commented Clare, who was in fact working on this project with Joan. 'Saves all the bother, gives us a good return, and releases a few more people for the general work pool. As Sister Margaret says, we have to keep our resources flexible.'

'And I really do want to swell the numbers attending regular devotions,' said Margaret. 'It gives such a good impression. Mind you, I'm not sure everyone is getting the message about bowed heads and grave demeanours. That comes within Catherine's orbit, of course. What does the woman do with her time? Perhaps someone should be put in charge of decorum.'

'I'll see to it, if you like,' offered Beatrice. 'I'll soon smarten 'em up.'

Margaret considered the matter. Beatrice sprawling about in private could seem almost disreputable, but there was no-one to touch her for grace and style in public. 'If you could perhaps demonstrate what is required.'

'My pleasure.'

'Now, I can't wait any longer for Agnes. Think about Joan's idea, everyone; we'll discuss it next time. And remember, Imogen: nothing too challenging for tea.'

When she had gone, Clare drew Beatrice aside. 'I know you think highly of that Sister Hope, but Sister Prudence is at her wits' end with her. At my request she put her in charge of the souvenir prayer cards. But really, Sister, she's just not suitable. Sister Prudence says she's a perfect pest. Sorry, but I told Prudence to use her judgement.'

'Fine,' Beatrice said easily. 'I was just impressed with her work, that's all.'

'Oh, apparently she's a good enough artist, but she upsets people.'

The door opened and Agnes came in.

'Too late, duckie. Business all over. That was a nice little talk you gave the plebs.'

'Yeah,' said Agnes. 'Noticed you lapping it up.'

Sister Kirsty, weighing out potatoes in the shed, was suddenly taken by a wave of wistfulness. She put down the bowl and took up a pink pockmarked potato. A patch of black earth had dried on it, the very earth Kirsty had until recently tended. She raised the potato to her nose and sniffed, then touched the earth with the tip of her tongue. She stared into the gloom and imagined sunlight on the crests of rain-sodden furrows, and the squelch of her feet in muddy pools between; she smelled the sharp nourishing tang of the steaming earth and felt hunger stir inside her.

All behind her now, she recalled sternly, and tossed back the potato. No use sorrowing. Steam these days smelled of detergent and she had better like it.

Quick footsteps tapped across the yard. Kirsty peeped out. It was Sister Florence, and she was alone.

'Sister?'

'Oh, my goodness!' Sister Florence clasped her throat.

'Have you – you know – seen about it?'

'I'm sorry?'

'About me being kitchen staff, regular. You said you'd see about it.'

Sister Florence's face fell. 'I'm sorry to disappoint you, Sister, but I had a word with Sister Imogen and I'm afraid it's out of the question. It's not the policy to attach people anywhere permanently now. They want everything kept flexible, so that whatever needs doing can take priority. Oh, don't look so devastated. Look on the bright side. At least you get plenty of variety.'

'I don't want variety, I want to *belong*,' cried out Kirsty. 'Sorry, Sister, but you don't know what it's like, not belonging somewhere.' Kirsty grabbed a fold of her skirt and began kneading it rapidly. 'It's terrible being passed from pillar to post. Some don't want you; they get mad 'cos you don't know their ways. Then Sister Imogen says go somewhere else and they put in a complaint 'cos you didn't have time to finish a job. People look down on you. They stop talking when you come in. And it's terrible waking up in the morning, not knowing where you'll be. It's a really terrible feeling, that. You feel like you can't hardly bear to get up.'

'Come come, Sister. Aren't you being a touch dramatic? And in any case—' She was about to repeat Sister Rachel's complaint about Sister Kirsty's slipshod ways, but the look in the young woman's eyes made her change her mind. 'I'm pleased with your work, but—'

Spotting a gleam of hope, Kirsty snatched at it. 'So if they change their minds—'

'Most unlikely, I fear.'

'Oh. Well. Thanks, Sister.'

Kirsty watched the senior housekeeper go, then went back into the shed. For a few moments she stood there, keeping still; then, as blood rose and sang in her ears, crouched in a corner and let her hot tears come.

Night air ruffled the sycamores. Beatrice pressed closer to the window pane, watching without expression the striptease taking place under the light bulb on the other side of the glass. She bit into an apple; bit, munched, watched.

The apple, the first of the season's orange pippins, had a stimulating acidity; the striptease on the other hand was bland and predictable. Think I'm getting bored with Hope, she decided after a time. Was this because she had discovered a new diversion? The question made her suck in her breath, for the very thought of her discovery, her new 'game', made her nerve-ends sing. In the room, Hope unbuttoned her shift. Beatrice chewed and watched, and because the spectacle lacked zing, played through the game in her mind. There she was, gliding silver and white towards her victim – the gentleman in room eleven, perhaps? – beauteous, desirable, and for ever out of reach. Demurely she extended her hand, softly uttered words of greeting: Had the journey been exhausting? It was her fervent hope that the visit would prove restorative. This last remark accompanied by a hand pressed anxiously to the bed's counterpane, testing for restfulness. Then a walk across the room to sniff the bowl of flowers on the table, a turn, a reminder that visitors were most welcome at the sisters' devotions, and a smile to show that the fairest blooms paled beside her loveliness. And all the time the knowledge of eyes unable to leave her, of a pulse quickening. It was a sharper thrill than any conjured by Hope's writhings.

Beatrice tossed away the apple core and reflected that it was perhaps just as well she had Hope to fall back on, for the game depended upon her own inviolacy, and one could not stay in the clouds for ever.

She went silently along the path, passing other decorously curtained windows. At the heavy oak door, she turned the handle and stepped inside.

In her room, Hope had drawn the curtains.

'I think you're losing your touch. That performance left me stone cold,' Beatrice grumbled, sitting down on the side of the bed.

'That's because you're in a mood. I can always tell. Come here.'

Beatrice shoved her off and bent half-heartedly to undo her shoes. 'And another thing: why did you have to mess up the new job I got for you, chucking your weight around, getting up people's noses?'

'I didn't.'

'Yes, you did. Apparently, you're not fit to be in charge of a hencoop. Don't ask me to put in any more words. You're going to be demoted, by the way.'

Hope pummelled the bedclothes. 'No,' she shouted. 'They can't!'

'Shut up, you fool,' hissed Beatrice, smothering her with a hand. 'Do you want to raise the corridor?' And when Hope still struggled wildly: 'I won't let go till you're quiet. Ouch!'

Hope had bitten her finger. Beatrice released her and examined the wound.

'Don't let them, Beatrice. You can make them do as you say.'

'Of course I can't. And I'm not going to damn well try.'

'Right then.' Hope sat up and looked grim.

' "Right then" what?'

'I'll make trouble.'

'How? No-one would believe your ravings. You're a well-known hysteric.'

Hope looked at her with glittering eyes. Then: 'But wouldn't they love to hear how we tricked Sister Catherine; indeed to goodness?'

15

'Come and have tea with us,' Monica said, slipping her arm through Catherine's. 'It's ages since you did, and you're looking peaky. Isn't she, Cecilia?'

Cecilia came tripping down the corridor. She had just waved to Beatrice across the cloister and received a dazzling smile in return. 'Isn't she what?' she cried gaily.

'Looking peaky. I've asked her to tea.'

'Oh good. We'll tell Anne and Elizabeth.' If the joint directrix sanctioned tea in the needlework room, who were they to object?

When they reached the needlework room, Cecilia went through to the gallery where tapestries were weighted, and called: 'Elizabeth? Anne? Come on. We're going to have tea. And don't pull faces; Catherine wishes it.'

A sister, overhearing this, looked furtively about, then slipped away in search of Sister Agnes.

In the main workroom they arranged themselves in chairs. 'Do you think you might be run down?' Monica asked, examining Catherine's hand as if it might yield a clue to her state of health.

Cecilia, setting out the Rockingham tea service, gave a sniff. Privately, she considered Catherine to be suffering from a prolonged bout of nose-out-of-joint. Catherine had once been the priory's star, but Beatrice, with her brighter beauty and her courage, had eclipsed her. Cecilia had mentioned this theory to the Prioress, and for once the tiresome old thing had not argued.

Cecilia leaned forward and raised the lid of the teapot, inserted a silver spoon and stirred.

'Were they pleased with the reredos at St Peter's?' Catherine asked.

'Oh, delighted,' enthused Elizabeth. 'It caused quite a stir. The publicity's bound to do us good.'

'Our order book's full to bursting already,' Anne said, taking her cup from Cecilia. 'Thank you, dear. I must say, this is nice. Horrid cups in the Blue Sitting Room, almost as thick as the refectory ones.'

They were murmuring their contentment with the thinness of the Rockingham china when the door opened and Agnes came into the room.

'My, this is cosy.' She smiled – always an unnerving sight – and sat on the arm of Elizabeth's chair.

'Do you want something, Sister?' Cecilia enquired frostily.

'Oh, don't mind me. Just carry on.'

'Perhaps Sister Agnes would care for some tea,' suggested Monica nervously. 'I'll fetch another cup.'

'Now that would be nice.'

An awkward silence fell. Only Agnes appeared at ease, waiting calmly for her tea, taking it, remarking in a mild voice on its acceptability. 'I didn't know you got up to such things in the needlework room,' she commented with heavy jocularity.

Elizabeth rushed to explain. 'Usually we don't. That is to say, Sister Anne and I go to the Blue Sitting Room, of course, but as Sister Catherine—' Her voice trailed away.

'Well, well,' said Agnes. And then, holding her cup at arm's length as if noticing it for the first time: 'This china is very unusual. Tell me about it.'

'Rockingham,' snapped Cecilia.

'Indeed?'

'It was my mother's.'

'Now isn't that interesting?'

'It was left to me.'

Agnes raised an eyebrow.

Catherine, beginning to grasp the situation, said hurriedly, 'Sister Cecilia passed it over to the priory, of course; but I suppose it was felt there was no particular use for it. I must say, I'm surprised, Sister Agnes, if you haven't seen it before because Sister Cecilia has often served her fellow sisters from these cups.'

'Perhaps she didn't cast her invitations widely,' smirked Agnes.

'I've used the china on many occasions, and I know I'm not alone.'

'No doubt. Still, it's a pity more of us haven't had the pleasure. Though I suppose it's very old and shouldn't come out too often.'

'Quite,' encouraged Monica. 'It has to be washed very carefully. You insist on doing it yourself, don't you, Cecilia?'

But Cecilia, who had turned pale, said nothing.

'I've just had an idea.' Agnes held her cup and saucer up to the light and moved her head about to view the china from several angles. 'Wouldn't the service look splendid in a display cabinet? In the visitors' sitting room, perhaps. And then, when Sister Margaret had to entertain an important guest, it would be there to hand. Do you know, I think it's even prettier than the Reverend Mother's service?'

Cecilia's mouth opened then closed. This was no time to disparage the Prioress's Royal Worcester. But thinking of the Prioress, she gave a sigh of relief. 'The Reverend Mother wouldn't hear of it. She thinks very highly of her own china.'

'You know, I'm not sure it's up to the Reverend Mother. I'm not sure we shouldn't see what the sisters in general think about it. The china does really belong to us all. Well, pleasant as it is sitting here chatting, I shall have to get on. Some of us have work to do, you know.'

Catherine hurried after her and caught her at the door. 'It's only a small thing. It means so much to Sister Cecilia. Is it worth causing her distress?'

'Distress? Now why should it cause distress? Really, Sister Catherine, you seem to see distress everywhere these days.'

Facing the Prioress were Catherine and Cecilia. Cecilia was too good to cry, however much she needed to. Her forbearance impressed upon her companions the severity of her pain.

Catherine doubted whether her presence here would help matters. If she had lost favour with the Prioress, as she feared, her opinion could be of scant value. Nevertheless, to satisfy Cecilia she had agreed to come. She had always viewed the inveterate tea ceremony with amusement, as an enjoyable little vanity of Cecilia's; but between these two old friends, she guessed, lay a deeper understanding; for them the tea parties stood for something: tradition, family, the past. She pitied the Reverend Mother, who would not care to be publicly associated with a breach of their vows, however venial.

The Prioress, having had the difficulty explained to her, sat in disgruntled silence. 'Never did like the cut of that one's jib,' she growled. Her companions frowned enquiringly. 'Sister Agnes,' she said.

Each pictured Agnes's unpleasing features. Finding themselves no further forward, they sighed.

'I don't know. Suppose they'll be after the Royal Worcester, next.' The Prioress spoke as if it were a progression in ascending order of merit. Cecilia felt for her handkerchief and fiercely blew her nose. 'I suppose you haven't any bright ideas, Sister?' the Prioress asked Catherine.

'Only that you might appeal to Sister Margaret, Reverend Mother.'

'On what grounds?'

'You might broaden the question: beyond that of the china, I mean. Ask her to consider whether ends are always justified if the means cause distress. Plainly, the china is of limited importance to the priory as a whole, compared with what it means to Sister Cecilia. But I think it would be wrong to limit an appeal for tolerance to this one case. There is also the issue of some people being treated cavalierly, as if some are of less consequence than others. Could you get her to consider taking things more slowly, perhaps? She might be asked whether so-called successes are indeed successes, if people have to suffer for them. The trouble is, she refuses to concede that people *are* suffering, which seems to me to compound the wrong being done to them. Ask if we can't find another path to success: a less direct path, but wide enough to take us all.'

'We seem to be getting away from the china.'

'It would be encompassed by a more charitable attitude all round, without begging favour for this one case. Do you see?'

The Prioress was not sure she did. But plainly an attempt must be made to explain the subtleties of life to these people, people like Sisters Agnes and Margaret, people from that sort of background. I suppose it all comes down to what you've been used to, she imagined herself patiently explaining. When you're used to drinking from nice thin china, tea doesn't taste right from crockery. I dare say there are people who feel just as strongly the other way round.

'Will you talk to Sister Margaret, Reverend Mother?'

'Oh, *will* you?' asked Cecilia, twisting her handkerchief.

'I suppose I must,' the Prioress sighed.

*   *   *

'Come in.'

Fussily, Margaret closed the door, then came across the room. The downward tilt of her head which obliged her to peer upwards gave her a look of penetrating watchfulness, though as the Prioress had noticed on previous occasions, she tended to avoid direct eye contact.

'Oh, how pretty,' Margaret remarked, extending a hand in passing to some rather nasty mauve chrysanthemums arranged in a vase this morning by Sister Lazarus. (The Prioress had spread old cloths extensively before allowing Lazarus to begin.) Margaret took the chair indicated, having first pulled it nearer to her hostess's side.

How healthy the woman looks; she quite glows, the Prioress thought enviously, and at once her opening line (I know Sister Cecilia can be a bit of a fusspot) flew out of her head.

Margaret took prompt advantage. 'I've brought something to show you.' She passed over a large notebook. 'Council meeting minutes.'

'But,' began the Prioress, who had been present herself at many of the meetings.

'I want you to look at the past dozen or so voting figures. I've pencilled stars in the margin to guide you. Do look; you'll find them revealing.'

Dully, the Prioress turned the pages.

'A most striking consistency, don't you find?'

'Oh, very.'

'Every proposal passed by a thumping majority. And the same tiny vote recorded against on each occasion. This does bring home the almost universal support my measures enjoy; have enjoyed for many, many months. The support for Sister Ca— I mean, of course, for the other side – has been virtually negligible. In view of this, Reverend Mother, is it not time to come to a decision about the future? People are of the opinion

131

that there is a quite unnecessary question mark hanging over it. A decision now would underline our success. And I am sure you agree we have been astonishingly successful?'

The Prioress clapped shut the notebook and handed it back. The woman had a nerve, instructing her to pronounce on the succession, no less. 'There are also religious considerations, however,' she said coldly.

'Of *course*,' breathed Margaret. 'I'm so glad you brought that up. It's something I'd hoped to discuss.'

'My province, I think,' snapped the Prioress, wondering how on earth she was to introduce the subject of Cecilia's tea service. 'I don't doubt you're doing splendidly on the money side, but you may safely leave spiritual matters to me. Interesting chap you brought to tea the other day,' she improvised desperately.

'Oh, but Reverend Mother, you should have told me you were unwell and I'd have put him off.'

'What?'

'A giddy turn, was it? I was *so sorry*. Never mind. In future, please don't hesitate to say if you're not quite the thing. I can manage very well in the visitors' drawing room, specially now we have the Rockingham china: that pretty stuff Sister Cecilia gave the priory, you know. Do come and see; it looks splendid in the display cabinet.' She smiled, sank back a little and clasped her hands prayerfully. 'But we were discussing the religious aspect. You know, that's another thing I've found rather disappointing. When Catherine showed so little aptitude for the practical requirements of leadership, we suggested, and she agreed, that she should have responsibility for improving our religious observance. It has proved an uphill task, I'm afraid. I've had to ask Sister Beatrice to assist her. I know you will feel as strongly as I, because, as you said, spiritual matters are very much your concern. As a matter of

132

fact, some of us have been considering how we can bring your role home to people: perhaps inaugurate a little ceremony in which you set us an example.'

'Example?' spluttered the Prioress.

'Sister Joan – such an inspirational thinker – came up with a suggestion. From your chair— Perhaps we should move it for the occasion to the centre of the chancel. From your chair you would ceremonially wash the feet of the postulants; to remind people of the virtue of humility; to remind them that however diverse the ways in which we are called upon to serve, no-one is greater than the rest, for we are all equal in the sight of God.'

'*Out of*—' Ejection of the words with which she intended to complete her wrathful cry – *the question* – was stymied by the Prioress's disobliging teeth. They fell about and clacked together, half in, half out of her mouth.

'Following, of course, Our Lord's example,' Margaret added, bowing her head. When she looked up, her eyes were moist. 'Moving, don't you think? Dear me, is something wrong, Reverend Mother? Let me get you a drink.' She bustled to the sideboard, found a glass and filled it from a water jug. 'I should sip it slowly.'

The Prioress sipped it very slowly. But no obvious course occurred to her. She decided she needed time, and when she handed back the glass, said plaintively, 'I need to rest. I do get rather stiff, you know.'

'Allow me to help you.' Tenderly, Margaret led her to the couch.

16

Outside, rain patted the window. Inside, were the lulling hum and intermittent gurgle of water pipes. Sister Imogen, arranged in queenly state upon the seat of a large lavatory in her favourite cloakroom, required to empty neither bladder nor bowel. She required to think. Nevertheless, it was a naked haunch she had applied to the rosewood, for thus there could be no hint of duty evaded or of rest unofficially taken. Swift to denounce slacking in others, she would never countenance the same fault in herself.

Her thoughts, simmering incoherently, took some time to surface. She stared at a majestic basin, tracing the paths of veiny cracks, dwelling on a stain that no amount of rubbing with Vim would shift. Armitage Shanks, she read thoughtfully, pondering the lettering above the overflow hole as if it were Holy Writ: Ar-mi-tage-Shanks.

At length, the overflow hole and the inscription receded, were replaced by the face of Sister Clare. Sister Imogen glowered. Lately, Sister Clare had assumed a dominating position within the inner circle surrounding Sister Margaret. Allied with Sister Joan, she was chock-full of confidence, outlining and promoting their ideas. It was all very well for Sister Clare; she had the leisure in which to work on these schemes, having overall charge of the money-making departments, each supervised by a capable head of its own. Imogen's burden, on the other hand, could not be laid down so lightly. She was in charge of areas of consumption: housekeeping and the general running of the place; there was no end to the demands upon these. And now Joan and Clare were set to win further accolades with their plan for the disposal of the old vegetable fields. But the production of vegetables for the house seemed to Imogen to impinge on her territory; though Clare, in her quest for self-aggrandizement, was unlikely to be stayed by scrupulousness. How satisfying, then, thought Imogen, if she were to discover some crippling snag. Perhaps discussions with Sister Martha and Sister Florence would prove instructive. Encouraged, Sister Imogen rose, reorganized her clothing, and rinsed her hands under the basin tap.

Over coffee cups in the office adjoining the kitchens, Sister Florence and Sister Imogen assessed the allure of home-grown vegetables. The type of visitor they proposed to encourage would expect no less from a tureen, Sister Florence considered. Strengthened by this, Sister Imogen rose from her chair: but was detained.

'One moment, Sister. You know, I don't see why we shouldn't take on some more regular staff for the kitchen. It seems pointless relying so heavily on temporary staff, and it's not as if the workload's likely to decrease. There's a particular sister, such a keen little thing—' Sister Florence had been unable to put from her mind the memory of Sister Kirsty's pleading.

'It's not policy.'

'So you said. But I don't understand; not when the work's there to be done. Why rebuff those eager to do it?'

'To keep everyone on their toes. To make them see it's a privilege to have a permanent position. There was a lot of slackness, a lot of choosiness before. Their attitude's much better now, people are working harder and with no argument. And when Sister Margaret needs a good show in the chapel she can rely on it.'

'But it's causing great unhappiness.'

'Good grief, Sister! Here we are working day and night to put the priory back on its feet' – Margaret's phrase came naturally to Imogen's lips – 'and people moan about unhappiness. If I weren't so busy I might get cross.'

Sister Florence, as if demonstrating the scarcity of her own leisure, sprang to her feet and began to wash their coffee cups.

Sister Imogen left, and made her way to the far greenhouse where Sister Martha proved even more enlightening than Sister Florence.

'Couldn't be done,' she declared, when the new proposal was explained to her.

'But it works with the milk. We buy milk produced by cows grazed on our own land from the people who lease it,' pointed out Imogen, testing Clare's theory in order to arm herself.

'Vegetables is different. Cows'll only give milk.' Martha waved a hand towards the vegetable field. 'That land'll grow anything, up to a point. You can't tell your commercial grower to plant a few hundred-weight of this and a few hundredweight of that. He'll plant a *field* of potatoes, a *field* of carrots. We can buy from what he produces, but to get variety we'd have to buy from outside. You'll only get all home-grown if we keep a field for a kitchen garden.'

'I see,' said Imogen.

Martha was surprised at her taking it so well.

How to make the best use of her knowledge now engaged Imogen. She quickly rejected quiet words in the ears of Joan and Clare, lingered over the prospect of confiding in Agnes whom she rather admired, then settled on the irresistible idea of an approach to the top.

Margaret, at first reluctant to relinquish Joan's brain-wave, became anxious at the prospect of unsettling the visitors with vegetables of doubtful provenance. 'So Sister Martha thinks it can't be done. Well, she should know, and it's not as if it's her own patch she's protecting: her job has already changed. In fact, between you and me, I think the flower garden might do a lot better if Martha were head gardener and Lazarus her deputy, instead of the other way round.'

'Or if Sister Lazarus gave up altogether,' Imogen put in daringly. 'She's got frightfully scatty lately.'

'Mmm, not a bad idea. Look into it, Imogen. Now, about the vegetables: I'll tell Joan and Clare to think again. And thank you. That was a useful initiative on your part.'

Pink with pleasure, Imogen stole away to await developments, and, as a diversion, to propose retirement to Sister Lazarus.

Clare was furious. There were too many 'Imogen says' in Margaret's new instructions. Joan, who was used to the world's inability to accommodate theoretical ideas, gave in with an air of fatality. But Clare feared ascendancy passing to Imogen. 'I'm not at all convinced,' she declared.

Margaret was astounded. She was also, as ever, in a hurry. 'Fortunately, it's not necessary for you to be convinced,' she said from the doorway, 'just to do as you're told.'

But as she hurried away to go over the accounts with Sister Veronica, a small doubt crept up on her. She listened to the chief accountant's explanations, but with only half her attention. 'I don't know,' she suddenly burst out. 'Sister Martha's not one of the world's

137

thinkers. Do something for me, will you, Veronica? There's a problem about the disposal of the vegetable fields. I'd like you to investigate the matter for me. On the quiet, you understand.'

In the potting shed was a wild and wounded animal. Wooden slats, straining ironmongery, seemed unlikely to hold. Hearing the bellowing within, Sister Barbara looked fearfully across to Sister Martha, who beckoned her to a further and safer distance.

Sister Lazarus was scarcely aware that she was inside the potting shed. She was nowhere; a stranded creature. Tears poured from her eyes and ran into her mouth. She heaved air into her lungs in rib-straining snatches to fuel convulsive plangent howls.

When Sister Imogen had delivered the sentence, thoughts of her own ineffectualness hit her like blows. Standing like a found-out child before an accusing teacher, Lazarus had suddenly seen that while re-awakened disease had afflicted her limbs, only fear had paralysed her mind. A shot of courage might have saved her. Now it was too late. She had stumbled towards the potting shed with her great weight of pent-up misery, and had waited in the dimness for anger to bring its release. She had pleaded for its arrival, enticed it with thoughts of Martha and Imogen, and when it came, gloried in it: pulled open drawers, hurled their contents to the wall; scuffed a row of pots from a shelf, beat them with a trowel to terracotta chips; grabbed a hand fork, stabbed open a sackful of compost, hurled dirt, sent the fork flying at the window. And all the time howling, raging.

The sound of shattering glass alerted other toilers. They joined Martha and Barbara. Warily, a small crowd approached the shed.

From among the scattered contents of the worktop

drawer, Lazarus selected the budding knife. She opened the blade, and as the steel flashed, opened her heart to a darting lust: *others should feel her pain.* Stabbings, slashings, gougings – approximations of her agony – flashed, blood-red, through her mind. Clenching the budding knife, she rushed from the shed.

At first she saw only Martha on the path, fat, open-mouthed Martha with her feet apart and her hand raised defensively. 'Traitor,' shrieked a voice in her head.

But then came a disturbance. Now she saw others, a whole crowd, and Catherine pushing through. 'You!' she screamed, racing forward. And as she lunged with the knife: 'You should have *stopped her.*'

Faces, faces, peering faces; faces sorrowful, anxious, embarrassed.

Perhaps she was in Mercy's bed, Catherine thought, and raised her head a couple of inches in an attempt to see. Mercy's or the one next to it, she decided, sinking back against the pillows. She wondered if Mercy had felt as she did now: like an unprepossessing object on general show.

She recalled Margaret's official face peering down. She recalled Margaret's voice: 'Oh, how dreadful. But what a mercy it missed her eye. Tell me, Sister Luke, how is she? It's just shock then, is it? And the wound, of course. How many stitches? I see. Splendid, splendid, one is relieved to find her in such capable hands.'

She recalled Angelica's concern. 'Catherine, oh, Catherine. I heard it was your eye, I was nearly sick, it didn't bear thinking about. Thank heavens it won't affect your sight.'

She recalled a visit from Monica and Cecilia. 'How unspeakably dreadful, Catherine. Whatever came over the woman? She must be possessed. We couldn't believe it, could we, Cecilia?'

'It's going to leave a scar right down her cheek. And it was Catherine's special type of beauty, that unblemished look.'

'Hush, Cecilia.'

She recalled Martha at her bedside. 'For one mad moment I thought it were me she were after. But then she lunged at you. It were lucky I caught her arm, else she'd have had yer eye out. Poor old Laz. Oh, don't get me wrong, I know it were a terrible thing she did. But you see, I'm her friend. She's come to depend on me, like. I 'spect they'll more or less confine her from now on, but I'll still keep an eye on her. 'Cos over the years I've learnt how to handle Lazarus. Oh yes, between you and me, I've been carrying her, job-wise, for months. I've more or less been running the show. Now if Sister Imogen had let *me* put it to her, tactful like, instead of coming right out wi' it—' The self-satisfied voice droned on in Catherine's memory. She pitied Sister Lazarus that she had been condemned to daily doses of it. No wonder she'd gone mad. Oh—

All at once Catherine understood what had happened. It was *Martha* Lazarus had intended to wound. She, Catherine, must have jostled Martha, and Lazarus had been unable to redirect her lunge.

It was an explanation which, for the moment, brought Catherine peace.

Catherine and Angelica crossed over the footbridge and entered the wood. 'Take someone with you,' Sister Luke had insisted, 'if go you must.' Leaping ditches, dodging low branches and trailing briars, choosing a route from a maze of criss-crossing paths, a lightness came over Catherine. She moved easily, dexterously among rooted things, the odour of stillness touching her light breath. They were moving towards Beechy Knob, a small hill near the wood's centre. Climbing it,

Catherine imagined a bird's eye view, a breast-shaped mound of tree tops. At the summit there was a platform of well-drained ground, crumbly between the tree roots and full of cracks and gaps where unseen badgers dozed. She resolved to return one moonlit night, to stand perfectly still and watch badgers' games.

'We came here in the snow. Was it last year?' Angelica asked.

'No. The year before.' (The year before, when there were merely hints of trouble ahead, but these easily dismissed because the Reverend Mother and Sister Mercy had secured promises of funds from outside. The year before, when it was certain that life would go on as before, and Catherine one day would lead their unchanging community.)

'I remember,' Angelica was saying, 'that we climbed up here and stood looking down through the trees. We saw a thousand white-topped branches like arms raised to the snow. And the stillness; it was a forest of petrified angels. Do you remember, Catherine? We gazed and gazed.'

'We were happy then,' said Catherine.

Angelica turned and looked at her, then turned away. 'I don't see why we can't still be happy,' she said, 'if we're sensible. There's so much to enjoy.'

'Not for everyone. How can we enjoy ourselves with misery in our midst, misery that we can alter?'

'We can't alter— Anyway, I think you're exaggerating. And I'm not going to argue about it.' She set off with a jolting downhill stride.

As the grey-clad figure descended, Catherine imagined – for a nun's habit confers anonymity – that it was her own body leaving the wood and the part of her left behind, motionless and scarcely breathing, was rooted here and virtually eternal. Day and night, changing seasons, and still she remained, just being, with no possible power to affect events. Then a bird flew startlingly from a tree overhead. Her heart leapt, and she saw again the flash of metal, felt the blow, heard Lazarus's cry: 'You should have *stopped her*.'

At the bottom of the slope Angelica paused. She turned and called, 'Are you coming, Catherine?'

'Yes. I've just remembered. Wait.' Catherine scrambled down, catching at tree trunks as she went. 'I've remembered what Lazarus screamed. And she *was* aiming at me; I'd half thought she meant to attack Martha. You should have stopped her: that's what she yelled. She meant I should have stopped Margaret.'

Angelica frowned. 'Catherine, for your sake, for my sake, for all our sakes, will you please drop it?'

A draught cut through the trees. The wood turned darker.

'Come on, you've been out long enough.'

Heavier-bodied than a few minutes ago, Catherine lumbered after her.

'How dare she?' fumed Margaret.

Beatrice, looking in, observed Margaret's heightened colour and made to withdraw.

'No, come in, Beatrice, and listen to this. Clare has taken it upon herself to circulate details of Joan's plan – you know, the one about the vegetable fields – among the members of Council.'

'Cheeky,' Beatrice commented, joining Margaret, Agnes and Imogen at the table.

'And of course, the figures sound most attractive, far better than the return from letting the land for sheep grazing, for instance. But there's another side to this. If we're going to serve our own vegetables – and we certainly are – we must hang on to that one key field, which puts the kibosh on letting the land for horticultural purposes, apparently. I put Veronica on to it, and it's all here in her report.' She passed a sheet of paper to Beatrice. 'But if Clare's whipped up feeling, we're going to have to go over it all in Council. And they're so argumentative, and so slow to grasp the point. What a wicked waste of time and effort. Blow the girl. I couldn't be more annoyed.'

'Show this to Clare.' Beatrice tapped the report. 'Better still, get Veronica to write one of those stiff letters she's so good at. "My dear Clare, I must caution you that should you persist in overstepping your brief—"'

'How would it be,' wondered Agnes, 'if Veronica's letter to Clare – containing a judicious ticking-off – somehow managed to circulate among Council members; sort of neutralizing Clare's effort? Might save us a lot of grief.'

'Veronica wouldn't like it,' mused Beatrice. 'She plays by the book.'

'We can handle it.'

'Of course.'

'Mm.' Margaret rose. 'I think I shall leave this in your capable hands. I shall ask Veronica to write to Clare: a copy to me, of course. I'm sure you'll act for the best.' She gave a self-deprecating smile and slipped tactfully from the room.

'To the blind man, Imogen,' explained Agnes. And when Imogen still looked blank: 'A nod is as good as a wink.'

'Oh,' breathed Imogen. 'She meant, Go ahead.'

'Right. Only she's got her position to consider. So get your hot little hands on Veronica's letter, and take it from there. Off you go, there's a good girl. I want a word with Beatrice.'

When the door closed, Beatrice swung her feet onto the table and settled back in her chair.

Agnes craned towards her and leered. 'Guess what I've been hearing.'

'Back off, will you? Your breath's particularly foul this morning.'

Jerking away, Agnes narrowed her eyes. 'I warned you to stop messing about with that Hope woman. Well, you've done it now. She's started blabbing. You've upset her, it seems.'

'Oh, she'll soon calm down. I'm working on it.'

'But there's open gossip,' said Agnes, rapping the table. 'I may find I owe it to Margaret—'

Beatrice sprang to her feet. 'Go and boil your head, Agnes. I told you, I'm dealing with it.'

17

Sister Veronica was regarded as an excellent woman, though a bit on the stodgy side, not someone you would enjoy a joke with. Some thought her too rigid in outlook, a little lacking in imagination; but all conceded she was fearsomely clever, especially at mathematics. Veronica knew she was clever, she was confident of her abilities and judgement. Just every now and then some little thing happened, or someone made a suggestion or a remark, and all at once she felt at sea. What she hated, couldn't deal with, was ambiguity. Given alternative explanations of a dilemma, she grew uneasy. But which one is *right*? she would cry to herself.

When the priory's fortunes took a lurch towards disaster, she had sought diligently for the most certain and rapid solution; and when this had come from Margaret – who was at that time her assistant in the accounting office – she had promoted it with courage and generosity, for there was nothing mean about Veronica. She took enormous satisfaction from watching her erstwhile helper – now directrix – turning round the priory's fortunes. Any idea of plotting or deviousness behind the scenes was beyond her visualizing. Things were going well, praise the Lord, because good sense and firm management prevailed. When it was suggested that some people had been made miserable and insecure by the reforms, she accepted Margaret's word that, if this were so, it was unfortunate but unavoidable, and that in the long term the benefits to the priory would trickle down and encompass everybody.

This morning she was on her way to her one-time protégée's office, dutifully armed with a copy of her letter to Clare.

'Veronica,' Margaret cried gladly, rising and walking across the room to a filing cabinet where she began to rummage through a drawer. 'Lovely to see you, but I've a thousand and one things to do.'

'I've brought you a copy of the letter I've sent to Clare.'

'Mmm?'

'You asked to see it, Margaret.'

'So I did. Thank you, dear, you're as meticulous as ever. If only the same could be said of everyone. Put it on my desk, will you?' She waved an arm abstractedly. 'Oh dear, where *is* that report?'

Veronica laid the copy of her letter on Margaret's desk. She stood back and regarded it doubtfully. 'You'll put it away?'

'What? Yes, yes. And thank you for being so prompt. I'll pop in on you later, shall I? Right now I'm trying to lay hands on the report of the Restoration Committee. I wonder if Agnes has borrowed it.'

'I can see you're busy. I won't keep you. I hope my letter solves the difficulty.' And she closed Margaret's door, closing her mind to the matter of Clare's letter also, feeling her duty to be done.

Hope was clearing up in the art room. She rinsed and dried brushes and pens, rubbed at a stain on an easel, tidied cards and paper on a work table. Now and then she took sly sideways steps to peep frowningly at her colleagues' work.

Outside in the dusk, Beatrice was looking through the lighted art room window. She watched the scene intently, noting with interest her mounting dislike for Hope: it was a physical thing, like indigestion or an itchy scab. When Hope moved towards the door, she sped into action; ran inside and collided with her in the corridor.

'Hello, stranger,' she said, gripping Hope's wrist with steely fingers.

Hope stifled a shriek.

'Get your cloak. We're going for a walk.'

'Oh no we're not.'

'Don't be so silly. How can I help you, if you won't even talk to me? Your curtains are always drawn these nights, and I rather think you push your bed against the door. Now be a good child and get your cloak.'

'I've said all I've got to say, Beatrice.'

'But it's not as simple as you make out—' She relinquished Hope's arm as a nun went by. 'We can't talk here.'

'Oh, all right. I'll meet you in two minutes round the corner by the lilac tree.'

Waiting in the half-light, a feeling of depression came over Beatrice. She had nothing new to say to Hope, nothing to bargain with; this was to be a final attempt to make her see reason.

'Shame for us not to be friends,' she remarked insincerely when Hope arrived.

'It's *you* who's not friends. If it was the other way round and you were the one who'd been pushed out of your job, made a fool of in front of your colleagues, I'd move heaven and earth to do something about it.'

'I keep telling you. There's nothing I *can* do.'

'Course there is. You're Margaret's chief aide. Margaret can do what she likes. Look, I'm not going to stand here arguing.'

'Let's walk, then.'

They began to walk down the path towards the back of the house.

'You'd better get one thing straight,' said Beatrice. 'It wouldn't do either of us any good to bring Margaret into this.'

'It might. After all, it'd reflect badly on her if our affair got out. You and she have been friends for years; everyone knows that.'

'You're off your head.'

They had turned in to the kitchen yard, and seeing the scullery door ajar and light flooding from the windows they hovered uncertainly by an outhouse.

Hope shivered. 'I'm not hanging about, I hate it out here. Just understand that I meant what I said. Fix it so that I get my job back by the end of the week, or I'll tell everyone about us, *and* how we tricked Sister Catherine.'

Beatrice controlled a desire to throttle her. Instead, she turned to look behind her, hissing: 'What's that?'

'What's what?' Hope asked sharply.

'That noise. Like a little creature scrabbling—'

Shrieking with terror, Hope gathered her skirts and raced from the yard.

Beatrice slipped into the deeper darkness behind the outhouse, out of sight of sisters running from the scullery to investigate. That was sheer self-indulgence, getting you absolutely nowhere, she reproved herself, and lolled back against the wall, trying to summon constructive thought.

'So you see,' Imogen was explaining to the half-dozen sisters she had detained near the notice board, 'Sister Clare has overstepped the mark. Those figures she passed round were based on an inaccurate premise. It's all here in Sister Veronica's letter.'

'It's quite a ticking-off,' one sister commented.

'Mmm. Really puts her in her place,' said another, peering at the letter over her companion's shoulder.

'The point is,' Imogen said patiently, 'it'd be a waste of time hearing her going on about it in Council.'

'Quite. I say, Sister Anne, come and take a look at this. It's a really crushing rebuke from Sister Veronica to Sister Clare.'

'Yes, do come and read it, Sister, then you can convey its gist to other members of the needlework department. If we can all be agreed in advance, there'll be no reason for Sister Clare to waste our time in Council.'

They cleared a passage for Anne, who duly began to read. 'But I don't understand,' she said when she had done so. 'What a funny thing that Sister Clare is. If it were my letter, I certainly wouldn't put it on show.' And she went on her way, leaving behind her a rapt hush.

Like all true budding powermongers (as opposed to those, like Imogen, who imagine they can secure a position at the heart of things by unswerving attention to their superiors' wishes), Clare had cultivated a following. Rather as the young Margaret had drawn Beatrice, Agnes and Joan, Clare inspired devotion in a group of her peers and encouraged them to look to a time when Margaret would be prioress and obliged in her turn to name a successor. Clare had spirit. 'Little Clare' was Margaret's affectionate term, denoting youth and energy rather than size, for Clare, in fact, was quite tall. She moved freely, almost impetuously, jumping up with excitement as an idea struck her, and spoke enthusiastically, whether in praise or scorn. Her eyes were blue, with a suggestion of a cast about them, her brows straight, her mouth wide, her chin firm. Clare was impressive, her close friends found.

It was one of these who brought her the news: Imogen had pinned up a copy of Veronica's letter to Clare and it was now being read by all and sundry. Clare and her friend went charging over to the refectory. They found Imogen gone, but the letter being gleefully studied by a huddle of sisters.

Imogen be blowed, thought Clare. It was Sister Veronica, with her weighty authority, who had undermined her. She ripped down the letter, dismissed her supporter and went alone to Veronica's office.

Veronica was utterly bewildered. It proved hard work getting her to understand what had happened. 'There must be some explanation, an accident, a draught scattering Margaret's papers,' she conjured wildly. 'But why would anyone pin it up? Why not return it to you or me?' Her cheeks burned at the indelicacy of the situation. 'I can only apologize. I assure you, I hadn't an inkling— Make free with a piece of private correspondence: why, it's the last thing I'd do.'

Clare saw that this was so. 'I accept your apology, but the damage has been done. What are we going to do? The matter can't just be left.'

'Indeed not. I shall investigate at once.' And Veronica with her flaming cheeks set off on a quest for enlightenment.

Sister Margaret was not available, a sister at the filing cabinet informed Veronica; she was escorting prospective visitors on a tour of the priory.

'Then I shall wait for her,' Veronica declared, seating herself beside Margaret's desk.

An hour later she was still there. Margaret came in and noticed her with annoyance. 'Not now, Veronica, please. I've simply masses of things to attend to—'

'This cannot wait,' said Veronica severely. 'The copy of my letter to Sister Clare that you requested has found its way onto the refectory notice board. By now half the priory is aware of its contents. I require an explanation.'

'I don't think I follow,' said Margaret.

Patiently, Veronica repeated herself.

'Well!' exclaimed Margaret, sitting down. 'It's beyond me. I remember glancing at the letter on my desk. Oh, and then I was called away. The pressure of work is quite daunting at times.'

'Then evidently someone removed it from your desk. You had better try to discover who. I intend to write again to Sister Clare, expressing my regret for what has occurred, and I shall put that letter also on the notice board. Furthermore, when the full circumstances are known, I insist they are made public.'

Margaret stared at the floor and shook her head sadly from side to side. 'Believe me, Veronica, I'm devastated by this. Certainly, I shall investigate, and if I discover wrongdoing the culprit will be punished. No stone will remain unturned: you have my word.'

'Thank you, Margaret,' said Veronica.

It was teatime in the Blue Sitting Room. Centrally seated were Sisters Anne and Elizabeth who, between sips, were pronouncing as they found.

'Shocking,' said Anne. 'An appalling breach of good manners. And to think they pressed me to read the thing.'

'How I feel for Sister Veronica! She is the last person to be associated with loutish behaviour,' declared Elizabeth.

Gradually other sisters were drawn in. In matters of etiquette Sisters Anne and Elizabeth knew what was what. They were respected for this, and so, in matters of propriety, where hopes of being similarly well regarded were entertained, it was from Anne and Elizabeth (and Monica and Cecilia) that people took their cue.

'I must say, I went hot and cold when I heard about it.'

'Ghastly for Sister Veronica.'

151

'Not very pleasant for Sister Clare. I'm glad I didn't read the thing.'

'It's unheard-of.'

'It lowers the tone. I just hope something is done about it.'

Agnes dropped four sugar lumps into her cup and strolled over to join them. 'Something the matter?' she enquired, and was soon tut-tutting with the rest.

'But, but,' spluttered Imogen, drowning in Agnes's easy chair, 'you said, "A nod's as good as a wink." You said—'

'Oh dear me. I hope you won't go jumping off the Albion Tower if I recommend it,' said Agnes humorously. 'We're all grown up, I hope; we all take responsibility for our actions. Now I dare say *your* action may turn out, in the long run, to have done us some good. And due credit will then be given, of course. In the meantime, it's put us in a bit of a spot. Susceptibilities' – Agnes pronounced the word wryly – 'have been affronted; people are such tender plants. So it's up to you to get us off the hook.'

'Perhaps if I say I misunderstood—'

Regretfully Agnes shook her head. 'Not good enough, I'm afraid. You and I are just cogs in the wheel. The thing that matters is the whole machine: and as we all know, only Margaret can drive that. So not a hint of this can be allowed to touch her. No, I'm afraid you must be a good soldier and take it on the chin. Every bit of it.'

'But what—? How—?'

'Resign from the Forward Planning Committee. Make a humble little speech to Council regretting your indiscretion. Say your enthusiasm carried you away, if you like, so long as you make it crystal clear you acted off your own bat.'

'But it doesn't seem *fair*.'

'My dear Imogen, when was life fair? Chin up. In a few months' time it'll all be forgotten, then we'll heave a sigh of relief and come begging you to help us again.'

Silence: while Agnes flicked out a lazy doodle and Imogen clasped, unclasped and reclasped her hands.

'It's the only way, you know,' Agnes said, peering kindly over her half-moon spectacles. 'But as I said, it'll only be a temporary setback. In due course Margaret will want to show you her gratitude.'

'Well, I suppose, in that case—'

'That's the spirit. We'll say Friday's Council meeting for your resignation speech, shall we?'

Imogen nodded.

'Fine. Close the door after you, there's a good girl.'

Half an hour later Margaret entered Agnes's room. She sat on the edge of the bed. 'Well?'

'Imogen'll put up her hand to it. As a token of regret she'll resign from the Forward Planning Committee.'

Margaret let out her breath.

'The beauty of it is, we can still put a veto on Clare bringing up the vegetable field thing in Council.'

'And you think the fuss'll die down?'

'Over the letter? Yes.'

'Good.' Margaret slapped her knees and rose. 'Well done, Agnes.'

'Just a minute, Margaret. Maybe you'd better sit down again. I'm afraid there's something else.'

18

Beatrice returned to her room from her bath and sat in her shift brushing out her long damp hair. As it dried, it began to separate in a pale gold mass. Eventually, she rose, hid the hairbrush in a box of religious pamphlets at the bottom of a drawer, and went to the window and drew the curtain back a short way so that she could see herself mirrored against the darkness. She studied her reflection intently, drew her hair forward, tossed it back, turned this way and that. Then she raised her hands and loosened the neck-tie of her shift and pulled it down over one shoulder. Quite distractingly lovely, she thought, turning a little, raising the bare shoulder to her mouth. After a moment's further contemplation, she sighed and closed the curtain.

A knocking jolted her; she sped across the floor and jammed the door shut. 'Who is it?'

'Joan.'

'What d'you want? I'm not decent. I've just come back from my bath.'

'Well, make yourself decent and come to Agnes's room. Margaret wants you.'

While Joan was gone in search of Beatrice, Margaret and Agnes found nothing to say to one another. Agnes leaned over some papers on her desk. Margaret watched her and wondered for how long she had kept this information to herself. The difficulty was, one never knew how far Agnes was working for the general good (as Margaret thought of work done for

154

herself) and how far for Agnes. It would be just like her to ferret out information and then store it away for her own purposes. And yet Margaret clearly recalled asking Agnes to tell her if anything transpired about Beatrice that she, Margaret, ought to know. Of course, Agnes had her uses, as Margaret would be the first to admit; take the way she had just dealt with Imogen. Like herself, Agnes was stout in combat and no respecter of persons. But whether Agnes was entirely trustworthy was another question. She'd never really liked her, it was impossible to feel real affection for her, the sort of affection one could feel for— *Joan*, Margaret told herself, swiftly substituting Joan's for the name her thoughts had been leading to.

But then, warily, she allowed Beatrice to stand in her mind. There was no doubt about it, Beatrice had brought a touch of genius to their campaign. It was Beatrice who had schooled Margaret to deepen her voice in order to sound authoritative: a refinement that would not have occurred to Margaret herself, or to Agnes or Joan. It was Beatrice who had shown her how to flash her eyes when under attack, thereby implying a commitment beyond her inquisitor's comprehension and causing the attack to seem thoroughly impertinent. Above all, it was Beatrice's daring on the night of the Albion Tower, and then her disarming recitation of a prayer to safely conclude a tricky meeting, that had allowed them, when their popularity was down, to live to fight another day. Where Margaret and Agnes could argue and batten, Beatrice could weaken people with the sheer magnetism of her presence. People were charmed by her, loved to admire her. Now we just might have something there, thought Margaret, seizing on the idea that Beatrice might charm even this difficulty away.

Joan returned. 'She's dressing,' she reported. 'Just had a bath. Look, do you really need me here?'

'Yes, Joan, we do. I know this is unpleasant, but we need all the help we can get, all the brains we can muster.'

'I can't see what I can do,' Joan muttered. 'Absolutely beyond my understanding.'

'It's beyond us all. That's why it will take a concerted effort to deal with it.'

'I've never felt entirely comfortable with Beatrice,' Joan grumbled.

Margaret opened her mouth to comment, but then closed it again.

Agnes was doodling, as usual, and she said nothing either.

They waited in silence.

In her room, Beatrice had pulled on her robe and hidden her hair in her veil. Her heart had begun to knock. Keep cool, she urged herself, putting on her shoes. She breathed deeply once or twice, then set off along the corridor to Agnes's room.

'Well, well; the old firm,' she commented, entering. It was such a familiar scene: Agnes sitting at her desk scribbling, Joan hunched in her chair looking twitchy as a landed fish, Margaret sitting composedly on the side of the bed – though her cheeks were decidedly pinker than usual. She grabbed a pillow and flopped down on the rug. 'What's to do?' she asked amiably.

'Beatrice,' Margaret said, then sighed and began again. 'Beatrice, I could certainly do without this piece of nonsense at the present time.'

'The Clare thing, you mean?'

'I mean on top of the Clare thing. I mean the, um, Hope thing.'

'Ah. That's too bad. I've been trying to keep the lid on that one.'

'We are not surprised,' said Joan.

156

'The point is,' said Margaret, 'is there any truth in this ugly rumour?'

Beatrice looked at her pityingly. 'Probably,' she admitted. 'Not heard any rumour myself, but then I wouldn't have, would I?'

No-one answered her.

'I'm presuming,' went on Beatrice, 'Hope's been hinting at an affair between us.'

They did not trouble to confirm it.

After a while, Joan said, 'I suppose these things — I've no way of knowing, of course; this is an entirely uneducated guess — I suppose these things can't very well be *proved*.'

They looked at her.

'So I suppose Beatrice could deny it. "Woman off her head" sort of thing.'

'A denial won't stop up that woman's mouth,' said Agnes. 'There'd be no end to the fuss. It would drag on and on.'

'Then I suppose Beatrice must resign from Council,' said Joan.

Beatrice plucked at the rug. 'Trouble is—'

'Yes?' pounced Margaret.

'Trouble is, there's a bit more to it than that.'

'More? You mean, worse?' she all but squeaked, her deep voice deserting her as she tried and failed to conjure a more damning scandal.

Beatrice looked into Margaret's eyes. 'Do you remember the service of dedication at the Albion Tower? How Catherine was seen at the window? Well, it was Hope who helped me fix that up. Now, don't look so amazed. You must have realized I had an accomplice.'

'Rather an unfortunate choice though, wasn't it?' asked Agnes, who prided herself on the management of her own coterie.

Beatrice ignored her. 'The point is, she's threatening to blab.'

157

'But this is serious!' cried Margaret, fighting the panic rising inside her.

'Well yes, I'm afraid it is,' Beatrice sighed. 'It puts Catherine in the clear.'

'It is vital we silence this woman. There must be something we can do.'

'We can't bribe her, if that's what you mean. She wants her job back, and Sister Prudence would resign rather than give it her. In fact, it wouldn't surprise me if the entire department threw down their paintbrushes. Hope's a talented artist by all accounts, but she's not cut out to be in charge of people.'

Joan gripped the arms of her chair. 'I think I've got it,' she cried. 'You say she's a good artist, Beatrice?'

'So they say.'

'Well, why not recognize it? Let her work on her own, producing small paintings of the place: a corner of the garden or cloister; the old courtyard, the little bridge into the wood: the sort of souvenir picture a visitor might like to purchase. Present the idea as a mark of her expertise.'

'Gosh, yes, she'd like that. It'd make her feel important.'

'And she'd be out of everyone's way. Brilliant, Joan,' boomed Margaret. They could tell from her voice she'd begun to recover. 'We must put it to her at once.'

'I'll handle it,' said Agnes. 'Best if Beatrice keeps her distance, and I dare say I'll put it over more succinctly than Joan: that the job's hers for as long as she keeps her mouth shut.'

'Agreed.'

'So, it appears we can breathe again,' said Beatrice sunnily.

'It's going to be a very, very testing time. We must just tough it out. In view of the rumours, Beatrice, you had better resign. Make a speech to Council – Hope's not a member, thank goodness – admit only that you have inadvertently, um, aroused feelings, and you propose to take a back seat as a mark of penitence.'

'Penitence,' repeated Beatrice. 'Mm, yes. I'm sure I can do penitence beautifully.'

'If all goes well I can reinstate you: in the New Year, perhaps; as a mark of forgiveness, allow you to make a fresh start.'

'That's really big of you, Margaret,' said Beatrice, feeling her way into her new role.

19

'It was dreadful. I was ashamed,' confessed Anne.

'Quite appalling,' Elizabeth agreed.

Cecilia declared that the priory had been disgraced, and Monica regretfully agreed with her.

Outrage was not confined to the needlework room; all over the priory sisters were muttering and voicing disquiet, for nothing like it, they assured one another, had been known to happen before. They could recall the odd tiff, an occasional breast-beating in public, a resignation on the grounds of ill-health, but such incidents were rare and had not in any case reflected on the orderliness or dignity of Council. Yet during today's meeting, within the space of one hour, two sisters had confessed to wrongdoing and tendered resignations (Beatrice and Imogen) and one (Clare) had stormed out in a huff.

'Catherine, you must go and speak to the Reverend Mother,' Cecilia said.

'Oh, I'm not sure about that.'

'But you must. The feeling's tremendous.'

'Catherine, dear, you are directrix,' Monica reminded her.

'Jointly with Margaret.'

'Sister Margaret,' Cecilia retorted, 'should be relieved of her position.'

'That's up to the Prioress.'

'Then go and see her. Sometimes, Catherine, it is necessary to take a stand.'

'If she sends for me, I'm ready,' said Catherine,

thinking that she couldn't be seen rushing to take advantage of Margaret's discomfort. 'But you four have always been close to the Reverend Mother; why don't you approach her?'

They were disappointed in her. She could tell from the way they dropped their heads.

In the corridor outside the needlework room, Sister Christa was waiting. 'We want to talk to you,' Christa said, seizing Catherine's arm and leading her away.

Six young sisters were crowded into Christa's room, perched on the bed or squatting on the floor or leaning upright against the wall. The one easy chair had been saved for Catherine. She sat in it uneasily.

Christa came straight to the point. 'What are you going to do? This is our best chance yet to stop her.'

The words, reminiscent of Lazarus's, came as a shock. Unconsciously, she touched her scarred cheek.

'Most people will be behind you. They're outraged by the trickery and back-stabbing.'

'Yes. Sister Margaret's really up against it.'

'They're discredited. It's our big chance.'

'Well?' asked Christa.

'I propose that everyone who feels strongly, says so: to the Reverend Mother, to Sister Margaret herself. I'll speak to the Reverend Mother when she sends for me.'

They looked at her in disbelief.

'You really think it'll be as easy as that?' Christa asked. 'You think Sister Margaret will give up without a fight?'

Catherine stared at the crucifix on the wall. Diffidently, she explained that she had already tried everything she could think of – argued for a slower, more sensitive course, described people's suffering, asked people to search their consciences – with the result that the Reverend Mother now entertained doubts as to her fitness, and assumed Catherine to be sulking because she hadn't been appointed sole directrix in the first place. All Catherine's arguments were read as a sign of bad grace.

There was a moment when they all spoke at once. Then Christa brought order. 'The point is, you've got an advantage over the rest of us. You are at least joint directrix. Presumably, you have some power to do things.'

'Do what?'

Christa spread her hands. 'Call one of those briefing meetings. Sister Margaret calls them at the drop of a hat, whenever she wants to rally opinion behind her. Why shouldn't you?'

Catherine had never thought of such a thing. The meetings were Margaret's creation. 'I don't even approve of these so-called briefing meetings.'

'For *heaven's sake*,' cried Christa. The meetings had been brought into existence, so why didn't Catherine use them? Why didn't she call Margaret's bluff: say she was calling a meeting to allow people to voice their worries and decide what they wanted to be done? It would be perfectly open and above board. What could possibly be Catherine's objection, given that it remained her opinion that Sister Margaret's methods were causing anguish and ought to be modified?

Of course this was still her opinion, Catherine confirmed.

'Well, then. *We* can't call a meeting.'

This was true. And so Catherine saw that she must.

There was a danger of her falling between two stools, Catherine thought. Cecilia and co. wished her to rid them of ugly scenes and horrid behaviour; Christa and her friends, however they presented it, were urging her towards a putsch. She walked through the night-filled cloister where the scuttle of a dry leaf in the wind resounded like running feet, and imagined the consternation in Margaret's camp tomorrow when they learned of the meeting. Clare, Imogen and Beatrice would rally to Margaret, whatever the difficulties, and Joan and Agnes would gear themselves up to be razor-sharp. Margaret would be full of fury, but would hide it well.

Music was coming from the chapel. Light shone in the organ loft. She did not go up to see Angelica, but slipped into the chapel. She prayed for grace to use the opportunity well. According to Thy will, she added.

It was a day of rain. The sort of day, Catherine reflected, staring out at the courtyard where brimming puddles merged to form a shallow lake, when the story of Noah seemed not altogether fabulous. She turned from the window and went on towards the refectory, dreading the closeness of eighty damp nuns and the odour of faintly steaming serge; trying to repress the thought that, had fate been kind, the day would be bright and bracing.

Margaret was already seated in her usual dominating position on the dais facing the rows of chairs. I suppose I ought to sit up here when *she* has called the meeting, Catherine thought, learning the lesson tardily. She nodded to Margaret and pulled up a chair beside her.

'I do hope this won't take long,' Margaret said. 'My time is precious. This priory does not run itself, you know.'

'Sisters,' called Catherine, and clapped her hands. 'Many of you have expressed dismay at the events of the last meeting of Council. I think it would be healthy if we voiced our disquiet openly so that we can agree on future action. Who would like to speak?'

Sister Veronica made a short and dignified statement. She regretted what had occurred. She accepted

163

Sister Imogen's apology. Above all, she exonerated Sister Margaret whose behaviour had always been exemplary, and trusted that the unpleasantness would swiftly be forgotten so that Sister Margaret's good work might continue unhindered.

Margaret graciously inclined her head.

Well schooled, Sister Veronica, thought Catherine; and called, 'Anyone else?'

Sister Cecilia bobbed up. It was all very well for Sister Veronica, but some people looked back to a time when such things were unheard-of. Before these new ideas of Sister Margaret's had come along – ideas which, incidentally, seemed to elevate financial considerations above all else – the sisters had conducted their affairs with courtesy and integrity. How she deplored the new roughness of speech, the lack of deference to older colleagues, the brushing aside of cherished traditions. Why, when Cecilia was a young nun—

The point was eventually rescued by another senior sister, and a general deploring of present-day conduct broke out.

Sister Christa hovered between sitting and standing.

Not yet, Catherine's quick frown warned; she feared a radical outburst might frighten off the support they were getting from traditionalists. 'Well,' she broke in. 'I have noted your comments and will pass them on to the Reverend Mother. I am sure your anxieties are not lost on Sister Margaret—'

'Might I interject?' Sister Agnes asked mildly. 'You know, Sister Cecilia spoke about a decline in our standards. She bases this decline, apparently, on one Council meeting.'

'I do not,' cried Cecilia. 'I complain about the general attitude: people being pushed aside when they're no longer needed, senior sisters treated as if they are of no consequence, the lay sisters bullied—'

'Oh dear, are we to hear it all over again? If I might just get in a word? The point about the Council meeting is that those sisters who resigned did so after publicly admitting their fault. Now isn't that preferable to *hiding* one's faults and pretending to be blameless? How many of us know, for instance, about Sister Cecilia's little fault? Not many, I'll warrant; she took pretty good care of that. But for years and years she kept a very nice tea service belonging to the priory for her own private use and enjoyment. Indeed, she would be using it still had she not been discovered. And I don't recall any public apology from Sister Cecilia.'

There was much stirring in seats. Most people knew the facts about Sister Cecilia and her Rockingham tea service, but they had never before seen them quite in this light. Murmurs broke out.

'I just think we should be careful before we start accusing one another of poor behaviour,' Agnes concluded reasonably.

Cecilia had turned pink. Catherine found herself at a loss. Into the hiatus jumped Sister Christa with a passionate denunciation of the system of allocating jobs. And when she paused for breath, Sister Kirsty wailed her agreement: 'It's awful not having a permanent place. You don't know where you are. You don't seem to belong.'

'Not *belong*?' Margaret queried wrathfully. 'May I remind the young sister that she belongs to the Albion Priory? *This* is where she belongs. This is where we all belong.'

Relieved applause greeted this.

'Nevertheless,' Catherine insisted, 'it can't be denied that within the community some people are placed less favourably than others. This has led to a new feeling of insecurity, and while I acknowledge the finances of the priory are now on a firmer footing, I do query that aspect of the new policy. It seems to me that when we come upon snags and disadvantages, we ought to make adjustments.' There were cries of agreement. 'Furthermore, I'm disturbed that certain people have been accorded quite unnecessary privileges. The system of the Blue and Green Sitting Rooms, for instance: they set people apart, create divisions, reward those in favourable positions as if their good fortune were somehow a virtue.'

Margaret sprang to her feet. 'I am sick and tired of people knocking success. Yes, there are problems. It would be wonderful if there were not. We are sorry if some people feel left out. But at a time when the priory is fighting for its very survival, it is important to reward those who make a special effort. Have you *seen* the order book for our tapestries? Have you *noticed* the massive increase in the work of the art department? Do you know that our visitors are making bookings *six months ahead*? Can we please stop all this talk of problems and difficulties and start being glad that some of us are achieving things? *Can we please applaud success?*' she roared.

Members of the Blue and Green Sitting Rooms, who had begun to feel alarmed, were happy to oblige.

Christa, red in the face and back on her feet, began to shout, stabbing the air with a forefinger as she did so to emphasize key words. 'Not a word, you notice, about *when* we shall do away with injustice. I doubt very much whether Sister Margaret *intends* to do away with injustice. I rather think injustice is part and parcel of her methods. What about the east wing? Sisters, the condition of the east wing is a scandal. I went there myself this morning and found water sheeting down the walls. It was damp, cold, quite disgraceful. Three lay sisters have been hospitalized already this winter. How many more will we put up with?'

'And we always prided ourselves on looking after

the well-being of the lay sisters,' put in Sister Monica, as Christa paused for breath.

'I think,' said Catherine directly to Margaret, 'you cannot ignore this feeling. Success is all very well, but worth precious little if it is got at the expense of our fellows. I put it to you that you must address the other side of the coin. If, as you indicate, we are prosperous, it is time to be generous. Many of us *do* see injustices. Let's find a way of putting them right.' There were cries of agreement, and Catherine, scenting victory, allowed her face and voice to relax. 'Now, I suggest we draw up a list of those items we feel should be examined first—' But Agnes, seeing that an effective diversion was required, quickly and loudly cut her off.

'Of course, Sister Catherine sees many things that are a mystery to the rest of us. Perhaps it does funny things to your eyesight watching others succeed where you've failed. And talking about generosity and nice feelings: where was Sister Catherine on the day of our triumph, the day of the dedication of the restored Albion Tower? I'll tell you where. She was ill in bed. Not so ill, though, that her curiosity couldn't get the better of her. Several people saw Sister Catherine – too ill to join our celebration, mind – spying on us from an upstairs window. I think anyone as mean-spirited as that should think carefully before accusing other people.'

'Sister Catherine is *not* mean-spirited,' called Sister Anne, her several chins quivering.

'And she was very ill that day,' Sister Luke confirmed. 'She was hallucinating. She thought Sister Megan had called on her for assistance.'

'I think,' Margaret said gravely, rising from her seat with a magisterial air, 'this has gone on long enough. There is work to be done, and I, for one, cannot squander precious time arguing. However' – she raised a hand detainingly – 'I have been attacked and'

– her voice rose to drown a denial – 'I will defend myself. No,' she told a protesting Christa, 'you have had your say; please allow me to have mine. Sister Catherine said a very misleading thing. She said we are prosperous. But we are not prosperous *yet*. We are working *towards* prosperity. If we falter now we shall fail. That is why I appeal to everyone: summon the spirit we applauded on the night of the Albion Tower. We conquered adversity then. We shall do so again. Sister Beatrice—Where are you, Sister?'

Beatrice rose and hung her head.

'Hiding herself, you see,' Margaret pointed out unnecessarily but affectingly. 'Some of you witnessed her apology the other day, an apology for an *innocently* incurred mistake.' (At this point Agnes sent Hope a hard look.) 'Let us not forget she was our heroine on that historic night. Sisters, words have been spoken in anger. I think it would be healing if Sister Beatrice now had the final word.'

'Thank you, Sister Margaret,' Beatrice all but whispered. 'Dear Sisters, there can be none so humble as I, a penitent, a sorrower. But I dedicate myself to this priory, to the work that lies ahead; and I ask every one of you to join me. With God's help we shall succeed.'

'Amen,' roared Margaret, climbing down from the dais, going purposefully to the door.

'Amen,' they echoed in their different ways: thankfully, robustly, uncertainly, resentfully.

'I can't tell you how I loathed it; even loathed myself. I detest all this arguing, all this word-twisting and scoring points.'

Catherine and Angelica were sharing the organ bench. Angelica had been playing a fugue, but Catherine had not assumed her former indulgence of pulling out the stops. Their friendship was less easygoing these days. Even so, Catherine couldn't resist the chance to speak honestly to a trusted friend.

'Then why don't you give it up?' asked Angelica. 'If only you knew how unpleasant you look, how unpleasant you sound. It really doesn't suit you. Do as I do: attend to your work. This is mine.' Angelica caressed the lower manual. 'I do a good job to the best of my ability. If everyone did the same there'd be less trouble.'

'You have a very rewarding job,' Catherine couldn't hold back from saying.

Angelica pressed her lips together. After a time she said in a tight voice, 'I understand you're responsible for our religious observance. Plenty to occupy you there, I should have thought. And very worthwhile.'

'Religion is more than observance.'

Angelica heaved a sigh and turned the pages of her music. 'There's no reasoning with you, Catherine. Now will you excuse me? I want to practise this piece for my recital.'

As Catherine went down the steps, a toccata poured out. Because it was late in the evening, Angelica had selected light thin stops, but the brilliance of the piece, the pattern of tumbling notes sharply punctuated by dissonant chords, could not be muted. Reaching ground level, Catherine turned into the chapel to hear it through. At one point Angelica broke off to practise a complicated passage on the pedals, and Catherine marked her gathering expertise. At last the toccata ended. Catherine was about to steal away when a new piece began, which she immediately recognized as one Angelica had composed herself several years ago on the death of her teacher and predecessor. It was a quiet lament. A middle passage rose in a crescendo, but soon returned to the final farewell: a three-note phrase played over and over, suggesting the reluctance of leave-taking.

We were such friends, thought Catherine. Who would have thought a difference could divide us? She imagined taking Angelica's advice, and 'giving it up', becoming engrossed in perfecting the worship of the priory. The idea drew her; she almost yearned for it. And why should her conscience object, for what work could be greater than glorifying God? And it came to her that were she not joint directrix such a life could be hers at once. Suddenly, the prospect of defeat seemed alluring. Bolstering this line of thought, she reflected that it was doubtful whether she'd ever make a success of leadership, for it seemed an appetite for conflict was needed, the sort of appetite enjoyed by Margaret and Agnes; that fired Christa's agitation. No, Margaret was the able one; let Margaret be directrix, let Catherine be free to pursue a path more suited to her temperament.

She felt more tranquil, having settled the future. But later, preparing for bed, doubt crept up on her, and when she lay at last in the dark, she knew Angelica was right to abandon her, for she could not give up the fight. An affronted sense of justice wouldn't let her.

Joan burst into Margaret's room. 'That's torn it. The east wing ceiling's collapsed. Oh, Margaret, I begged you to do something about it. Now we'll be blamed. And just as we've survived our greatest trial.'

'But this is splendid news,' cried Margaret, rising from her desk. 'I had begun to think the wretched place would hold out for ever. This will get the lay sisters out. The east wing's far too good for them; the best view in the priory is to be had from those windows. Now we'll be able to do as we like with it.'

Joan sat down. 'But where would they go to?'

'I've got it all worked out. The rooms over the kitchens.'

'Impossible. They're in a terrible condition.'

'It's just a temporary measure. We'll turn them into proper living accommodation later on, once it's understood that the lay sisters will not be returning to the east wing. Now, I suppose people need assistance?'

'It's chaos out there.'

'Well, come along. No, wait; I've an idea. Fetch Sister Hope, she can sketch the operation. Make sure she does one of me with my arm round some poor old dear. Pass me a blanket; blankets look so comforting, I always think. And you can write a stirring account of it for the *Bulletin*, Joan.' She was in the corridor now, and bursting into Agnes's room. 'Wake up, Agnes. The east wing's gone. And bring Beatrice. This could prove as helpful to us as saving the statue. A godsend.'

20

'I don't feel I'm able,' protested the Prioress. 'These sharp winds play havoc with my sciatica.'

'They won't if you're well wrapped up,' Catherine insisted, holding out the Prioress's cloak.

'It'll do you good,' Cecilia said. 'You've been stuck in this room for weeks. Besides, what has happened to the lay sisters is truly dreadful, and how can you tackle Sister Margaret if you haven't seen it with your own eyes?'

'I can picture it.'

'Really, Reverend Mother,' exclaimed Monica.

Grumbling to herself, she nevertheless allowed them to wrap her in the cloak and lead her into the draughty corridor. 'And the *stairs*,' she groaned.

'We'll take them slowly,' Catherine said ruthlessly.

It was a day in spring, bleak with a spiteful wind. The weather suited Catherine. Her anger had grown over the past few months, not hotly, but bitterly. She welcomed it, for it hardened her resolve. The soft temptations that had once briefly come to her seemed remote as an infantile dream.

As restoration work on the east wing progressed, it became apparent that the heavy expenditure and elaborate refitting were not intended to compensate the lay sisters for past pain and inconvenience. They were intended to lure yet more and even richer visitors. The abominable area over the kitchens continued to house the lay sisters. It had been treated to a coat of whitewash, an application of linoleum, the installation behind flimsy boarding of lavatories, basins and showers, and pronounced refurbished.

'It should be perfectly warm, being right over the stoves,' Margaret had said brightly.

'But a *dormitory*. There's no privacy,' Catherine and a few others had protested.

'When our financial position is secure we can consider a more luxurious arrangement. In the meantime it is absolutely vital that we live within our means.'

'But huge sums are being spent on the east wing.'

'As an investment. The east wing will generate income. If we spend money like water before we've earned it, we shall soon be back where we started. We must all make sacrifices.'

'Who must? The lay sisters?'

An impatient wave of the hand and she was gone. It was always the same; impossible to pin her down. Questions beginning Who, Why, When, Where, were simply ignored. A daily issue of the *Bulletin* hammered out the correct line and provided the more comfortably placed sisters with easy rejoinders to criticism. 'Throwing money at problems isn't the answer', 'These things take time', 'It's a question of priorities', the satisfied ones echoed gratefully.

BULLETIN for the third of March.

'WE ARE PLEASED TO DO OUR BIT,' SAYS LAY SISTER PAULINE

'The dormitory is clean and bright and we are glad to be out of the old east wing,' Lay Sister Pauline said yesterday. 'Of course, it would be nice if we had separate rooms, but we understand it's a question of priorities. Putting the priory back on its feet comes first.'

It is good to hear that message getting through at

last. And what a pity the whingers and moaners don't take a leaf out of Lay Sister Pauline's book. Do we want to go back to the bad old days of cadging our living? Of course we don't. We, the sisters of the Albion Priory, are made of sterner stuff. We intend to hold our heads high and earn our keep.

'What a coup, Joan, getting a quote from that lay sister.'

'Yes, it was rather. She's a sensible sort. Agnes has put her in charge of the dormitory.'

'And it's an excellent piece of writing.'

'As a matter of fact, Sister Verity wrote it. The *Bulletin* has become too much for me on my own.'

'You mean that stocky, fierce-looking nun?'

'I suppose she is a bit. But her heart's in the right place.'

'Evidently. I like her style. Committed. We can use her, Joan.'

The Prioress walked stiffly between the rows of beds. At the end of the room she looked back. 'Like a hospital,' she grunted.

Cecilia shivered. 'Only, it isn't a hospital. This is where the poor things live.'

'Come and see the bathrooms,' said Catherine. 'There are just the two. Try the doors.'

'Most insubstantial,' the Prioress found.

'And not enough room to swing a cat.' Cecilia waved her arms to demonstrate.

'And the draughts,' called Monica. 'Did you notice? Feel over here.'

Glumly, the Prioress felt. She had a nasty feeling that demands were about to be made on her. 'I hardly think Sister Margaret intends this to be a permanent arrangement,' she said, so as to forestall some of them.

'I think you'll find she does. She talks vaguely of improving this and adding that, but with no indication of *when*. Personally, I find it outrageous that there are no plans for the lay sisters' return to the east wing.'

'Ah. Now that may be impossible. I gather from Margaret that the rooms there are appointed in a very superior fashion, far beyond what is suitable for a nun, with a bathroom attached to every bedroom. And there is a library, and a writing room—'

'Reverend Mother, you do see what Margaret's done? She deliberately allowed the east wing to collapse so that an entirely new facility could be put in its place: one that fits in with her concepts. She does like to preclude the tedious difficulty of opposition whenever she can.'

The Prioress detected an alarming note of sarcasm in Catherine's voice, alarming because out of character. She turned her face from the blazing eyes and recalled Margaret's hint of a certain irrationality in her co-directrix's recent behaviour. Possibly, she had not exaggerated.

'Reverend Mother, will you tackle Sister Margaret about these conditions?' prompted Cecilia.

'I shall talk to her, certainly,' she said huffily, and conceded as the cold penetrated her cloak, 'I must say I'm not heartened by what I have found.'

'We knew you couldn't be,' said Monica.

They were walking in the garden, Sisters Catherine, Christa and Gabrielle. They held their cloaks tightly to their bodies, oblivious of the bravely flowering daffodils, of the scent of narcissus, of swelling buds and catkins overhead. They kept their eyes to the ground and envisaged the bleak dormitory scene.

'Well, I got her to go and see,' Catherine reported.

'She was visibly shocked, but whether she'll rouse herself to actually do anything—'

'Everyone should see it. There'd be an outcry,' said Gabrielle, who was one of Christa's supporters.

'If there's one thing I've learned it's that people avoid seeing what they don't want to see.'

'People should be compelled to make a visit,' Christa said.

'How? We can't take the dormitory into the Blue and Green Sitting Rooms. And we can't drag their members into the dormitory. Of course, there've been a few honourable exceptions: the senior needlework sisters regularly visit the place: they're disgusted by it; Sister Florence has been, so has Sister Luke; and to give her her due, so has Sister Veronica.'

Beyond the yew hedge and the greenhouses, Sister Kirsty stood gazing over the old vegetable fields. There I would be, she remembered, cutting the first of the purple sprouting. She pictured herself bent double between the rows, her hands flying, her feet shuffling, her breath hot and wet on her face in the sharp March wind. Sister Beth working on the far side of the field would call, 'Sticky going, isn't it?' And every so often Sister Martha would yell, 'Time for a break. Come on, you two, or you'll fetch up like fish hooks.'

We were a team, thought Kirsty. But we never knew how lucky we were.

'You with us, Sister?'

Kirsty swung round. It was Sister Martha. 'I was just thinking: this time last year we were cutting the Purple Wonder.'

Martha came up and stood beside her. 'So we was. Ah well, it's pastures new these days; don't do to dwell. Now, I want you to carry on planting them sweet pea seedlings. I have to leave off for a while: business indoors.' A hollow feeling had attacked Martha; she felt in need of a restorative Blue Sitting Room tea.

'Right you are, Sister. Oh, Sister,' called Kirsty, 'did you ask again about having me permanent in the garden? And Sister Beth, too. We're desperate to be settled.'

'If it were up to me, Sister,' said Martha, shaking her head. 'I told Sister Imogen, you need proper gardeners in a garden; folks as know what they're doing, I said. It wears me out having to stop and explain to these newcomers every five minutes. There's some as don't know a trowel from a dibber. It's a blessed nuisance, Sister, I said.' Martha sighed and concluded wonderingly, 'Don't ask me why, but for reasons best known to theirselves, they're agin it.' She heaved round to face the house and screwed up her eyes to scan the niftiest route to the tea table. 'I'll have to go or I'll be late. If I see Sister Imogen, I'll mention it again. But I shouldn't get yer hopes up,' she called, setting off along her chosen path.

By the garden wall, Kirsty discovered the sweet pea patch. It was marked out with lines of taut string. Nearby were boxes of seedlings and a trowel. On the far side of the garden, Sister Catherine and two other sisters were pacing. I wonder if she knows, thought Kirsty, and on an impulse, ran out onto the path.

'Excuse me, Sister Catherine, but I wondered if you knew we've got to move out of our rooms and go into the annexe.'

'Who has?' Catherine asked, feeling bewildered.

'All of us unattached ones. There's me and Sister Beth and five others in the north wing, and about a dozen in the south wing. Ten sisters with regular jobs are moving out of the annexe into the wings. The ones with no permanent jobs have got to make room for them. It means we'll have to share two to a room.'

'But why? Who said so?'

'Sister Imogen told us this morning. She didn't say why, just that after evensong we've got to move our things. It's going to make it really stick out that we're the ones without a regular position. Why are they picking on us, Sister? It doesn't seem right.'

'Oh, Sister Kirsty,' said Catherine, spreading her hands.

Gabrielle became alarmed for one of her friends. 'This'll affect Sister Rose. You know? – she used to be the cheesemaker.'

Catherine put her hand on Kirsty's arm. 'I'm going to look into it. Don't move your things until you've heard from me.' She turned to Christa. 'We'd better do something quickly, or it'll be the lay sister saga all over again.'

If only she can, thought Kirsty longingly, as she returned to the sweet pea patch.

'Of course I agreed,' snapped the Prioress. 'A perfectly straightforward arrangement.'

She spat out the last three words, wild with herself for having adopted a ludicrous posture in an attempt to ease her sciatica, wild with Catherine for having discovered her. Painstakingly the Prioress had built a wall of cushions on the couch, in agony had lowered her spine to the flat of the couch and raised her legs to lie over the cushion wall. The tricky bit had been managing her skirt; she had gathered up a great knot of it and stuffed it between her knees. All to no avail. Almost at once had come a knock at the door, and in her hurry to rise the cushion wall had collapsed and pain so seized her jolted limbs that she had fallen back unable to move a muscle. No doubt she presented a pitiful spectacle. There was no end to the humiliation.

'What do you mean "straightforward"? Why should they move from their rooms to share accommodation in the annexe? What possible reason could there be?'

About this the Prioress was hazy. The chief thing she

recalled from her interview with Margaret was a repetition of the proposal that she publicly wash some postulant's feet: a thing she wished fervently not to do. Passiontide would provide an appropriate opportunity for the ceremony, Margaret considered. By the Prioress's fevered reckoning that lay a mere three weeks away. The idea made her feel more than ever singled out for punishment and pain. 'I cannot recall her precise reason. As you see, I am suffering greatly. That excursion to the lay sisters' dormitory has inflamed my sciatica, as I warned you it might.'

'Where would you like these?' Catherine bent down to retrieve the cushions.

In her imagination the Prioress airily indicated that they might lie at the foot of the couch, rose to her feet with dignity and went to sit in her high-backed chair. As it was, after a pause, 'Under m'knees,' she mumbled.

With some embarrassment, Catherine slid an arm under the bony limbs and inserted two cushions. 'Nothing under your head?'

'Perhaps one. A thin one.'

'Is that comfortable?'

The Prioress grunted.

Catherine drew up a chair and sat down. 'Now, whatever Margaret's stated reasons may have been, I should like to explain to you the consequences of moving the unattached sisters to the annexe.'

The Prioress sighed.

'All the sisters without permanent attachment to a place of work will now be isolated from the main body. They will lose the comforts – and the comforts are considerable these days – enjoyed by the majority. With the lay sisters, they will be set apart.'

'Margaret said nothing of that. Something to do with refurbishment. Or was it ease of organization?'

'Whatever. It really doesn't matter. The consequences

will be as I've described, which, since Margaret is an intelligent woman, I think we must assume she intends.'

'But why should she intend any such thing?'

'It's how her system works. She creates an unprivileged group at the bottom of the pile to keep others on their toes. Some of the Green Sitting Room lot would find themselves in that unfortunate position if, for example, she were to close down bee-keeping, or cut down the number of artists. And the more comfortable life becomes as a member of a Sitting Room, the more terrible becomes the prospect of losing it. So they praise Margaret to the skies to show their hearts are in the right place and reassure themselves by believing their privileges are thoroughly deserved. The more comforts they acquire, the more indispensable those comforts seem. The same goes for members of the Blue Sitting Room. She has built a pyramid of "success", with losers at the bottom to frighten people into line. People feel anxious to safeguard their own individual welfare, and it soon becomes clear that in order to improve the lot of the unfortunate ones, some of their privileges would have to go. People are no longer thinking of the general good, you see, but of what's best for themselves.'

In spite of her pain, the Prioress had listened. Indeed, so novel to her was Catherine's view of the status quo that for a moment she quite forgot her sciatica. And she found herself persuaded. After all, it explained the Sitting Room nonsense, and the strutting airs some senior sisters now affected. The trouble was, the Prioress privately and ruefully acknowledged, she would soon forget the reasoning behind it; she so quickly lost the thread these days. And anyway, what could she do: old, frail, painracked? She had appointed Catherine to *do* things. 'What do you suggest?' she asked gruffly.

'That you forbid it. Prevent the move. But do it quickly. Do it now.'

Demands. Instructions. Do something about the lay sisters. Stop this move to the annexe. Make a spectacle of yourself washing some gel's great feet. Thinking of this last, the Prioress closed her eyes. It was the worst requirement because so glaringly public. She supposed she could bear to do something about the other, summon Margaret, order her to think again: but it might be prudent to put her instruction in writing and thus save argument. Though there'd still be a fuss. Would the sisters obey their prioress, even? Catherine, of course, would set an example, and Monica and Cecilia— Wait a minute. If she were to make Catherine sole directrix there would be an end to Margaret's power. And Catherine would soon put a stop to feet-washing tomfoolery. 'Do you know,' she asked, watching carefully for Catherine's reaction, 'they want me to wash a postulant's feet, make a ceremony of it in the chapel?'

It was utterly unexpected, quite off the point. 'What?' barked Catherine.

'Margaret's idea. To symbolize how we are all equally great and equally humble in the sight of God. As if God needed to be reminded.'

'Typical,' Catherine exploded. She leapt wrathfully to her feet and paced up and down. 'She deliberately creates new inequalities, exploits those that already exist, then dreams up some sentimental symbol to pretend the opposite. Talk about hypocrisy! You won't do it, of course,' she cried, returning to the couch and towering over it.

Fear showed in the Prioress's eyes.

'It's empty, vulgar. In the present circumstances it's a blasphemous lie.'

'She's trying to improve our spirituality.'

'Reverend Mother, I implore you: put a stop to all

this.' She fell to her knees and brought her hands down hard on the couch.

Jarred, the Prioress groaned. 'The slightest movement and I'm sick with pain. I can't *think* now. Perhaps— No; I couldn't stand the fuss, and I'm not sure they'd back us. Oh, how can I think when I'm suffering so?'

'Our Lord in His death agony thought of others.'

'Our Lord,' said the Prioress through gritted teeth, 'was divine.'

Catherine rose from her knees and went to the window. In the courtyard below, groups of visitors were strolling. Two nuns hurried by, their heads bowed and their hands clasped in the manner demonstrated by Sister Beatrice.

'Please go,' pleaded the Prioress.

'Will you tell Sister Margaret to stop this move to the annexe?'

'I shall pray for strength and guidance.'

Catherine didn't trust herself to say more.

21

'It's high time we isolated Catherine,' Margaret said.

Agnes had recently arrived in her office with details of Catherine's busy afternoon: how she had escorted the Prioress to the lay sisters' dormitory, aided and abetted by Sisters Cecilia and Monica; had taken part in an ambulatory conference with those hotheads and troublemakers, Sisters Christa and Gabrielle; had finally dashed to the Prioress's room where she had been closeted for nearly an hour.

'She's pretty isolated, already,' Agnes observed. 'Sister Angelica has very little to do with her, same goes for the Sister Precentor. It's just those two old needleworkers; and that radical lot, of course.'

With care, Margaret plucked a tiny scrap of fluff from her habit. 'I'm sure the threat she poses is minimal, more theoretical than actual, because the Reverend Mother wouldn't dare— All the same, she's a nuisance. She's become a rallying point for the malcontents. Without her they wouldn't have a hope. I'm tired of pussyfooting around the Sister Catherine factor.'

'Time we got tough?' suggested Agnes.

'Time she was isolated,' Margaret said.

Then most beautifully intoned the Sister Precentor: '*Lighten our darkness, we beseech thee, O Lord; and by thy great mercy defend us from all perils and dangers of this night; for the love of thy only Son, our Saviour, Jesus Christ.*'

Never had Kirsty sung Amen so earnestly. Perils and dangers of this night seemed particularly apt, for Sister Rose, the erstwhile cheesemaker, friend of Sister Gabrielle, had proposed that they stage a protest. If Sister Catherine failed them (as seemed likely, for she had sent no message and Kirsty was almost sick with the struggle to repress her hopes) they would refuse to leave their rooms. And if their belongings were then packed for them in the laundry bags lent for the purpose by Sister Imogen, they would sit with their baggage in the north wing corridor and refuse to move to the annexe. With trepidation, Kirsty and Beth had agreed to the plan. None of the other disaffected sisters were likely to join them, for the wrath of Sister Imogen was a daunting prospect; indeed, Kirsty secretly wondered whether her own courage would remain intact. During the next hymn, she turned and looked hopelessly towards Sister Catherine, whose lips seemed scarcely to be moving, so feebly was she singing.

Now came further prayers. Cecilia's knees creaked as she descended to her hassock. Not getting any younger, she warned herself, thinking of stiff joints and dodderiness. Which put her in mind of the Reverend Mother, who had not come down for evensong. Perhaps this was just as well; the side pews were full of visitors, and ten to one the Prioress would drop her prayer book or her spectacles, and pronounce her part in the proceedings grudgingly. Cecilia put a clamp on her thoughts and began to concentrate, for this, the prayer of St Chrysostom, was her favourite.

'*Almighty God, who has given us grace at this time with one accord to make our common supplications unto thee; and dost promise, that when two or three are gathered together in thy Name thou wilt grant their requests*—'

At this point, Cecilia usually allowed one or two small requests to hover discreetly in the forefront of her mind. 'Amen,' she warbled at the prayer's end, then waited with a beatific smile for the Grace.

The sisters, schooled by Beatrice, filed out correctly.

Margaret took note of this and reflected that her friend had done a first-class job on them. At last it could be said that the priory's practices were becoming to God. This gave her deep satisfaction, for the establishment of things that are pleasing to God had been her life's quest. Fortunately, Margaret had been blessed with an instinctive understanding of Godly preference; not for her the breast-beating, heart-searching agony afflicting so many of the would-be holy. As a little girl she had seen that her obedient industry and calm good sense delighted her father. And similarly, as an adult, she aimed to please her Heavenly Father, determined that when He looked down on her it would be with untroubled eyes. All the more distressing, then, to discover her sisters in Christ not so meticulous; their sloppy, self-indulgent habits had shamed her for her Lord's sake. Happily, she could now offer up another job well done: decorous, reverent conduct.

Margaret left the chapel and turned into the cloister. There she caught sight of Sister Cecilia and recollected a more mundane task awaiting her attention. She hurried forward and took hold of Cecilia's arm.

Cecilia jerked her head back an inch or two, thus preserving that necessary distance between herself and a person of a lower class. So ingrained in her was this habit that she performed it unconsciously, and few of those on the receiving end understood its significance, for her enquiries as to a person's health or opinion of the weather were full of good-natured concern. Nevertheless, when poor taste on the part of the interrogated permitted a reply of some length, a blankness would veil her eyes, shutting out her former interest. 'Dear, dear,' or 'Never mind,' she would interject firmly while backing away. Now, faced with a close-up of Margaret, she assumed a look of deep discouragement.

Margaret failed to notice it. 'A word with you, Sister. There's a little job you can do for me: or rather for the priory. Can you spare the time to step into my office?'

'I suppose I can,' Cecilia said reluctantly. 'Does now suit you? I've promised to visit poor Sister Lazarus later on.'

'How kind. Yes, now is perfectly convenient. Come along.' Margaret led the way. In her office, she waved grandly towards an armchair. 'Do sit down.'

Cautiously, Cecilia lowered herself.

Margaret sat at her desk, leaned her forearms on it and clasped her hands over it, and craned forward. 'Yes. You have exactly the right qualifications.' (Cecilia's nose twitched suspiciously.) 'Our visitors come for peace and quiet, of course. Nevertheless, some do rather enjoy having a special fuss made of them. I try to entertain them to tea at least once during their stay. Normally I do the honours alone in the visitors' sitting room, sometimes upstairs with the Reverend Mother, but' – Margaret lowered her voice, and confided – 'her *condition*, you know, and those rather unfortunate teeth. So I'm afraid the duty invariably falls upon me. And the demands on my time, Sister Cecilia, are simply endless. It suddenly came to me during evensong. (Wasn't it a delightful service? The Sister Precentor has such an elevated tone.) Yes, it came to me in a flash: Sister Cecilia is the very person to relieve me of my little chore. No messy pourings out from her! And, of course, no fears for the delicate Rockingham china. In Sister Cecilia's company, I told myself, the most retiring visitor will feel at ease, and the highest of the high quite at home. What do you say, Sister? Will you be responsible for entertaining the visitors to tea?'

'Good heavens,' cried Cecilia. 'Well. It would have to be thought about.'

'Not for too long, I hope. I can't stand indecision. Either the idea appeals, or it doesn't. It's a responsible position; I set great store on making our visitors feel at home. And naturally it would entail membership of the Blue Sitting Room.' She paused for a full ten seconds, allowing Cecilia more than adequate time to consider. 'Well, you disappoint me. I wonder whether the position would be of interest to Sister Monica?'

Cecilia's head began to wobble. 'I was about to get to Sister Monica. She and I are used to working together.' Indeed, from their schooldays, Monica had done much of Cecilia's work.

Margaret clapped her head as if struck by a brain-wave. 'Of course, the two of you! What an excellent idea, for sometimes there is quite a little crowd requiring tea. That's settled. You are both appointed.' She rose and went to clasp Cecilia's hand. 'And don't forget: this means you are both eligible for member-ship of the Blue Sitting Room.'

'As to that, I'm not sure we shall care for it,' Cecilia warned. 'Nasty thick teacups, I hear. Though I dare say we shall put in an appearance now and then; to be sociable, don't you know.'

Cecilia's little feet scampered through the corridors. Just wait till she told Monica— But what a blow! Monica was not in her room. Where was the woman? In the needlework room, perhaps.

Monica was indeed in the needlework room. She jumped guiltily when the door flew open, for she was engaged on an illicit piece of work of her own, an embroidery depicting a milkmaid and her swain dallying in a flower-stippled meadow.

'Oh, you'll never guess, Monica,' Cecilia cried.

Monica rolled up her work and dutifully offered her friend her attention. 'Then you had better tell me, Cecilia.'

Cecilia's face, flushed and shining, wore an expression Monica remembered from their schooldays when Cecilia had wangled some treat or advantage. And this was how she now presented Margaret's offer. She had crafted a victory. Her social poise, her innate superiority had been conceded and was to reconcile her with the beloved Rockingham. 'In the end, you see, breeding tells. Apparently some of the visitors are more *our sort*. But I don't suppose the others will be too bad. In any case, *we* shall set the tone. Won't it be fun? I shall quite revel in it. And on the strength of it we're to become members of the Blue Sitting Room: though as you can imagine, I soon let her know what sort of honour we think *that*. All the same, I shall enjoy breezing in and putting a few noses out of joint. Oh, Monica, what a triumph!'

Oh dear, thought Monica, sensing danger, but hating to pour cold water on her friend's enthusiasm. 'It sounds attractive, but we shall have to go into it carefully. We'll ask Catherine first.'

'First? What first? I said we'd do it and that's that. Oh, don't worry, I know what you're thinking, but rest assured I didn't show eagerness. Not at all, I kept her dangling for quite a time. Ultimately I gave in, because we wouldn't have wanted her to change her mind.'

'You misunderstand me, Cecilia. I suspect there may be more to this than meets the eye. Consider, dear, how we have urged people to go and see how the lay sisters are placed. We even took the Reverend Mother to the dormitory this afternoon. We have made an issue of it, and I don't suppose Sister Margaret is pleased. This may be her way of buying our silence.'

'Rubbish.' Cecilia sprang to her feet. But Monica saw alarm in her eyes and understood how her delightful new world had trembled. She watched as Cecilia marched up to the work table and began to untidy a pile of paper patterns. 'I refuse to believe even Sister Margaret could be so devious. Really, Monica.'

She stayed at the table fiddling with the patterns for some moments. When she turned and wandered back it was because, Monica guessed, some promising line of argument had occurred to her. 'No, I really believe the poor gel, finding herself a little out of her depth, has had the honesty and good sense to pass the job on to those who are equal to every occasion. Give credit where it is due, if you please. Sister Margaret is a pain and a bore, and I don't deny it; but in this I salute her. It would be churlish not to help her out. No, I am quite clear about it, Monica: this is our duty.' And she sank in triumph into her easy chair.

Monica sighed, thinking what a burden it can be to know another person too well. She had anticipated Cecilia's every thought, could have completed her every sentence. 'Well, at least let us tell Catherine what has occurred.'

'Tomorrow, or whenever we see her, we will,' Cecilia agreed airily; 'but now,' she went on, bringing a note of vigorous virtue into her voice, 'we must go and visit Sister Lazarus. We promised.'

'So we did. And, dear one, do try not to talk *at* the poor creature. Be gentle. Try to draw her out.'

'But I do, Monica. I do my very best to be cheery and uplifting.'

For the past two months, Imogen had entertained hope. Her longing to be taken back on the Forward Planning Committee was so intense she was afraid even to mention the Committee in case in doing so her voice should crack. When it was referred to in her hearing she became violently hot and had to turn away to hide any give-away blushes. Recently, Margaret had congratulated her on her handling of the business of the lay sisters' accommodation. 'Your quiet good sense has seen us through what otherwise might have been a very tricky situation.' Those were Margaret's very words. Imogen repeated them to herself every night on retiring, and when in need of a boost during the day locked herself into her favourite cloakroom and sat on the rosewood lavatory seat to linger over them some more. They must mean that forgiveness was near, forgiveness for publicizing Sister Veronica's letter to Clare. They surely indicated how very much in Margaret's thoughts were Imogen's talents, and how sorely they were missed by the Forward Planning Committee. At length, having thought of all this and stoked her impatience to screaming pitch, Imogen would stuff her knuckles in her mouth. 'Soon, very soon,' she would promise herself.

But now, at half past eight on this Thursday evening in March, her hopes lay in ashes along the north wing corridor. At intervals on the brand new blood-red carpet, Sisters Kirsty, Beth and Rose squatted with their bulging laundry bags, each outside what had been until an hour ago her room, and was now very definitely not her room but that of some other sister newly moved in from the annexe.

Sister Rose was their spokeswoman. Sisters Kirsty and Beth merely nodded or shook their heads and stared about them with fright-filled eyes. Sister Christa and others stood about in the corridor, lending support. The sisters who had recently moved in from the annexe kept opening their doors, popping out their heads and protesting a willingness to return from whence they came.

'Stay where you are, and keep your doors closed,' Imogen commanded again and again.

But that did not budge the rebels. Whatever line she

took, whether she cajoled or threatened, Imogen found they were implacable. They would stay in the north wing corridor unless and until they were restored to their rooms.

'Your rooms are in the annexe now,' Imogen repeated wearily.

Not so, they insisted, and waited for Imogen's next move.

The redness of the carpet seemed to run and spread. The corridor rocked. Imogen expected the floor to give way, the walls to crumble, sulphur to seep in and choke them all; hell, she felt, could not be far away. She was beside herself with impotent fury and dread lest Margaret should arrive and discover the impasse.

But it was Margaret's co-directrix who arrived and began talking in an undertone to Sister Christa.

'Sister Catherine,' Imogen cried, and was relieved to hear the tight control of her voice. 'I trust you are here to lend your good offices to an immediate evacuation of this corridor. These sisters have accommodation waiting for them in the annexe.'

Sister Catherine, it appeared, intended to ignore her. She moved along the corridor to where Sister Kirsty was squatting, knelt down and questioned her.

Imogen, straining to hear, caught nothing. Near to her, Sisters Christa and Gabrielle were talking in rude, loud voices. Sister Catherine rose and went to speak to Sister Beth. At last she came to Imogen.

The corridor fell silent. Catherine looked into Imogen's eyes. 'They are doing as their conscience dictates. We must all do that,' she declared, and went quickly away.

Several sisters now disappeared into their rooms, and soon returned bearing rugs and blankets.

'Here you are, Sister Kirsty, you can sleep on this.'

'This will do for you, Sister Rose.'

'Sister Beth, take mine.'

'Good job there's this new thick carpet.'

They were setting up camp like a bunch of eager Girl Guides, thought Imogen. Giddiness shook her; she put a hand to the wall, then turned and went slowly through the corridor, picking her way through the cinders of her dear dead hopes.

'All night? You mean to say they stayed in the corridor *all night*?' Margaret was almost apoplectic. 'Whatever was Imogen thinking about? How could she allow it? And you say Catherine actually came and did nothing to stop it?'

'Gave it her blessing, more like.'

'Right. That does it. No holds barred from now on. I've been patient. I've put up with a lot of time-wasting nonsense. But now she'll discover what sort of fight she's got on her hands. Joan: the *Bulletin*. I want something – and make it crystal clear this time – to the effect that Catherine is stark staring mad.'

'Help, Margaret! I can hint at it: because I suppose approving of people sleeping in the corridor is hardly a rational response for someone in authority, is it? But I'm not a doctor. I can't state it as proven fact.'

'Oh, stop wittering, woman, and go and get Sister Verity. She'll know what I want. There are ways of saying these things. And Sister Verity says it with *punch*.'

Hurt and crestfallen, Joan went in search of Sister Verity.

'I must say, I'm disappointed in Imogen,' Margaret went on to Agnes.

'What could she do? – apart from hoisting 'em over her shoulder and carrying 'em off to the annexe. Anyway, this morning she had the presence of mind to remove their belongings from the corridor while they were all at work. They'll find they have to go to the annexe tonight, unless they propose to stay in the clothes they've got on indefinitely.'

'It's most unsatisfactory,' Margaret said.

Sister Verity arrived. She was a stocky, jowly creature, with bulging brows and a pessimistic countenance.

'Ah, Sister Verity. You others may go. Sister Verity and I have a great deal to discuss.'

BULLETIN for the tenth of March.

IS THIS THE BEHAVIOUR WE EXPECT?

Three sisters spent last night in the North Wing corridor rather than in their perfectly good beds in the annexe. Disgraceful, we hear you say. But we have even worse news to report. Our joint directrix (not — need it be said? — Sister Margaret) actually encouraged these sisters in their outlandish behaviour.

Sister Catherine is becoming more and more strange. There have been whispers about her. There are even fears that she is losing her mind. If this is so, we pity her. But can we afford instability in a leader? The answer is a resounding NO. For the sake of our priory, Sister Catherine must now resign.

22

At the foot of the organ loft stairs, Catherine caught up with Angelica. 'Don't know about yours, but my hair needs a trim.' Most sisters paired with a friend to keep one another's hair to the regulation shortness.

'Sorry. I'm expecting a pupil.'

'Oh, I don't mean right now necessarily. When you've time.'

'I should ask someone else. As a matter of fact, Sister Theresa and I cut each other's hair a few days ago.' Angelica ran up the stairs.

A pulse hammered in Catherine's throat. She leaned against the wall. When the organ sounded, she gathered herself together and hurried away. She decided to get her hair-cutting over with.

In the bathroom, she sat in her shift on the stool and peered into a dingy mirror. A stranger stared back, or, rather, a familiar face unseen for some time. Terrible things had happened in the interim. The face had become gaunt, the skin lustreless, there were violet wells beneath over-bright eyes. A scar running vertically from left cheekbone to jaw, and dark clumpy hair threaded here and there with grey, reinforced an impression that here was an inmate of some prison camp. Horrified, she rose and went closer to the glass, and loosened the drawstring at her neck. Bones jutted, hollows were deep, collarbones and ribs had the merest covering of skin. Unable to bear the sight, she pulled up and secured her shift, draped a plastic cape round her shoulders and began methodically to slice away her hair.

When the job was done, it occurred to her that she might be anaemic. She went right up to the mirror and pulled down her lower eyelids. As she'd suspected, the inner skin was bloodless. She bathed, then dressed, and set off for the hospital.

So run off her feet was Sister Luke that for the time being Catherine forgot about her anaemia. A virus had attacked the lay sisters. Lying in their freezing dormitory, many of them had become ill. The hospital was full to overflowing, and Sister Luke had been granted only one extra pair of hands.

'You should have sent for me,' cried Catherine, rolling up her sleeves. She tied on an apron.

Many hours later Catherine sank into a chair and mentioned her own problem. 'I shan't bother the doctor, Sister, but let me have some iron tablets, will you?'

'Oh, but I think you should. You've looked pinched for months.'

'Later on perhaps. In the meantime, see what you can find for me.'

Just before suppertime she left the hospital, promising to return in the morning.

'There you are,' Christa cried, hurrying towards her through the cloister. 'I've been looking for you. Sister Imogen took their belongings to the annexe this morning. Rose intends to camp again in the corridor, but Kirsty and Beth seem to be weakening.'

'They must do as they think best.'

'Hang on. The other thing is— Well, you'd better come and see for yourself.'

Christa led her to the refectory notice board. On it was pinned the latest *Bulletin*, and Catherine discovered she was advised to resign. She read the piece slowly, and then read it again, aware of curious glances towards her as nuns came in for supper.

'What do you think?' Christa asked.

'I think I shall draw up a dossier of all that is wrong with this place. Then I'll pin it up next to this. One can at least learn from one's enemies.'

'Great idea.' Christa was encouraged by Catherine's resilience. She really is coming on, she thought, recalling how Catherine had required prompting and urging in the past. These days Catherine's blood was up. She clapped her on the back. 'If you need any help,' she offered.

Catherine sat at her desk. Christa leaned over her. Behind them, Gabrielle lolled in the easy chair.

'As a result of the ill effects of their atrocious accommodation, two-thirds of the lay sisters are ill, many so seriously that they are confined to the hospital,' Christa suggested.

'No, no,' Catherine said. 'We must think how *they* would write it.' She put her head in her hands.

'Don't forget to mention the annexe business,' Gabrielle put in.

'Shh.'

Catherine began to write.

Ten minutes later, Christa took the paper from her and read what she had written:

'AT OUR WITS' END,' SAYS SISTER LUKE.

It was a grim scene yesterday in the hospital. Sister Luke and her staff were exhausted. 'Every bed is taken, and many more are sick in the dormitory,' she said. 'Two sisters have pneumonia. Most are too ill to do a thing for themselves.' This state of affairs is unprecedented in the recent history of our priory. We demand to know WHY.

'Gosh, yes, that's really good.'

'It's hateful. But that's the way it's done. Give it back. I'll list the faults of the dormitory next, then ask why they put the lay sisters there in the first place.'

'Then the annexe business,' Gabrielle reminded her again.

'No. I think a different topic each day. One sheet of the dossier put up at a time. More of an impact, don't you think?'

'You're right. Come on,' Christa said to Gabrielle. 'We must go and give Rose moral support.'

'And Kirsty: I managed to persuade her to stay in the corridor for another night. But Beth's dropped out, unfortunately.'

Catherine looked up. 'Don't put pressure on Sister Kirsty. She's unhappy enough as it is.'

Late that night while her sister nuns slept, Catherine crept through the corridors to the art room. She found a lamp on a desk and switched it on, collected paper, Indian ink and a pen. Painstakingly, she wrote out a sheet of her dossier, then, to save herself trouble on future nights, composed two more, one dealing with the compulsory move to the annexe, another entitled *WHAT IS THE PURPOSE OF THIS PRIORY?* In a desk drawer she found a box of drawing pins. Taking these and her finished work, she left the art room and went back along the corridor. Then she turned right and entered the cloister.

The wind had dropped. There was only freezing stillness. As she tiptoed between wall and open arches, afraid almost to breathe, she was struck by the independence of the place itself. For without anyone to see or know, the stones oozed dampness, dust consolidated, and secretive spores bloomed in the grass. She started as a black shape swooped across the pale navy of the quadrangle. A bat, she thought, straining to see; but it merged with the denser darkness of a hollow between two pillars.

On the refectory notice board, she pinned the first sheet of her dossier against the side of the *Bulletin*. In her exaggerated wide-awake state she couldn't leave it, but read it through compulsively again and again. At last she turned away and went through the corridors to her room, and soon lay with her racing thoughts in bed.

Agnes burst into Beatrice's room. 'My God, has she seen it?'

Beatrice, who was lying on her bed with her eyes shut, chose her words carefully. 'If I said, incandescent with rage, would it answer you?'

Agnes groped for a chair.

'You'd better watch out. I thought you were supposed to be her eyes and ears. 'Fraid you've rather slipped up, Aggers.'

'That blasted Catherine! I'd like to pin her to the proverbial wheel.'

'What an awful thing to say.'

'She must have got up in the night to put it on the notice board. Clare says it was there first thing.'

'Clare, eh? And she didn't come running to warn us? You'd think she'd try to earn her passage back, like good old Imogen. Now if it had been Imogen who'd spotted it, she'd have come panting like a good doggie to lay it at Margaret's feet. Sweet, I always think, the way poor Imogen tries.'

'Should I go and talk to her, do you think, or keep out of the way?'

'Depends how strong your stomach is this morning,' said Beatrice, recalling her own interview with Margaret.

Beatrice had been the unfortunate bearer of the news. The trouble was, she had rather enjoyed Catherine's spunk; it was so unexpected. A worthy paragraph describing the lay sisters' woes and a heavy-handed rebuke aimed at authority were the sorts of the things one would have anticipated from Sister Catherine. Instead, she had cheekily imitated Sister Verity's style. It was possible, Beatrice conceded, that she'd allowed a degree of amused admiration to colour her account of the outrage. Whether she had or not, Margaret had fairly hit the ceiling; leapt from her chair, arms flailing, eyes swivelling; had been all for marching on the notice board then and there and ripping it down. 'But Margaret,' Beatrice had protested, 'that'd be so undignified. Better to ignore it. I should disdain even to look at it if I were you.'

'Shut *up*,' Margaret had yelled. 'Don't you understand? I WANT IT REMOVED NOW.'

It was the first time Margaret had rejected Beatrice's advice: and with such unpleasant passion! 'Well, don't look at me,' she'd said huffily.

'Clear off, then. Scram. Where's Agnes? It's her job to prevent things like this. Send for Joan; p'raps she'll talk *sense*.'

Margaret, Beatrice recalled with a shudder, had been as imperious and unlovely as a Chinese emperor.

When Agnes saw that she was unlikely to get further information from Beatrice, she left and set off cautiously for Margaret's office. The door to it stood open. Joan was in the doorway, wringing her hands. From where she was standing, Agnes was unable to see Margaret; she could hear her, though: 'Ridiculous suggestion. You're losing your touch, Joan. Send me Sister Verity.'

Joan came sightlessly past Agnes. And Agnes, not liking the sound of things here, decided to leave also. She decided to go and sound out Sister Clare.

Soon, Sister Verity came plodding to Margaret's door.

'Come in. Thank goodness it's you, Verity. Have you heard?'

'Heard what?'

Steadying herself, Margaret told her. 'What do you think we should do?'

'Rip begger up. Pardon, I'm a plain speaker, me.'

'Quite understood. And then?'

'Hit back.' She punched a fist into the palm of a hand.

Margaret's breath eased out. 'My feelings exactly. Do it at once, Verity. Then come back here and we'll work something out. By the way,' she called, as Verity went to the door, 'I've decided to make you my communications secretary.'

Catherine's anger was like an engine. *She* did not power her legs, this force drove them, on and on. The dislodged remainder of her body floated above them in a haze of indignant disbelief. Light-headed, she burst into Margaret's office. Her eyes, which were also supercharged, pounced on the dossier (*her* dossier) in the wastepaper basket; they reported other images also, in sharper than normal detail: she noticed the thread veins spoiling the whites of Margaret's eyes, and that her hand, stilled by her surprise, hovered like a hawk's talon; she noticed the open pores on Verity's nose, and that her hanging dinted cheeks trembled slightly, perhaps with startlement at Catherine's abrupt arrival, perhaps with annoyance at it.

'So there it is,' cried Catherine when she had done surveying them. She swooped on her brutalized handiwork. 'How dare you remove it? How *dare* you?'

'How dare *you*?' Margaret countered. She rose and leaned across her desk. 'How dare you write such stuff, accusing me, blaming me?'

'That's rich. You had the nerve to ask me to resign.'

'I? I had the nerve? I do not write the *Bulletin*. You, on the other hand, produced that scurrilous sheet yourself.'

'Whether or not you personally write what goes into it, it gives your point of view.'

'Because my point of view, dear Sister, happens to coincide with the best interests of this priory. It is I who have set this priory back on its feet. You and your nasty broadsheet seek to undermine everything we've built up. That is why I had it removed. Quite simply, it is against the priory's interest.'

'I see. So freedom of speech is expendable.'

'Don't talk to me about freedom,' bawled Margaret, by now very red in the face. 'The day we get trial by broadsheet is the day that freedom dies!'

'Are you saying,' Catherine asked quietly, 'that you will prevent me from putting my point of view on the notice board?'

'Certainly. In the interests of the priory.'

'Right. Then I shall call a meeting and explain the situation to everyone.'

'We won't fret about that,' Verity put in. 'Folks know which side their bread's buttered. They'll back us, you'll find.'

'Yes, call a meeting,' Margaret agreed, after a slight hesitation. 'You can put your side and I shall put mine. Then we'll call for a show of hands and that must be an end to the matter. I can't allow us to be diverted by dissension. There's work to be done around here, and I intend to see it's done.'

The mere thought of arguing in public yet again with her co-directrix, Margaret found wearisome. She did not enjoy argument of any sort, considering it a waste of time. And it seemed particularly futile to spend time wastefully in its pursuit today when so many fascinating and important matters awaited her attention. However, she had agreed to this meeting and must see it through. Sighing, sometimes heaving with impatience, Margaret waited for Catherine to finish speaking. She paid scant attention, merely took in key words here and there which might trigger her own pet phrases. The word she latched on to now was 'freedom' – actually, 'freedom' preceded 'of speech', but Margaret didn't notice that. Freedom was a word she could use. She focused on it, and her pulse quickened.

When Catherine sat down, Margaret jumped up smartly. Without any preliminaries, she barged straight in. 'Catherine talks of freedom,' she said. (There were no protests.) 'Shall I tell you what is the best guarantee of our freedom? Success. Material success. For if the priory fails, where is our freedom then?' And then she was away, heading for the sure safe ground of just rewards for the hardworking, and as she launched upon this she sensed an exhalation of relief from the audience; Catherine's remarks had unsettled the sisters, they wished to be made comfortable again. It buoyed Margaret up, this knowledge of their need. 'There is nothing wrong with making our priory wealthy,' she soothed. 'Wealth allows choice. It is what we choose to do with our wealth that is important.'

But suddenly, to Margaret's chagrin, she was interrupted by Catherine.

'But it also matters *how* our wealth is created,' she shouted (rudely, Margaret thought). 'It matters very much when it is created at the cost of someone's impoverishment. Our so-called success has been achieved by deliberately excluding some members of this community. Can the lay sisters choose to return to the east wing? Can the sisters in the annexe choose to do the sort of work that is well rewarded? They cannot. They are denied choice. An inferior mode of living is imposed on them. So where is *their* freedom?' she demanded, sitting down.

Furious now, Margaret decided it was time to tell a

few home truths. 'Very well. Let me make myself plain. The fact is, there is *no regular work* for the lay sisters and the annexe sisters. This priory had become inefficient. Too many things were undertaken merely to keep people occupied or to indulge inclinations. We could not go on in that fashion. We needed to work purposefully, to *earn* our living. To that end, some areas of work had to go. Others had to be made lean and fit. Some areas, the profitable ones, were expanded: needlework and art, for example. More people were needed to clean and cook for our visitors; but as I am sure you are aware, the number of visitors staying with us at any one time varies considerably. Therefore it is necessary to vary the number of people working to serve them. Which is why we need a *flexible* workforce.

'But I must be frank with you. In spite of the visitors, we still have sisters whose labour is surplus to our requirements. In other words, they are *passengers*, because the rest of us, those doing necessary and profitable work, are obliged to carry them. Now, I put it to you: would it be equitable if these *passengers* were placed in exactly the same position as those who *earn* their privileges? Of *course* it would not.

'You know, I think a sense of gratitude wouldn't be too much to ask. I have been disturbed to hear that certain sisters who should properly reside in the annexe have refused Sister Imogen's request to go there. Instead they have set up camp in the north wing corridor. Sisters, I find such behaviour deplorable. How *dare* they complain about their circumstances? Do the sisters who are obliged to support them complain? I say to Sister Rose and Sister Kirsty: end this outrageous disobedience now! Be grateful for the generosity of your peers; show respect for authority. Above all, try to be worthy of the name of Albion!'

The applause was deafening, relieving a pent-up

atmosphere. Catherine, leaping up and bellowing to be heard, felt she was expending the last dregs of her strength.

'Wait. Listen. Our lot may have improved, but we're forgetting how to live as a community. We're forgetting why we are here: not to be stokers of some machine called the Albion Priory—'

'Disgraceful!' yelled Agnes. '*Some machine* is a disgraceful way to describe—'

'Then what about *passengers*?' Christa screamed.

Someone shouted back at this, but the voices of individuals were soon drowned by roars of distaste from the main body of the audience.

Thrown by the eruption, Catherine lost her thread. She gripped the dais in front of her. 'My point is, what I'm trying to get over, um, to put to you today— Well, let me ask you a question. Can't we agree to include every sister in our improved circumstances? Can't some of us give up a little – one of the new sitting rooms perhaps, some of those new offices and bathrooms – so that everyone can be decently accommodated? Can't we forgo one or two luxuries for the sake of less fortunate sisters? Would it hurt us so much? Let's vote on it,' she cried, encouraged by the listening hush that had fallen, and feeling that this was the moment to tie Margaret's hand.

Margaret, scenting danger, got hastily to her feet. 'I was about to suggest a vote myself. I'm sick and tired of going over and over the same old ground. Let's put an end to the argument, once and for all. You are voting,' she warned them sternly, 'on whether you wish the priory's affairs to continue in my hands. Do you wish to consolidate the progress we have achieved, or risk losing it for the sake of Sister Catherine's scruples? Those who wish things to continue as they are at present with *me* in charge, raise your hands.'

A singing came in Catherine's ears. Too late now to establish the correct motion, to shout, No, put your hands down, that is not what I said. She watched a hundred arms rising, and in her dazed state thought of plants shooting after a rainfall.

But Margaret was not altogether satisfied. 'Interesting to see who is behind one,' she mused.

Cecilia, holding her hand in the air, kicked Monica's ankle. 'Put it up,' she hissed.

'But Catherine—'

'Do you want to lose us the tea-party job? Put your hand up, Monica, or I'll never forgive you.'

Miserably, Monica raised her hand to shoulder height.

Elizabeth was experiencing a similar difficulty. 'Please, Anne,' she whispered.

'No, I don't know—'

'You'll be out of the Blue Sitting Room: the only one of us not a member.'

Anne's arm also rose.

'Hmm,' said Margaret. 'Over to you, Sister.'

Catherine's face was as grey as her habit. Her pallor, and the scar on her cheek and her dark eyes, gave her a fanatical appearance. But her voice came out firmly. 'So be it. You want Sister Margaret to remain in charge.' She took a deep breath, sensing a last chance coming. 'But will you ask her to moderate her policies? Will you show willingness to forgo just a few of your privileges for the sake of the less fortunate? Raise your hands, please, if you agree to that.'

Now the hands of Christa and her friends flew up. One or two of the annexe sisters – including Rose and Kirsty, whose cheeks still flamed from Margaret's rebuke – daringly voted in their own interests; but most of these were too embarrassed to raise their hands, conscious that it was not they who were called upon to make sacrifices. (The lay sisters, of course, were not eligible to be present.) There were rustlings, murmurings, head-turnings.

'Don't dare,' Cecilia whispered sharply to Monica, 'I meant what I said.' For Monica had again begun to raise her hand. The rise ended at her mouth. She bit on her knuckles and thought how dearly she loved Catherine, and then how dearly she loved Cecilia. In the end, love for Cecilia, her friend and companion since childhood, prevailed. Her hand fell into her lap. She bowed her head.

Anne was thinking that of course Catherine was right – as Jesus is right, and the Scriptures. If this were a morality tale of her own invention, she would make Catherine triumph. But there was also to be considered her prized Blue Sitting Room membership. Blow it, she *enjoyed* the Blue Sitting Room. Was that so very wicked? It was plain there'd be no consensus to forgo it; why should she be holier than the rest? And as Elizabeth's sidelong glance now warned, if she were to defy Margaret and raise her hand, sure as eggs were eggs she would find herself somehow excluded. Tears sprang to her eyes as she thought of Elizabeth, Cecilia and Monica tripping merrily away at half past three, and she left solitary in the needlework room. She clamped her hands between her knees and waited tensely for the moment to pass.

Silence fell like a blanket, smothering people's thoughts. In an agonizing prickle of suspense, they waited.

Margaret broke the stillness. 'Pretty decisive, wouldn't you say?' she asked, turning to Catherine.

But Catherine was running from the room.

Margaret contemplated Verity, and did so with affection. The pleasure of victory was the more intense because she had secured it without assistance from

Beatrice, Agnes or Joan. Hitherto, when drawing up strategic plans, it had been assumed among them that contributions from all four were necessary. This afternoon Margaret had demonstrated otherwise. In a moment she would call in the others and accept their congratulations, for it would be gracious to appear magnanimous. At this moment, though, Verity's forthright attitude suited her mood.

'To all intents and purposes,' she mused, 'that vote should have settled the issue of the succession. I'm sure it has, as far as Catherine's concerned. Did you see how she scuttled away? No, it's just a matter of bringing it home to the Prioress.'

'Done any work on that?' Verity asked.

'Mm, lots. In fact, I'm about to bring matters to a head. Did I ever tell you about the new ceremony we're to have; the washing of a postulant's feet?'

'Go on.'

'It's part of my campaign: *mission*, I suppose, is a better word, because that's how I feel about it, Verity: I'm engaged in a mission to deepen our spirituality. I thought how fitting it would be if our spiritual leader were to follow our Lord's example when He washed the disciples' feet.'

'All of 'em? Take a dickens of a time.'

'No, no. One will suffice, it's the symbolism we're after. I had thought the newest postulant's feet would be suitable, but I've discovered she's a great buxom thing. That little novice Sister Fay will suit the part to perfection, so I shall say "one of the postulants' feet" and in fact see that Sister Fay is chosen. We'll have the ceremony in the chapel where the visitors can watch. I think they'll find it moving.'

'But the Reverend Mother won't like it, you reckon?'

'The Reverend Mother, Verity – now please don't be shocked, and please accept that it pains me greatly to say so – the Reverend Mother is a thoroughly selfish and indolent woman. She cares only that the priory is run with the minimum of trouble to herself. What a tragedy it is that those who bear responsibility for our religious life take their duties so lightly. I may be primarily concerned with our material welfare, but I do care deeply for the spiritual side. I shall insist on the Reverend Mother pulling her weight. She shan't get out of it.'

Verity attempted a grin, but as always on these rare occasions her weighty dewlaps proved a handicap. 'But you reckon she'll have a darn good try? Make you her successor and tell you to get on with the feet-washing yourself?'

Margaret's eyes glinted. She wanted to assure her new friend that she herself would be perfectly comfortable to perform such an act; indeed, would perform it with grace. But she chose instead to stick to the point: the task of persuading the Prioress to see where her duty lay in the matter of the succession. 'Not *necessarily*,' she answered. 'Rome wasn't built in a day. However, the proposal will test her commitment. For I shall make it plain that more, much more will be expected of our spiritual leader in future. After all, as we grow materially stronger it is vital to have a corresponding growth in our spiritual development. This little ceremony of the feet-washing is only the start of things. But we mustn't waste time chatting. About the *Bulletin*, Verity. I'm very keen to keep up the pressure. It's obvious that Catherine is a spent force, but it needs to be said again and again until the Prioress makes it official.'

24

Across the concourse, holding her thumb against the head of a drawing pin that was pressed through the second sheet of her dossier with the point protruding, Catherine came striding; head and shoulders held unnaturally stiff, eyes fixed on her goal.

It had cost her a great deal to come here at this busy time of day, but if she had come at a quieter time, early this morning or late last night, the prompt removal of her dossier would have ensured ignorance of its existence. They would remove it in any case, she had no illusion about that; but its arrival and removal would at least be noted by this lunchtime throng, and a few braver sisters might read it. She wondered if the sisters gathered here were thinking her foolish, messing about with her sheets of paper, after yesterday's verdict. But there was such a thing as bearing witness, she had told herself as she sat on the edge of her bed trying to muster courage. Her unnatural gait and her set expression were unconscious outward signs of the degree to which she was shrinking inside.

Unknown to Catherine, her strange appearance gave credence to sentiments expressed in today's issue of the *Bulletin. We are alarmed to note signs of eccentricity in Sister Catherine's demeanour of late.* The sisters making way for her to pass fell awkwardly silent. When the dossier was in place, and Catherine turned on her heel and strode away, they let out their relief. How embarrassing it would have been if she'd paused to inspect the *Bulletin.*

In the kitchen Catherine learned that the meals she had come to collect for patients were not yet ready. Promising to return in ten minutes, she went outside, away from the stench of food cooked to death in vast quantities and incongruous variety, gratefully taking the fresh air.

At that moment, Sisters Rose and Kirsty arrived outside the refectory. 'Doesn't look as though they're ready. What's the matter with them in the kitchen?' Rose grumbled, and turned away to push through the crowd to the notice board. Kirsty kept close to her, not because she wished to read the notices, but because the public scolding she had received from Sister Margaret had left her nervous, and Rose, who was friendly with Sister Christa and her crowd, was sure and strong and made Kirsty feel safe.

'I say, Kirsty, look at this.'

Reluctantly, Kirsty looked. It was the piece written by Sister Catherine, and it was about the plight of the annexe sisters. Kirsty glowed as she read it. 'She really understands,' she commented to Rose. 'Though I don't suppose it'll do us any good. Still, it's nice to know someone's bothered.'

'Oh, my goodness, though, look here.' Rose pointed to the *Bulletin*.

Kirsty read it and grew hot. She hoped Sister Catherine wouldn't see it. But then, reading further, her heart came to a standstill. *The two annexe sisters still camping in the north wing corridor are becoming a couple of pests.* As her heart raced to make up for its missed beat, a particular word caught her eye. For a moment it transfixed her. Then she gave a cry, and turned and ran until she found herself in the open air.

'Whatever is it, Sister?' asked Sister Florence, who was walking across the yard.

Kirsty leapt into the shed and jammed the door shut with a sack of potatoes.

'Sister?' cried Florence, as an unseen Kirsty gave vent to her fear and indignation. Sister Florence pummelled the door. 'Open up, please, Sister. Sister Kirsty!'

Hearing the commotion, Catherine came running.

'Sister Kirsty has shut herself in. She sounds dreadfully upset.'

Catherine put her mouth to the edge of the door. 'It's Sister Catherine here, Sister Kirsty. Please tell me what's the matter.'

Kirsty was becoming exhausted. Her shaking legs gave way and she slipped to the floor and leaned back against a potato sack. Sister Catherine's voice came through to her. 'Scroungers,' she called in answer. 'It called us scroungers.'

'What did? Where?'

'The *Bulletin* on the notice board. It says there's no proper work for us and the rest have to keep us. We're scroungers moaning for better conditions.'

Sister Florence broke the silence. 'The poor thing. You know, they really do go too far. It's not their faults. It's the way things are run nowadays—' Her voice trailed away as Catherine turned to stare at her.

'I didn't notice your hand raised in their support yesterday.'

Sister Florence turned pale.

'I'll stay with her,' said Catherine. 'I expect she'll come out in a minute. Will you see about the trays for the hospital? I was about to do that myself.'

'Of course,' mumbled Sister Florence.

When her tapping footsteps were no longer to be heard, Kirsty removed the sack and opened the door. 'I was a bit upset. It was the shock. Sorry,' she said, shamefaced.

'Come on. Let's go somewhere quiet and talk.'

*   *   *

212

'I used to come here a lot,' Catherine said, leading into the deserted cowshed.

'Is it all right? Are we supposed to come in here?' asked Kirsty.

'I'm sure they won't mind. It's a couple of hours yet before milking. In the old days, when they were short-handed, I used to help out with the milking. That was how I got to be friendly with Sister Mary John.' Catherine arranged herself on a bale of hay, and after a moment Kirsty joined her.

Out of the sharp keen air, the cowshed struck warm. It was not quite silent, but faintly hummed and stirred: a lulling sort of place, scented by hay and dung and milk. A cat stole from the shadows. 'Come, puss, come,' Catherine called, putting out her hands. The cat jumped into her lap and nestled down, purring.

After a time, Catherine asked Kirsty whether she thought she would be able to weather the unpleasantness.

Kirsty looked blank, then began to weep. But this time she cried softly, and as she did so, tried to explain what it was like, going into the north wing at night, preparing to camp down in the corridor. You got to dread it, she said. You got to feel that everyone was secretly watching. Rose would settle down outside her old room, and Kirsty would do likewise outside hers. Sometimes, Sister Christa or Sister Gabrielle would come and keep them company for a while, which made them feel less awkward. But it was still horrible to be doing it, you still felt like an intruder. However much you told yourself this was *your* room, *your* corridor by rights, you still felt you'd marched into someone else's place and just plonked down. It made you go hot and cold, feeling that.

Catherine remarked that it must do, and Kirsty found a handkerchief and blew her nose. Then, no longer weeping, Kirsty explained that it was even more complicated. Because after a while in the corridor, she'd start thinking of Beth, Beth who had given in and gone to share a room in the annexe. And it would come to her that she didn't want to finish up like Beth, going about with her head hanging down, too humble to speak to people. Kirsty would rather be like Rose, who was strong and stubborn and proud. Besides, Kirsty would hate to let Rose down. It had been frightening to be singled out in public by Sister Margaret. And it wasn't very nice when senior sisters like Sister Agnes and Sister Imogen came up and said things. And that name the *Bulletin* called her had come as a shock. But still: it wasn't as if it was just her on her own. As well as Rose, Sister Christa and Sister Gabrielle were backing her up. 'And you, too, Sister Catherine,' she added shyly.

'I think you're very brave,' Catherine said. She stroked the cat and thought over what had been said. It worried her to learn that Sister Kirsty was banking on her. 'You know, Sister, I suspect it's going to be a long, long time before the situation changes,' she warned. 'I'm not trying to dissuade you; if sticking it out with Sister Rose feels right, then for goodness' sake carry on. I know you'll be well supported. Sister Christa and Sister Gabrielle are strong-minded women.' She made a small self-deprecating sound before saying, 'I suppose they're the hope for the future.'

'Oh, but Sister Catherine. *You*'re the hope. You can change things. You're as high up as Sister Margaret.'

'Look, I'm going to be honest; it may help you decide what you want to do. You see, I doubt very much whether I can make a difference to what happens here. I'm no match for Sister Margaret. I never have been. In a way, I'm a part of what was wrong with this place and what allowed Sister Margaret to gain her toehold. I shall go on trying, but really I'm just—' She noticed her young companion's horrified expression, and laughed

214

ruefully. 'I'm just banging my head against a wall. Sister Christa's a leader for the next generation.' She laughed again, remembering how ill at ease she'd been at first with Christa, disturbed by her directness and her forthright manner; and that now she'd come to respect her. 'The thing about Sister Christa,' she explained, 'is her ability to distance herself from bruising confrontations. That's a very useful quality when you need to fight battles. I'm afraid I'm not made of the same stuff.'

Kirsty looked away, feeling embarrassed. She wanted to protest that Sister Catherine was wrongly running herself down; but she couldn't, because she'd suddenly seen that what Sister Catherine had said about herself, and also about Sister Christa, was true. All the same, her heart went out to the tired-looking woman smiling at the cat she was nursing. She longed to save her from further hurt. 'I wouldn't go reading things on the notice board, if I were you, Sister,' she hinted anxiously. 'I wouldn't bother. Stuff like that: well, it's better ignored.'

Guessing what lay behind this piece of advice, Catherine laughed and lifted down the cat. 'Come on,' she said, getting up and brushing herself down. 'You've cheered me no end. You've given me my appetite back. Let's go and see if there's anything left to eat.'

25

It's a pity I'm so fond of these, thought Anne, helping herself regretfully to a second cream puff.

When she had eaten it she detected no feeling of repletion or content. You see, she reasoned, hoping the lesson would be remembered for future occasions, a second one is no use; you could go on and on. Think how much happier you'd feel if you knew it was in you to resist temptation.

The knowledge that it was not in her made her gloomy, and she began to dwell on the vote taken at yesterday's meeting: another occasion when she had succumbed to the temptations of the flesh. Full of cream and sugar and self-disgust, she shifted in her chair and said belligerently to her neighbours: 'We voted out of sheer selfishness yesterday, you know. Selfishness and greed. It wouldn't hurt us to forgo this sitting room and all these disgusting cakes to help the annexe sisters and the lay sisters.'

There followed the kind of silence born of a social lapse. There was then a rush to dispel it.

'Oh, *Anne*,' said Elizabeth, conveying distaste and disappointment.

'What does the gel say?' Cecilia demanded of Monica, having concluded that her ears had misled her.

Monica was saved from replying by an outburst from Sister Martha, though in any case Monica could not have borne to repeat Anne's words for they rang alarm bells in her own conscience.

'Stuff and nonsense. Sorry, but I've never heard such a load of rubbish. Sister Margaret's doing a right good job, and as far as I'm concerned what she says goes. I'd back her to the hilt. Don't get me wrong, I'm sorry as the next person for the annexe sisters; in fact, I've done me darnedest for that Sister Kirsty, and I don't mind saying I felt proper let down when I heard about the stunt she's been pulling.'

'Poppycock,' declared Anne loudly, jamming a cushion into the small of her back. These low soft chairs played havoc with the digestion. 'You can say comforting words to yourself all you like, but you can't deny self-interest didn't come into it.'

Sister Faith drew herself up. 'I don't think this arguing back and forth is very pleasant.'

'It's not,' agreed Martha. 'But Sister Anne's talking through her hat.'

'Shall we change the subject?' asked Sister Joy. She turned pointedly to Sister Elizabeth (who was mortified that her friend should earn a reproof from such as Sister Joy or Sister Faith). 'Have you heard about the visitors expected today, two sisters from overseas?'

'I hadn't heard, no. How interesting. Do tell us about them, Sister.' And Elizabeth set an example by sitting up straight and raising her teacup daintily.

They were grateful for the diversion, and most of them assumed expressions of interest. Sister Joy endeavoured to pack her tale with fascinating detail. Sister Martha chewed a doughnut. Anne looked cross, a martyr to her ruined digestion.

Beatrice stopped staring out of the window, breathed on it, and with her finger drew a grid in the condensation. She traced noughts and crosses with the aimlessness of a boy kicking a can through the gutter, and with a similar purpose, the relief of tedium. For she was seriously and dangerously bored.

Life had gone flat. The fun of grooming Margaret for power was over. It was possible she had done the grooming too well, for Margaret behaved like an autocrat with no sense of gratitude; indeed, that she had ever been groomed at all seemed to escape Margaret's memory. Looking back, it seemed astonishing that people had expressed no surprise at the miraculous and instantaneous metamorphosis of Margaret, from bright but deferential nun into masterful creature with a ready-made plan to save the priory's fortunes. But people were like sheep: so accepting. Yet if it had not been for Beatrice's spotting the genius of the plan (originally Joan's, but argued for more cogently by Margaret) and painstakingly turning its proponent into a powermonger, where, she would like to know, would the priory be today? And where would Margaret be without Beatrice's secret work on her behalf: stage-managing the briefing meetings, planning how to trick and get the better of Catherine?

Particularly Beatrice missed the feeling of life being transacted beneath the surface, the glorious business of fooling people. Unlike Margaret who liked openly to wield power, Beatrice enjoyed power's secret side. It was as the hidden agent that she excelled, influencing events and determining outcomes. Secret power was the greatest thrill. She loved its paraphernalia, the late-night plotting, the deadly rivalries. She loved its never-to-be-spoken-of knowledge, and she loved smiling into people's eyes and thinking, Little do you know, but I've cooked your goose. She loved it when her pulse raced and her nerves sang, and loved having to mask these delightful sensations with a calm expression and steady hands. And I'm so darn good at it, thought Beatrice, impatient with the wasting of her talents, for Margaret in her new-found arrogance appeared to have no need for undercover work. Or could it be that someone else was now providing that service. Sister Verity, perhaps?

Frowning, she wandered down the corridor, a corridor on the first floor of the south wing. When she came to the wide landing, she paused. A rasping noise was coming from the bottom of the stairwell. Beatrice peered over the banister, and saw Hope below, making a drawing with charcoal.

Hope was sketching the old courtyard, a favourite scene with the visitors, especially as viewed through the ornately carved window against which she sat. A board with paper attached was propped on her knee. She stared out of the window, looked down and drew rapidly, looked up and stared again. For some moments Beatrice observed her. Then a smile crept over her face, and she raced back silently to the window she had breathed on and where she remembered having seen a large dead bluebottle on the window sill. She collected the fly and returned to the top of the stairs, leaned over the banister and extended her hand over the area of Hope's drawing board. The effect of relinquishing the fly and its soft ping upon the paper was predictable: a scream, a scattering of board and charcoal, a tumbling chair, a vanishing Hope.

Now Hope would be in a quandary, Beatrice guessed. She could not abandon her work, nor could she summon assistance for so nebulous a cause. Chuckling to herself, she pictured Hope in some corner below, trying to squeeze up courage. Sure enough, when Hope crept into view, her head, jerking like a chicken's, described her fear with every timid step. Beatrice was about to cast around for a second missile when she was distracted by a noise outside: the throbbing and whirring of giant wings. She gazed in anticipation through the window. Below her, Hope also gazed.

Dust blew up in the courtyard. A helicopter

descended and neatly came to rest. Then Margaret stepped up. She waited patiently to greet her visitors.

Beatrice recalled that Margaret had mentioned these visitors to her. 'I want you to help me entertain two nuns who are coming from overseas. You can be very charming when you put your mind to it, Beatrice. I want us to make a good impression because their organization is interested in putting money into the priory.'

'Good Lord, Margaret. You're not planning to sell us off?'

'Don't be ridiculous. Possibly they will invest in us, that's all. But I'm talking about a considerable sum.'

'Gosh, you *are* planning to sell the priory.'

'Just do your stuff this afternoon. Understood? You can leave matters of finance to me.'

Beatrice had gloomily anticipated a couple of worthy *religieuses*, fat, squat, bespectacled, even – such was her luck these days – moustached and bearded. But now— Oh my God take it back! Could these be they; these slender wonders clad in gold-coloured tunics and *trousers*? And with hair, unless she was very much mistaken. Yes, there was definitely hair showing under their veils, which were little more than gold-coloured headscarves. One sported shiny black curls against her nut-brown cheeks and fore-head, and from under the head-covering of the other jutted an auburn frizz.

She waited no longer. Raced down the stairs (nearly causing Hope to suffer a heart attack), along the corridor to the door, paused for breath, then swung out onto the gravel path.

'Ah, this is Sister Beatrice, Sisters. She is a valued colleague of mine. And Beatrice dear, here are Sister Diane and Sister Betty-Lou, come to visit us from the Convent of Eternal Enterprise in California.'

'Delighted,' smiled Beatrice. 'Charmed.'

Sister Betty-Lou extended her hand. 'Hi, Beatrice. Good to meet you.'

'It surely is,' confirmed Sister Diane.

It was late. Elizabeth and Anne were in the needlework room stretching a newly completed tapestry to save time in the morning. Monica and Cecilia had looked in to keep them company.

'What did you think of their get-up?' Cecilia asked. It went without saying that the get-up she referred to belonged to the Californians.

'Nasty cheap clorth,' Elizabeth said. 'Synthetic sort of stuff. Pull harder,' she exhorted Anne.

'I thought it a becoming style of dress,' Cecilia said in a faraway voice, 'at least, it was on them. They have the figures to carry it off. A get-up like that would go rather well on Sister Beatrice. It would have suited Catherine once, before she lost her looks.'

'Oh, not Catherine,' Monica protested. 'No, it would never have suited Catherine, not at all. Catherine has always been – otherworldly.' Her voice had gone choky.

'We have to move with the times.' This was a startling announcement from the mouth of Cecilia who was a great decrier of modern manners. Even Anne, kneeling over the damp canvas with her bottom in the air, twisted up her head to look at her. 'Progress,' Cecilia explained, waving an arm. 'Oh, yes. One of the guests at tea the other day, an *entrepreneur*' (she pronounced the word firmly in French) 'helped me to understand the importance of progress. A most en-lightening conversation.'

Anne snorted.

Elizabeth said: 'Well, I thought it wholly unsuitable attire. And I must say, that's a bit rich coming from you, Cecilia.'

'Stop talking and hurry up. My knees are going to sleep.'

'You know, Anne,' called Monica unsteadily, 'I've been thinking. There was something in what you said this afternoon, about us voting selfishly.'

Elizabeth groaned. 'Not that again, please.'

Cecilia looked closely at Monica and wondered about her. Senility did run in that family, she mused. Monica's Aunt Tilly had been spectacularly demented.

'But I think there may have been *some*thing in what Anne said—'

But Anne silenced Monica with a grumble to Elizabeth. 'My goodness, I wish you'd get a move on. The blood's gone to my head.' Though really it was not blood to the head that made her long to stand upright, but bile to the throat. Those horrible cakes, she was thinking. Never, never again.

26

'Mad' was a word sometimes heard, also 'deranged' and 'eccentric'. Catherine had overheard Christa reporting the use of 'mad' to Gabrielle, and Gabrielle agreeing that she'd heard it too. Once, when Catherine was walking behind some sisters who were on their way to the Green Sitting Room, she'd heard one say to another there was a rumour going round that Sister Catherine was deranged, and another reply that Sister Catherine was certainly eccentric. Cecilia had accused Catherine to her face of appearing to be eccentric. And only yesterday, entering a room and finding it charged with the pull of a slanderous conversation, Catherine had caught the word 'crazed', swiftly followed, of course, by silence. She'd almost chuckled at their embarrassment, but had foreseen in the nick of time that a chuckle would confirm her reputation.

Since the *Bulletin* continued to express concern for her state of mind, she concluded that this encouraged the speculation. Perhaps I *am* mad, she found herself wondering late one evening when her morale was low. It was probably insane of her to keep hammering out her arguments when scarcely a body listened. But neither the gossip nor the futility deterred her. When she felt impelled to speak out about something, she did so. As for example over the treatment of Sister Hope.

Christa had discovered it was the practice of some nuns to hiss when encountering Hope. She was following two sisters across the sloping lawn by the sycamores when, Christa said, they suddenly gave out like snakes. Christa couldn't think what was going on until she saw Hope at her easel starting up at the sound, then blushing and looking away. Christa had tackled Hope about it, she'd asked if it had happened before. But Hope wouldn't talk; had only shrugged and continued with her drawing.

Catherine had exclaimed over the unfairness of this treatment, particularly in view of the forgiveness shown to Sister Beatrice.

'What do you expect?' Christa had cried. 'According to the official line, Hope is the villain, *she* entrapped Beatrice. Though I must say it stretches the imagination when you come to think about it.'

Deciding that hissing wasn't to be tolerated in any case, Catherine had gone at once to Margaret's office. There, she reported her suspicion that Hope was being picked on, evidently because she'd been unjustly apportioned the greater share of blame. And Catherine had asked Margaret to appoint two or three impartial senior sisters to look into the matter.

Margaret's reaction had been instantaneous. 'Utterly disgraceful,' she'd cried.

'The hissing? I quite agree. But if someone looks into it—'

'*Your suggestion* is disgraceful. It's lucky for that girl she's still here. I find your remarks offensive and insulting. You had better go.'

So Sister Hope was added to the list of people Catherine held in her mind whose position she had tried to improve and failed. The first of these was Sister Mary John. Her heart ached whenever she remembered Sister Mary John. But it was no use brooding. Obviously she was unable to change things for the better, but at least she could comfort the casualties.

*   *   *

'What now?' Catherine asked, peeling off her rubber gloves.

She felt most useful in the hospital. The work was not especially congenial to her. The fact was she was squeamish. But she had learned to hide it, and the knowledge of her usefulness more than repaid the effort.

'Oh, you've done the sluicing. How kind,' Sister Luke exclaimed. 'Well, you could give Sister Lazarus some attention. You're so good with them, Sister.'

'Them' referred to the officially disturbed: Sister Lazarus and Sister Grace. It was possible she was good with them due to a natural affinity, thought Catherine, grinning to herself. But her face quickly straightened as she approached Lazarus's door. The disturbed were not all the same. Sister Grace was a sweet vague woman, Sister Lazarus was not. On good days Lazarus was lucid or withdrawn, on difficult days she was excitable or seething with incoherent rage. Catherine wondered if she had retained a lingering apprehension of Sister Lazarus. Sometimes, when Lazarus was excited, a nerve jumped in Catherine's scarred cheek.

'She might be persuaded to go outside,' Sister Luke called, and added: 'You'd need help, though. I can spare Sister Megan for half an hour later on. But at all costs keep her away from the garden.'

Of course. The garden, as a place and a topic of conversation, was treacherous ground for Sister Lazarus.

Catherine knocked on the door and immediately opened it. Lazarus narrowed her eyes as one of Martha's spies came in. 'How are you today, Sister?' Catherine asked.

I'll show her how I am, thought Lazarus, and shot out her hands. 'See?' she cried. 'Steady as a rock.' Catherine stared at the hands that convulsively jumped and twitched. Steady as a rock, she agreed solemnly.

That's given her something to think about, said Lazarus to herself.

Catherine racked her brain for news. Oh yes, the trouble getting this year's palm crosses, and Sister Winifred finding a bird stuck in the library chimney. As she talked, she went over to a table on which books, skeins of wool, a handkerchief, orange peel and other items were jumbled together, and began methodically to sort them.

Lazarus looked on. Soon as the woman had come in she'd known Martha had sent her. She wouldn't find it though, Lazarus comforted herself, let her turn the room upside down. Of this Lazarus was perfectly confident, not having been able to find it herself. Though what precisely 'it' was, Lazarus could not have put into words. Long ago she had forgotten its exact nature; she simply knew it was a highly desirable thing of her own, something she'd once set great store by. It had slipped from her grasp, very likely, due to the unreliability of her fingers. But at least Lazarus could rest easy that, so far, Martha hadn't managed to get her greedy hands on it: otherwise she wouldn't keep coming back to search.

Visits from Martha gave Lazarus a desperate time. Martha would sink into an easy chair and thrust out her legs and let her hands hang over the chair arms. 'How goes it, Laz?' she would ask. And Lazarus, tensely perched on the edge of her seat, would carefully say nothing. Martha never noticed, straight away she would launch into one of her word-spewings. 'I'm feeling peckish, Laz,' she might interrupt herself to say after a time. 'What yer got?' And Lazarus would hold her breath as Martha sauntered to the table and poked through her belongings, then opened a drawer or the bedside cupboard door and peered in there. 'Ah, them apples look nice. Ribston pippin, ain't they? You want one, Laz?' But Martha would keep her back turned to

Lazarus, grab up her skirt and give the apple a rub. Then it would be munch-munch through her words and all the time one of her fat hands would be turning over Lazarus's property. She never found it, though.

As well as coming herself, Martha sent her spies. They had no luck either. This one couldn't even find the Nice biscuits. 'They're in the cupboard,' Lazarus said slyly.

Surprised, Catherine lost the thread of her chatter. In any case, it had been talk for talk's sake, talk to cover a malevolent silence. She opened the cupboard door. 'These? You'd like a biscuit?'

'Not I,' declared Lazarus. Oh no, she was not going to be caught like that.

'The packet's been opened, I see.'

'It has,' said Lazarus, nodding grimly. And we know who opened it, she thought.

'I'll try to find a tin for them, later. Otherwise they'll go soft. Sure you won't have one?'

What's her game? wondered Lazarus. '*You* have one,' she retorted.

'No thanks. I've given up sweet things for Lent,' Catherine said lightly. She replaced the biscuits in the cupboard and came slowly back to Lazarus, telling herself to stop chattering inanely, to stop shying away from silence between them. If she gave Lazarus a chance, perhaps she would talk. She sat down and let her eyes slide casually over the floor, the wall.

Lazarus said nothing. Not a word.

After a time, Catherine said, 'I see you've started weaving. Sister Luke showed me your frame.' Someone had kindly made a simple loom for Lazarus in the hope that her fingers might manage to control a shuttle where they failed with needles and knitting pins. 'It'll be nice spending time in the work room with the other sisters, Grace and Ellen. It'll be company.'

Lazarus scowled.

'Doesn't it appeal to you?' asked Catherine softly, and leaned forward and daringly took one of Lazarus's hands.

After a time, Lazarus reached out with her free hand and shakily explored the scarred cheek.

Catherine held herself still.

'There's something on your face.'

'I know. It's nothing.'

A wave of incontinent feeling shook Lazarus. She remembered being shut in a dim place, earthy-smelling, with dirt flying about, and lots of noise, and metal flashing, and a terrible feeling inside her. She remembered breaking out of the dim place and rushing into the daylight. She remembered there were people, and running towards these people. She remembered yelling at them and raising her arm—

Catherine swallowed and instructed herself to keep as still as possible, given that her right hand, still in Lazarus's grip, was being shaken more and more violently, and consequently her right arm and shoulder.

'And then,' cried Lazarus out loud, 'then I, then—'

A sharp smell came in the room, like vinegar. Then the door opened and Sister Megan put her head round.

'Are we ready for our walk?'

Catherine let out her breath and recovered her hand. 'Shall we go out? Get some fresh air?'

'We daren't,' said Lazarus, suddenly tumbling to the fact that this wasn't one of Martha's spies after all, but Sister Catherine. Sister Catherine had a mark on her face, which was fortunate, because it made her easy to pick out. In future, when Lazarus saw the mark, she'd know she could relax. Martha wasn't stupid, she'd know it was no use asking Sister Catherine to do her dirty work. Lazarus leaned closer to Sister Catherine and whispered, in order to prevent the Welsh nurse who might not be equally trustworthy from overhearing: 'We daren't go out. They might come in while we're gone and find it.'

'I see,' said Catherine, nodding sagely. 'Well, I know what we'll do. We'll ask Sister Luke to let us have the key to this room, then we can lock the door behind us.'

'A key?'

'Yes. Then everything will be safe while we're gone. Will that do?'

Lazarus nodded, and Catherine went to the door to say quietly to Sister Megan that Sister Lazarus had wet herself.

While Sister Megan dealt with that problem, Catherine went in search of Sister Luke.

'Key? Oh dear, let me think,' said Sister Luke.

'If you can find one, it would be useful. I think it would persuade Sister Lazarus to leave her room more often.'

'Just a minute.' Sister Luke rummaged through a drawer of her desk. 'It'll be one of these, I should think. Go and try them. I'm glad you've solved the mystery of why Sister Lazarus hates to leave her room.'

Ten minutes later, Catherine, Lazarus and Megan set off arm in arm along the corridor. Carefully, they descended the chapter house stairs. At the bottom Lazarus freed her arm from the chatting Megan's and felt in her skirt pocket, finding the key safely inside. Such peace of mind, she exclaimed to herself thankfully.

At their approach, a group of nuns in the cloister fell silent. When they had gone by, the nuns stared after them, watching the gaunt wild ones and the gabby Welsh nurse go slowly by the arches, passing alternately through shadow and pale watery shine.

27

'You asked to see me, Reverend Mother?'

'Yes, Sister Catherine. Come in.'

The room was full of April sunshine. The Prioress was sitting by the window. Her hands held a square of canvas, a needle, and a length of pink embroidery silk. 'I've got some work on the go.'

Whenever the Prioress or Cecilia and her friends spoke in an intimate tone of work on the go, they referred, Catherine knew, to a piece of embroidery, such work being the only kind a lady permitted herself; unless it was gardening, of course, though somehow gardening, being an outdoor pursuit, was not work but recreation. 'That's good,' said Catherine politely.

'Yes, I think it's coming along.' She held it out at arm's length. It was a conventional flower spray, worked in *petit point*, which was the Prioress's favourite stitch because it covered the ground speedily. 'I'm trying to stir myself. This last winter rather got on top of me. Nothing like work for clearing away the cobwebs. Mmm, and, er, I've come to a decision.'

'Oh.'

'Yes. Sit down. No, not so far away. Bring up a chair. I'll just finish this row, if you don't mind. Tch, blow! That's got it. Mmm.'

The succession, thought Catherine. Ah well, she'd been expecting it.

'There.' The Prioress took a pair of scissors from a stool by her side, snipped the thread and jammed her needle into the back of the canvas. 'Of course, this will only make up into a cushion. I was much more ambitious in my youth. I worked that fire screen, you know.'

Catherine did know, but turned her head towards the screen.

'That was done when Jacobean embroidery was all the rage.'

Finding nothing more to say about it, the Prioress frowned, and thought how very peaky – no, worse than that, *overwrought* – Catherine was looking. Her appearance did not inspire confidence. No wonder every senior sister summoned to her room had without exception plumped for Margaret. Even Catherine's former supporters – Cecilia, Monica, Elizabeth, Anne, the Sister Precentor and Sister Angelica – had regretfully concluded that Margaret and not Catherine should replace Sister Mercy as sole directrix and prioress-in-waiting. Naturally, Anne and Monica had fallen over themselves to qualify their opinion. 'I think Catherine isn't well,' Monica had said, twisting her hands. And Anne had sarcastically declared that Catherine had always been up against it, trying to persuade people to act unselfishly. Monica and Anne had annoyed the Prioress with their comments, for she had clearly ruled out any discussion. 'Just give me a straight answer,' she'd told them. 'Sister Margaret or Sister Catherine?'

The decision, once arrived at, had released in her a surge of energy. She had started some work, and it must have been nine or ten years since she last took up a needle. She had renewed her interest in the chapel proceedings and found that she had to hand it to Margaret; there'd certainly been a pulling up of socks: no milling round the door after service, no ill-disguised yawning, no dashings in at the last minute, but everything calm, orderly and dignified.

231

She'd told no-one of her decision. Keeping it to herself gave her a pleasant feeling of being back in control. It occurred to her that there was no need to squander this feeling by making her decision known too soon. She could hug it to herself for a while and think carefully of the consequences and make sure of the right terms. And after all there was honour in this: hers to dispose and withhold, but also hers to deal justly, hers to ensure that the path be made smooth for the loser: and that everything was settled as she wished it to be for herself, of course.

There was no doubt that Margaret had forced the issue. Margaret knew perfectly well that the Prioress viewed her role in the coming feet-washing ceremony with distaste and dread. What a *shame* about the Prioress's sciatica, had said Margaret with her head sympathetically on one side, for sadly there was to be much leaning forward and bending down. Never mind. Next year, when the question of the succession would undoubtedly have been resolved, the prioress-in-waiting could relieve the Reverend Mother of the chore. Unfortunately, it seemed that this year she must make the best of it, for spiritual leadership was indispensable to the role of feet-washer. Margaret had gone on to describe the enviable conditions in which a semi-retired prioress would find herself: oceans of uninterrupted time for contemplation, for reading and for prayer. The important things, Margaret had added wistfully.

Message understood, m'dear, the Prioress had silently and grimly conveyed.

'Do think it over,' Margaret had murmured.

The Prioress had thoroughly thought it over. She had consulted widely, but the end result was always inescapable. There was heartache in recalling Catherine as she used to be and the hopes she had had for her. She shan't be made to suffer, the Prioress resolved. I won't have her belittled. Over her sewing she'd considered the matter, and as roses spread salmon pink across the canvas it had become clear to her that she must make a sacrifice.

'I think we'll have a nice cup of tea.'

Wearily, Catherine rose and went into the little pantry where there was a sink and a kettle. When the tea was made she left it to brew and returned to the sitting room to set out a tray. Then, sensing that nothing would be said until they were fortified by a sip or two of strong Earl Grey, she sauntered to the fireplace, above which was a portrait of the Prioress's predecessor. Hooded eyes stared down into Catherine's; the great lady appeared to sneer. After a moment, worried lest her scrutiny be misconstrued as the entertaining of false hope, Catherine hurried back to the teapot.

'Here we are.' She held the tray while the Prioress helped herself to milk and sugar. 'Now,' she said firmly, 'I think you have something to tell me.'

The Prioress puffed away the steam and drew carefully from her cup; then, jerking back her head, said gruffly: 'I've decided to appoint Sister Margaret as sole directrix – and my successor, of course.'

'Yes,' said Catherine, and sighed.

'However, I'll see you're not embarrassed. I'll keep the decision to myself for a month; that'll give you time to decide on a position you'd find congenial. Come and tell me when you've fixed on something, and I shall make it a condition of my naming Sister Margaret.'

'But Reverend Mother, there's no need for that. If I'm allowed to, I'll work in the hospital. If not, I'll join the annexe sisters and go where I'm bid day by day.'

The word 'annexe' made the Prioress jump. She slopped her tea. Catherine ran for a cloth, and blotted skirt and carpet.

'You'll do no such thing,' spluttered the Prioress. 'I

won't have it. Think how it would look. Think how it would have upset poor Mercy.' Her teacup rattled on its saucer. Tactfully, Catherine relieved her of it and put it down on the stool.

'I didn't mean to upset you.'

'Well, you succeeded. I have steeled myself to make a very big sacrifice for your sake, Catherine. If I were to name Margaret at once, I shouldn't have to go through with this feet-washing malarkey. Sister Margaret would do it herself. She good as told me so, providing I name her as my successor at once.'

'Then, Reverend Mother, please do so and save yourself the trouble.'

The Prioress was indignant. She had not braced herself for martyrdom to have it thrown in her face. 'You want to be a living reproach to us: is that it?'

'Certainly not.'

'Well it sounds suspiciously like it. Sounds like sour grapes to me.'

'All right, Reverend Mother, I'll do as you ask. I'll talk to Sister Luke—'

'Talk also to the Sister Precentor and to Sister Angelica. I'm sure they'll be delighted if you choose to work with them.'

'They'd be embarrassed. I'm sorry, Reverend Mother, but it's true. Entirely my fault, but there it is. You know, there's so much ill-health at the moment, it would be a blessing for Sister Luke if she could gain another pair of hands.'

'Mm, I suppose the hospital would do – if we can think of a suitable title. How about "Sister Almoner"? "Almoner" has a substantial ring. But think it over. The chapel was always your natural place. Come back in four weeks and tell me what you've decided.'

'I will. And thank you for your kindness, Reverend Mother. I'm sorry about the ceremony. I wish—'

'We won't talk about it. Drink your tea.' She took her

own cup from the stool and tasted the contents. 'Bah! Stone cold. Let's have some fresh.'

Catherine collected the cups, and the Prioress took up her sewing.

'I wonder,' she mused. 'Elizabeth said I should work the background in beige, but I'm rather inclined to blue. Always a cautious soul, Elizabeth. Blue might lift it, don't you think? Shall I be adventurous? Yes, I've made up my mind. A nice bright cornflower blue.'

28

There was a spring in Margaret's step. Bounce, bounce, she went through the cloister, smiling and inclining her head. Nuns thus acknowledged felt especially favoured, for Margaret's customary style was to bustle as though time were of the essence and to set her face in an expression designed to discourage anyone wishing to waylay her. When Sister Imogen met Margaret's sunny countenance, she caught her breath. And further wonders followed when Margaret, having passed Imogen by, suddenly turned and called after her. 'Oh, Imogen, just a moment, there's something I've been meaning to say.'

Imogen hurried to her side.

'I was so pleased to hear those tiresome annexe sisters have given up their silly protest at last. Your doing, I'm sure.'

Margaret referred to Sisters Rose and Kirsty who, having become worn out with lack of sleep, had taken to their beds in the annexe: actually, to recover their strength and plan further protests, though this was not known to Imogen and Margaret.

'You know, Imogen, it's high time you came back to help us on the Forward Planning Committee.' She spoke as if Imogen had been taking an unreasonably long vacation.

Imogen's heart began to race. 'Yes, yes,' she stammered.

'Good. Well done. We'll expect to see you at two

o'clock today. We need all the best brains: something big in the air.'

Imogen couldn't speak. Her heart was swelling to such a size that it jutted into her larynx. As Margaret bounced away, she folded her arms and brought them tightly in against her ribs.

A minute later, Clare came across her still rooted to the spot in the cloister. 'You all right, Sister?' she asked curiously, for Imogen was very red and had her arms pulled in to her waist. 'Got the jip or something?'

Imogen shook her head and looked secretive. Poor old Clare, she was thinking, still out in the cold. Whereas I, I— She lurched forward and discovered her legs had gone wobbly. She needed to rest. She needed to sit somewhere quiet and let what had happened sink in.

On her rosewood throne in the cloakroom, she began to breathe calmly. She felt her happiness, like a warm dog, turn and turn and settle down inside her. Water chuntered in the pipes and the sun peeped in. Oh blissful day, thought Imogen, that had restored her at last to the Forward Planning Committee.

So Margaret needs to muster support, concluded Beatrice, seeing Imogen at the table. She wondered what large scheme was now afoot.

Margaret bustled in and opened the proceedings. 'Things are moving,' she announced, and darted a look at Verity (a look registered jealously by Beatrice and Joan, and wryly by Agnes). 'It has come to my ears that the Reverend Mother has been taking soundings. However—' She paused and looked thoughtful. 'It seems she will go ahead with the feet-washing ceremony this evening as planned. But never mind that. I've received a letter from our Californian friends. They were very,

very impressed with our set-up here. For some time they've been looking for a chance to expand, and are now convinced they've found the right opening. They propose to build the new branch of their convent right here in the grounds of the Albion Priory. The point is, Sisters, where to put it? Any ideas?'

'I should have thought,' Verity put in promptly, her face empty of expression, 'the old vegetable fields would fit the bill.'

'Splendid, Verity. All that land lying idle. How satisfying to find a use for it at last.'

'I presume we gain some advantage from this?' Agnes enquired.

'Very considerable advantage,' said Margaret.

But Joan was uneasy. 'Hang on. If we're not careful we'll compromise our own interests. We can't afford to jeopardize our autonomy.'

'Can't afford to turn up our noses at darn good offers of new cash. They don't grow on trees,' growled Verity.

'But Agnes,' cried Joan, turning in appeal to her neighbour at the table. 'What about Clare's new plan?'

'Clare?' Margaret cried with annoyance.

'Yes, she's been working on a new project. It sounds very promising, doesn't it, Agnes?'

'I hardly think it would measure up to *this*,' Margaret retorted, jabbing her pencil into a sheaf of correspondence.

'But Clare's new project wouldn't be risky. After all, you're talking about foreigners actually occupying Albion territory; it could lead to all sorts of trouble. I think we should hold back.'

'Perhaps we should consider each option on its merits,' put in Agnes judiciously, 'weigh up the pros and cons.'

'Bet Clare's is worth peanuts,' scoffed Verity. 'Whereas this—'

'Is worth millions,' cried Margaret. 'If we let that land go too cheaply, someone else will reap the benefits. Mark my words: whatever the controls and restraints, that land will find its price. You can't buck the market, Joan.'

Joan groaned and put her head in her hands. Margaret ignored her. 'Can we be agreed at least to look at their proposal further? One of us will have to fly over there. I suggest you go, Beatrice. That reminds me: Sister Betty-Lou sends you her regards and says she hopes to return your kindness in California.'

Beatrice's smile had never been broader. 'Oh yes, Margaret, certainly. Definitely you can depend on me.' What a turn-up! she cried to herself, and beamed her happiness in an encouraging way round the entire table. 'Surely no-one's going to object to exploring this brilliant idea?'

'Much too attractive a chance to miss,' Imogen declared.

'Good, good. I knew you'd agree.' Smiling with particular warmth at Imogen and Beatrice, Margaret gathered up her papers and rose. 'Then we'll put things in hand. Come along, Verity: such a lot to do.'

The ornaments of the chapel – altar crosses, statues and portraits of the saints – were draped in the mourning cloth of Passiontide. A feeling of suffocation attacked Catherine. Trying to stave off panic, she reasoned that it was caused by all the black stuff about.

Before a congregation of nuns and visitors, Margaret was explaining the symbolism of the ceremony about to take place. She had a special voice and manner for religion, and she achieved it by making her mouth small, her face still, her eyebrows high and her glance directed downwards. Catching herself with these critical observations, Catherine heard in her head the Prioress's comment: 'Sounds like sour grapes to me.'

At that moment the Prioress was making a more pertinent comment in her own head, for soon the Sister Precentor would lead her to the throne-like chair placed in readiness at the top of the chancel steps. Cecilia was thinking that if the Reverend Mother upset the water, she'd die; she wouldn't dare look for fear of catastrophe. At her side, Monica was wishing that the Reverend Mother would look less cross. Fiddlesticks, Anne was telling herself, listening to Margaret's explanation. But Elizabeth was touched by it, and her eyes misted with tears. Beatrice was imagining herself beneath a Californian sun, clad all in gold, her flaxen tresses hanging a good six inches beneath a jaunty veil. In her pew halfway down the nave, Sister Veronica was thinking to herself that Margaret was a marvel: not only did she possess the brain and willpower to put the priory back on its feet, she had the spiritual imagination to create this ceremony. From her seat further back, Martha was able covertly to observe the visitors' reactions. They were paying rapt attention, seeming to be awestruck and moved. Martha felt her heart swell with pride, and this took her mind off a matter that had been bothering her earlier: the insubstantial nature of tea, due to the kitchen staff's being busy with preparations for the supper which was to follow the ceremony. At the front of the nave, Imogen with an unimpeded view of the water bowl was congratulating herself for having gone before she came out. She hoped someone had had the sense to take the chill off the water, otherwise heaven only knew what the effect would be on that poor girl. I shall catch my death, worried the postulant Sister Fay as she waited barefoot below the chancel steps.

It was time. The Prioress struggled up. For pity's

sake, may it be got over with quickly and safely, she prayed.

Catherine closed her eyes. To witness the Prioress in her present role would be to see personified her own great failure. For the thing that was about to happen was false; the Prioress knew it was false and was an unwilling participant; she was going through with it for Catherine's sake, to buy Catherine time. In every way she had failed, Catherine said to herself. All her battles were lost. Inside her, a great weight of hopelessness grew; grew and grew, ever heavier, ever more dense. Struggling to keep in touch with the faint part of her that was still sensible, she clung to the sound of the organ, willing herself to concentrate. Angelica had chosen well, she noted: a melody rippled evenly over a sustained anchorage with no modulation or massing of chords; all was light and airy and innocent, like angels dancing, thought Catherine, trying to picture it. But then a bass note, the foundation of the music's harmony, crept up one tone and plunged the notes above into dissonance; note pressed against note, squeezing, resisting, yielding—

Catherine, with sweat pouring off her, lurched to her feet and went crashing into the aisle.

Nothing is what it seems, she thought, leaning on Beatrice, who, with presence of mind, had caught her and led her from the chapel and was now supporting her to her room. Scratch an angel and it will wink and leer. Put up an image and people will cheer while the substance lies dead on the ground.

Beatrice took in that Catherine's lips were moving, also her eyes were going round and her skin burned to the touch. Concluding that she was probably delirious, she pushed Catherine onto her bed and went to fetch some water.

241

'Drink,' Beatrice commanded on her return. 'Come on. You're feverish.' She helped Catherine to drink, then laid her down. Catherine stared up at her without the least idea of who Beatrice was or even who she might be herself, Beatrice surmised, judging from the look of her.

As she returned the hollow-eyed gaze, an emotion stole over Beatrice that she experienced very rarely. She felt pity all of a sudden. 'Poor old stick,' she murmured. 'I suppose what it is, you've realized it's all over. Well, I'll say this for you, you didn't lose for want of trying.' She recalled Catherine's relentless objections and challenges, and the way, when beaten, she would still come back for more. But the cost was plain. If ever there was a case of being burnt out, Catherine was it. 'You're totally wrecked, aren't you?' she said sympathetically. 'Which is a shame because' – she sat carefully down on the edge of the bed alongside Catherine's legs – 'if you want to know the truth, there was never a cat in hell's chance you'd win. You were up against a champion. So don't brood, eh? Give yourself a break.'

Wonderment came into Catherine's eyes.

'You do know what I'm on about: Margaret and you? Look, I'll tell you something about Margaret. She's as sincere as you are about wanting what's best for the priory: and she probably wants it with more conviction. I bet you're the self-questioning type: am I right? Well, you won't catch Margaret dithering. Once she's made up her mind on a course of action, she goes for it.'

Catherine, trying to speak, choked instead. Beatrice hauled up her head and again held water to her lips. 'Go on. That's right. Take some more. Gosh though, you do look green.' As Catherine's head fell back, Beatrice resolved to send for Sister Luke the moment the service was over.

'I didn't mean to upset you, you know. Quite the reverse: I was trying to give you a lift. I was trying to explain that whatever you'd done, you'd have lost to Margaret.' Catherine's eyes looked unwaveringly into Beatrice's. And Beatrice read this as evidence of interest. 'You want to know why? Well, because Margaret's ideas made most people better off. They weren't going to say No to that, were they? And of course, her stroke of genius was making 'em feel good about it. Though it's easy enough, I suppose, to make people feel deserving. And religion came in handy there.'

Noise bubbled up out of Catherine. She painfully cleared her throat. 'Uh?' she barked.

'That's what religion's for, isn't it? At least, that's what it does: supports the status quo, legitimizes the division of spoils.'

Catherine now made a supreme effort. 'Christ,' she got out, 'was hardly about succouring the better-off.'

'Yeah, well there you go. It figures that you'd pick out Christ,' Beatrice said cheerfully. 'Christ the Saviour, Christ the preacher: fits your book. People always home in on the aspect that suits 'em. Margaret's a God person I'd guess, like most respectable, well-ordered folk. God, the old man in the sky. Comfortable people know in their guts He's on their side and fond of law and order and the profit motive. True, they'll indulge in a bit of hand-wringing over the poor from time to time, the deserving poor, who know their place and can be relied on not to threaten theirs. That's what I meant about religion coming in handy. It bolstered Margaret's line.' She hesitated, took on a dreamy look and confided, 'Though for me, personally— Well, I've always looked to Jesus.' She was thinking of her particular peccadillo and of Jesus's indulgence towards Mary Magdalene. 'But we all cling to what suits us, I guess. It's human nature.'

Catherine decided she was dreaming. Beatrice noticed her faraway look and gave her a friendly nudge. 'Hey, that's good, you're looking more relaxed. Maybe now you'll sleep.' She got off the bed, and looked down. 'Pleasant dreams. Just remember it wasn't your fault; Margaret had it all, the perfect hand.' On her way to the door, an idea struck her, and she turned round. 'Talking of cards: play yours right and you could still carve out a nice little niche for yourself. After all, you've got prestige, and between you and me, Margaret's a bit of a sucker, on the quiet, for prestige.' She winked, said Toodle-oo, and let herself out.

Beatrice felt more cheerful than ever as she swung along the corridor. Whatever had come over her, she asked herself humorously, to make her so considerate to that pain in the neck, Catherine? Her coming visit to California must have mellowed her. It must have inclined her to be supergenerous. And why not? The poor creature was all washed up. Whereas her own future had never looked more enticing. She went over in her mind all the goodies in store: air travel, sunshine, plenty of glamour; and some unfinished business with Sister Betty-Lou.

29

Bluebells were out in the wood. For the past few weeks
Catherine had monitored their progress from tight
green flower-heads to the first peeping of blue and
finally this intensely coloured flower-burst. As she
came over the footbridge she smelled their perfume.
She marvelled again at their comradely scent, unde-
tectable in a single flower, yet potent and heady from a
massed effusion. She went slowly along a winding
overgrown track and when, ahead, it dipped under
muddy water, took a semicircular diversion through
vegetation. At close hand the depth of colour was
striking, each flower so violently blue that colour
seeped like a bruise into the stem. In the distance
the blueness was softer, milky in the slanting light.
Between the trees, over banks where briars prepared to
shoot, and in flat clearings, waves of bluebells went on
and on. Trees canopied greenery above them, moist
greenery bedded them, and through them jutted stiff
young ferns with uncurled tips, ornate as bishops'
crooks.

The climb to the top of Beechy Knob made her puff
and blow. She sat on a log, listened to the rustling
wood and scanned the sky-coloured floor below.

Her enforced holiday was nearly over. 'You must
take a long rest,' the Prioress had ordered. 'Sister Luke
tells me you're unwell. She will be glad to have you
working with her in the hospital, but not until you've
recovered your strength. Until I settle matters with
Sister Margaret you are to do absolutely nothing at all.'

This evening Catherine would become the Sister Almoner and Margaret would become sole directrix and the Prioress's appointed successor. Catherine was glad. The way ahead was straightforward.

At length, Catherine rose and climbed down between the smooth trunks of the beech trees. At the bottom of the Knob, she turned along a path leading through coppiced sycamores. Their leaves were yellow-green in the sun. They trailed and brushed against her face as she ducked and weaved her way through them.

Arriving back at the wood's edge, she heard the chapel bell. Its sound came unevenly on the breeze. She stood still and listened, and the bell's ringing brought the priory to life in her mind's eye: the sisters about their work, thronging cheerfully in the refectory and decorously in the chapel, going singly to their rooms or in groups through the cloister; and hidden beneath their everyday demeanours an undercurrent of thought and emotion. Now, here, pressed to an ancient oak, the moist exhalation of plants on her skin and breath, the priory world seemed remote and impossible. But even as she thought this, she moved away, set off across the footbridge; and soon she quickened her step as if fearing to be late.

'I am up and down,' said the Prioress, turning her head to look bleakly out of the window. 'The winter was lowering. Spring was so late. Those nice few weeks we had at the end of April were a tonic, but lately there's been so much rain.'

'It's a glorious day today,' Margaret said briskly.

'I am not the woman I was,' the Prioress conceded.

Ah, thought Margaret. Are we getting somewhere at last? She crossed her legs and smoothed her skirt. 'There is no need for you to exert yourself, Reverend

Mother. You have earned a period of contemplation; indeed, I am sure the priory will be the better for your prayers and thoughts. As I pointed out—'

'Yes, yes,' said the Prioress irritably. 'Well, I've come to a decision.'

Silence fell in the room. Sounds from outside buzzed faintly and joined with the floating dust and faded fabric to cast a pervasive muzziness.

'Sister Catherine has been unwell.'

Margaret made her face sympathetic.

'She has overtaxed her strength, I fear.'

A bubble of annoyance rose in Margaret.

'I have spent some considerable time thinking about it, trying to decide what is best.' She stared at the cushion she had recently embroidered. 'It came to me that Sister Catherine can no longer endure the onerous role of joint directrix. However, some position must be found for her.' Here the Prioress leaned forward and peered at the very rose she had been stitching when reaching this conclusion. 'After all, Sister Mercy chose her for her assistant. That must count for something. There is the dignity of the priory to consider.'

'I am sure—' Margaret began, but was put off by the Prioress suddenly jabbing with her finger.

'Pass it to me, will you?'

Margaret stared at the empty chair beside her. 'You mean the cushion?' She got up quickly, preparing to apply it to the Prioress's back.

But the Prioress snatched the cushion and began closely to examine her work. 'What a relief. It must have been a trick of the light. I thought I'd missed a stitch.'

'You mean you made it?' breathed Margaret.

'I worked it. Sister Elizabeth made it up for me.'

'But it's lovely. If only I had the patience.'

'Do you think so?' the Prioress asked curiously. She herself was no longer convinced of its merit. Ready to defend her choice of a blue background to Elizabeth, who had lamely suggested beige, she had been taken aback by Cecilia's frank disparagement. Unlike Elizabeth, Cecilia could not be accused of liking to play safe.

'Oh, what a nasty shade of blue, Reverend Mother,' she had cried. 'Whatever possessed you? Were you trying to use it up?'

'Certainly not,' had protested the Prioress. 'Elizabeth suggested beige, but I thought blue would make a better background for the salmon pink.'

'Dear Reverend Mother, that cruel blue makes the salmon cringe. Beige, I grant you, would have killed it. But green— Now if you had chosen a pale sage green it would be an altogether different story.'

At once the Prioress had known Cecilia was right. It had ruined the cushion for her. Now she was wild to use up the rest of the salmon pink with some nice green thread she had discovered in her workbox. She regarded Margaret thoughtfully. 'You shall have it. It would be a fitting gift in a way, for while I was working it I decided to make you sole directrix and Sister Catherine—'

She got no further. Margaret's hand shot out and claimed her present. She clasped it to her breast, genuinely moved. In years to come she would point it out to guests: 'That cushion was worked by our former prioress; she made it specially for me, her chosen successor.' Just a minute, though; the Prioress had not quite said she was her chosen successor. 'Forgive me, Reverend Mother, I interrupted you. The fact is I was overcome.'

This surprised the Prioress considerably. She would never have suspected Margaret of sentimentality. She recollected herself. 'Yes, as I was saying, my successor must guarantee Sister Catherine's position. I am very firm about that.'

'Oh, absolutely. Something fitting—'

'She wishes to be attached to the hospital. This is a surprise, but there is no dissuading her. "Sister Almoner" is a suitable title, don't you think? She has no nursing qualification, but Sister Luke says her particular forte is soothing the patients down. Apparently, a great many patients these days require some soothing down.'

Almoner? Margaret experienced distaste at the word. It sounded suspiciously like 'social worker', a complete waste of time; and didn't it cast a rather doubtful aspersion on the priory? Still, if it satisfied the Prioress it would do for now. There was no saying what any particular sister would be doing a few years hence, for the changes had hardly begun. 'That sounds perfectly satisfactory,' she conceded.

'Good. It's settled, then. I also appoint you my successor, by the way. The announcement will be made tonight before evensong. It'll be the usual thing. I shall say my piece while you wait outside. I shall mention Sister Catherine, thank her for her work for the priory and describe her new position. Then the chapel doors will be opened and you will walk down the aisle to the chancel steps and say something suitable to the congregation.'

At last! And so casually alluded to. Margaret, one hand clutching the cushion to her breast, fell on her knees at the Prioress's feet. 'I shall do my utmost to prove worthy,' she murmured, her free hand drawing gnarled and reluctant fingers to her lips.

'Of course. Well, I am rather tired,' hinted the Prioress, in the hope of being rid of her.

Margaret went dreamily to the door.

'And if you see the Sister Almoner, tell her I'd like a word.'

*   *   *

Catherine came in.

'You are out of breath,' the Prioress remarked.

'I was in the wood. I came back and ran into Sister Marg— I mean, of course, the Directrix. I assume you've told her?' The Prioress nodded. And Catherine said gravely that the Directrix had told her the Reverend Mother wished to see her.

'Quite right, I do.'

But the Prioress seemed to be heavily engaged in turning out her sideboard. Drawers gaped open; assorted objects were heaped on the sideboard top, and several had fallen onto the carpet. Catherine stooped to gather items up.

'I've been looking for— Drat! Why is it always the last thing one comes across? And now it's stuck.' The Prioress tugged at a package caught in a crack between drawer end and drawer bottom. 'Got it,' she cried, and there was a tearing sound. 'Never mind, it's only the wrapping paper. Yes, here we are.' She uncovered a book and pushed it at Catherine. 'For you. Take it.'

Catherine was astounded. She turned the book over in her hands. It was a Book of Common Prayer splendidly bound in ivory, the title inlaid with mother-of-pearl.

'The Prioress – that is, my predecessor – gave it to me before she died.'

Then Margaret ought to have it, Catherine thought, and wondered how to suggest this inoffensively.

The Prioress seemed to read her mind. 'The Directrix has had her present: some small thing she fancied. So I'd like you to have that.'

Catherine turned the pages; they were tissue-thin edged sharply with gold. A delicious mustiness wafted. 'It's beautiful. I love it.'

The Prioress grunted, her offhand manner deliberately disguising the significance of her action. But she knew what she was doing. Her hand being forced, she had appointed Margaret to run this place. But the spirit of the priory— Ah, that she saw embodied in the prayer book which had been passed down to her and which she now passed on to Catherine. She stood quietly for a moment, committing to memory the sight of Catherine with the prayer book in her hands. Then abruptly turned away. 'What a mess I've made,' she grumbled, suddenly more than usually weary. She placed her forearm along the sideboard and scooted a heap of objects into the drawer.

'Let me do it. I'll soon make it tidy,' cried Catherine, putting her gift to one side.

The Prioress brightened. 'Will you, m'dear? That's kind. And when you've done, we'll take a small glass of wine. It will buck us up no end.'

Later, going down the stairs, Catherine remembered the Prioress saying that Margaret had had her present, and she suspected that the Prioress had been disingenuous. But why should she care? Margaret knew nothing of the tradition of passing on this particular prayer book, just as, until a moment ago, no other soul knew of it save the Prioress. And Catherine made up her mind that Margaret never would. It was her own small prize. She smiled to herself, and reflected that it was in fact the booby prize, for the Prioress had presumably intended it as consolation. She kept the prayer book hidden in the folds of her skirt all the way to her room.

Before hiding it away, she spent some time examining it. The ivory binding was out of fashion, she reflected. Quite rightly, ivory was frowned upon now. But the thought of things passing in and out of fashion, and not only things but ideas too, took hold of her imagination. She foresaw that one day even Margaret's rule would no longer seem exciting, that the worm would turn, that people would look at one another and ask what had happened to spiritual values. She foresaw that they would start to yearn for a kinder, more inclusive way of living and working together. Not in her day perhaps, but possibly in Christa's. It was a thought that she resolved to hang on to. A thought that she would remember whenever in private she opened her prize.

Although there was no-one to see her save her Maker, Margaret stood to attention outside the closed chapel doors. It was a solemn moment. The organ had stopped playing. The Prioress, unheard by Margaret, was now conveying to the congregation her decision. When two awe-covered postulants opened the doors, Margaret didn't hesitate; she had rehearsed every step, every look, every word.

She went briskly down the aisle. Delay would be inappropriate, for if ever an honour came tardily, it was now. Her smile, however, was forgiving. The muscles of her throat were flexed, ready to emit exactly the right sound of becoming sweetness and underlying authority.

Her words were also well prepared. There was to be no triumphant speech, no hectoring look at the future: these would keep for another occasion. Magnanimous in victory, she proposed to strike a conciliatory note. It had come to her in the quiet of her room as she sat on her bed with the Prioress's cushion in her lap, that she could do no better than repeat the charming prayer she had uttered at the time of her appointment as joint directrix. It might also serve as a reminder that a great deal of trouble would have been saved had she been created sole directrix and the Prioress's successor in the first place.

She reached the top of the chancel steps. Turning, she faced the assembly, tilted her head slightly to one side, and began: 'Sisters: in the words of Saint Francis of Assisi:

Where there is hatred, may we bring love;
where there is discord, may we bring harmony;
where there is doubt, may we bring faith;
where there is despair, may we bring hope;
where there is darkness, may we bring light;
where there is sadness, may we bring joy,
for Thy mercy and truth's sake.'

AMEN

Outside, Looking In
Kathleen Rowntree

'SPARKLING . . . A DELIGHTFUL COMEDY'
Cosmopolitan

Aston Favell had many features of which it was justly proud – the fact that it had come second in the Best Kept Village Competition, its listed houses, and Mrs Bullivant's bring and buy coffee mornings (there were, perhaps, too many of her crocheted pot holders but no one ever had the courage to say so). But now Aston Favell had something the inhabitants didn't really want – a Peeping Tom. First spying on a courting couple at Ellwood's farm, then on the ladies' exercise class in the village hall, the Peeping Tom sends a frisson of unease round the homes of Aston Favell.

To Kate Woolard the intruder meant more than unease. A young widow, slowly recovering from her husband's death and fighting against the trauma of loneliness-induced fear, the Peeping Tom nearly shattered her growing equilibrium. Courageously she tried to go about her normal life, part-time teaching at a local school, and helping her friend, Will McLeod, with the tragic problems of caring for his wife who has Alzheimer's. Will and Kate, both emotionally wracked, do not need extra stress in their lives.

Slowly, as the Peeping Tom – outside, looking in – observes the everyday events of the village, many private and domestic scenes are revealed, the most surprising being the finally discovered identity of Aston Favell's spy.

Rich in hilarious, poignant, and eccentric characters, *Outside, Looking In* captures all the tensions of contemporary village life whilst at the same time telling a story of great emotional impact.

'SEETHES WITH EVERYDAY HUMAN CONCERNS . . . POIGNANT COMEDY'
Madeleine Kingsley, *She*

0 552 99606 8

BLACK SWAN

Laurie And Claire
Kathleen Rowntree

'A BIG, BRAVE, INTROSPECTIVE BOOK TO SAVOUR'
Madeleine Kingsley, *She*

When they were children at Foscote an enduring,
unbreakable bond was forged between Laurie Stone
and Claire Haddingham. Tested by dawning maturity and
adult defection, the bond still held firm. For neither Claire,
nor Laurie – a talented TV performer and everyone's
favourite party guest despite his hidden conflicts – could
contemplate life without the other.

But then Lydia arrived on the scene. Strong and bold was
Lydia's style of beauty – hers was not the soft and gentle
kind. Danger filled the house and Claire felt this most
strongly. It emanated from Lydia's air of malign purpose.
Claire had long observed in herself a capacity for
ruthlessness where her love for Laurie was concerned.
The question became, how far would she go?

'THIS MOVING ACCOUNT OF AN UNCONVENTIONAL
LOVE AFFAIR THAT UNFOLDS OVER SEVERAL
DECADES MAY FINALLY WIN KATHLEEN ROWNTREE
THE EXPOSURE SHE DESERVES'
Options

'THERE IS A KIND OF LUSH ROMANTICISM TINGED
WITH BLACKNESS AT THE HEART OF KATHLEEN
ROWNTREE'S LATEST NOVEL . . . SOMETHING VERY
SEDUCTIVE . . . ROWNTREE IS A SLY AND WITTY
WRITER'
Marie Claire

0 552 99608 4

BLACK SWAN

A SELECTED LIST OF FINE WRITING
AVAILABLE FROM BLACK SWAN

99313	1	OF LOVE AND SHADOWS	Isabel Allende	£6.99
99564	9	JUST FOR THE SUMMER	Judy Astley	£6.99
99618	1	BEHIND THE SCENES AT THE MUSEUM	Kate Atkinson	£6.99
99648	3	TOUCH AND GO	Elizabeth Berridge	£5.99
99687	4	THE PURVEYOR OF ENCHANTMENT	Marika Cobbold	£6.99
99622	X	THE GOLDEN YEAR	Elizabeth Falconer	£5.99
99656	4	THE TEN O'CLOCK HORSES	Laurie Graham	£5.99
99611	4	THE COURTYARD IN AUGUST	Janette Griffiths	£6.99
99392	1	THE GREAT DIVORCE	Valerie Martin	£6.99
99688	2	HOLY ASPIC	Joan Marysmith	£6.99
99696	3	THE VISITATION	Sue Reidy	£5.99
99506	1	BETWEEN FRIENDS	Kathleen Rowntree	£6.99
99325	5	THE QUIET WAR OF REBECCA SHELDON	Kathleen Rowntree	£5.99
99584	3	BRIEF SHINING	Kathleen Rowntree	£5.99
99561	4	TELL MRS POOLE I'M SORRY	Kathleen Rowntree	£5.99
99606	8	OUTSIDE, LOOKING IN	Kathleen Rowntree	£5.99
99608	4	LAURIE AND CLAIRE	Kathleen Rowntree	£6.99
99672	6	A WING AND A PRAYER	Mary Selby	£6.99
99650	5	A FRIEND OF THE FAMILY	Titia Sutherland	£5.99
99130	9	NOAH'S ARK	Barbara Trapido	£6.99
99643	2	THE BEST OF FRIENDS	Joanna Trollope	£6.99
99636	X	KNOWLEDGE OF ANGELS	Jill Paton Walsh	£5.99
99673	4	DINA'S BOOK	Herbjørg Wassmo	£6.99
99592	4	AN IMAGINATIVE EXPERIENCE	Mary Wesley	£5.99
99641	6	A DESIRABLE RESIDENCE	Madeleine Wickham	£6.99
99591	6	A MISLAID MAGIC	Joyce Windsor	£4.99